SEAN M. TIRMAN

Hounds of Gaia

The Marrower Saga: Book One

For my wife, Tristen, who believes in me even when I don't, inspires me to be the best version of myself, and continues to tolerate my questionable sense of humor.

Many of the dangers we face indeed arise from science and technology — but, more fundamentally, because we have become powerful without becoming commensurately wise. The world-altering powers that technology has delivered into our hands now require a degree of consideration and foresight that has never before been asked of us.

—Carl Sagan

Acknowledgement

First and foremost, I want to thank my wife, Tristen, for everything. She's my first reader and editor, the person I go to first to bounce ideas off of, and my moral and emotional North Star. Without her and her endless support, this book simply wouldn't exist.

I'd also like to thank my brother Ryan, Mom, Dad (and Beckisue), Steve Bryant, Will Vega, and anyone else who read an early version of this book. Your insights were an invaluable, integral part of bringing this universe to life.

A special thanks is owed to Sereli Rodriguez, who has been one of my biggest supporters and best friends, a voracious and utterly reliable reader (for both this project and others I've worked on).

Thank you to Winston Blake Wheeler Ward, the mad genius behind both *Infinite Worlds* and *Infinite Horrors*. Those first two publishing credits gave me the confidence to move beyond just short stories and try something a lot more ambitious.

Credit is also owed to Anne-Marie Rutella, my editor, for helping turn my manuscript into something actually readable.

And I want to thank you, the reader, for taking a chance on a story that's extremely close to my heart. I hope you enjoy it.

Prologue

Survive.
  Move.
  Survive.
  Observe. Examine. Analyze. Extrapolate.
  React. Retreat.
  Survive.
  Dodge. Guard. Protect.
  Faster.
  Advance. Attack. Annihilate.
  Survive.
  Slash. Maim. Rip. Crack. Devour.
  Digest.
  Satisfy. Nourish. Sustain.
  Evacuate. Escape.
  Survive.

☿

"Where the hell is everybody?" Corporal Vasquez, a senior Deadwood Mining Corporation Security officer, said aloud.

"How should I know?" replied his captive, a gaunt, worse-for-wear man known around the station only as "Fink."

"Wasn't talking to you." Vasquez shoved Fink, sending the bald, slender man shoulder-first into one of the security substation walls. Fink tumbled to the ground.

In his four years working for DMC-Sec's boots-on-the-ground District Management Team, Corporal Vasquez had never seen a security substation so empty. Even for Deadwood—one of the smallest backwater mining asteroids, floating around the Kuiper Belt so far beyond the reach of the sun's rays—it seemed unusual, concerning even. There wasn't even an officer stationed at the reception desk.

"Hey, watch it, man," the prisoner whined, righting himself. He shook his wrists, jingling the cumbersome cuffs that kept his arms secured behind his back. "Kind of at a disadvantage here."

In the short time Fink had been in his custody, Vasquez had already begun to understand why some of his fellow officers chose to use violence as a means of keeping the rabble around the station in check. It wasn't his style. In fact, it was a point of pride to Vasquez that he never bent the rules when it came to enforcing what limited laws there were on Deadwood, but Fink had pushed him to his limits through sheer annoyance and indignation.

Vasquez had picked up Fink while undercover on a human trafficking sting. The skeletal man hadn't been the target, and the corporal had blown his cover by bringing him in, but Vasquez simply couldn't ignore the flagrance with which Fink had approached him. Worse, Fink was offering up children for sale. The conversation between them had lasted mere minutes before Fink was in cuffs and Vasquez was marching him back to the security substation for processing.

But now the pair stood in an empty lobby, and Vasquez was—for all his years of service—uncertain of how to proceed.

"Hello?" Vasquez called out, louder this time.

And then he heard the familiar sound of a heavy metal station door sliding open.

In unison, Vasquez and Fink turned to see a grubby man emerge from the rear of the substation, dressed in the drab, standard jumpsuit of a DMC-Sec officer. Except this one was covered in stains. He stopped in his tracks and stared at the pair of men standing in the lobby as he shoveled the last bite of the same fried junk food that already filled his cheeks into his mouth.

"My bad," he mumbled, crumbs cascading from his lips down onto his uniform. "Bathroom break."

"Officer Johnson," Vasquez addressed his subordinate with a sigh.

Fink laughed.

"Hey, Vasquez. Who's the perp?" Johnson continued, unconcerned with the dissatisfaction in Vasquez's voice.

"Phineas Ames," the corporal answered. "Goes by Fink. Tried to sell me some kids, so I booked him."

"Weren't you supposed to be undercover?" Johnson asked.

Vasquez nodded.

"Blew it all for this one guy, huh?"

"Say…" Vasquez ignored the jab. "Where is everyone?"

"Oh yeah." Johnson perked up. "Some shit went down in the bowels of the station near the old refinery…number twelve, I think. I don't have all the details, but I guess it's a pretty big deal. Got a whole sector cordoned off. Everyone that's not already on a job or doing rounds is down there…'cept me. Said I should send anyone else that comes in, too. I guess that

3

means you."

"Comms?"

"Nah." Johnson shrugged. "You know how it is down there, all that rock and metal makes shit go haywire. And the cams down there are all still out, too. You're just gonna have to truck it thataway and see for yourself."

"How long?"

"Uhh…" Johnson kept chewing.

"How long have they been down there?" Vasquez demanded.

"A few hours, maybe three?"

"You don't know?"

"Been a little busy here all by myself," Johnson scoffed.

"So it would seem," Vasquez sighed. "Anyone report back?"

"Not yet."

"And that doesn't seem odd to you?"

Johnson shrugged.

"You call it in to the guys upstairs?" Vasquez pointed up, suggesting the direction of DMC-Sec's orbital headquarters. "They know we're short-staffed as it is. Maybe they can send some guys from another district."

Johnson nodded, "Weir called it in before he left, but the request was…how did he put it? *Promptly denied*. You know how is with the fucking brass up there. We're not exactly high on their list of priorities."

Corporal Vasquez shook his head, took a deep breath, and shoved Fink forward. "Think you can handle this one?"

"I can put him in holding, sure," Johnson replied, still chewing. "But I'm not doing your paperwork. You can take care of it when you come back up."

"You're a real pal," the corporal retorted as he handed the man off to Officer Johnson.

Johnson tapped the panel on the wall and the door to the rear of the station slid open once more, locking into place with a loud *thunk*.

As Vasquez turned to leave, he glanced back over his shoulder one last time to see his prisoner, the man called Fink, give him a wry smile and a wink.

"Miss you already," Fink sang before turning his attention to the other officer, his voice trailing off as the pair shuffled deeper into the security substation. "Officer Johnson, right? I think you and I are gonna be great friends. Got any more of those snacks?"

☿

Corporal Vasquez marched through the dimly lit depths of Deadwood Station with purpose, veering around piles of discarded refuse and scrap, staying tight around the station's corners, and maneuvering through the labyrinthian corridors as only a true Deadwood resident could.

It wasn't always this way. When he had first arrived on the asteroid, Vasquez was baffled by the station's layout. As was often the case with colonies in the Kuiper Belt, Deadwood wasn't built with people in mind. It had originated as a mining colony and, as such, the pathways carved through the cold, hard rock were determined by where the most valuable veins of ore were located. It was hardly a consideration whether that was done in a human-friendly manner or not.

Vasquez had always likened the station's layout to the human circulatory system—the pathways seemed disorganized to the point of chaos when considered from up close, but a God's-eye view elicited a different feeling in him. When looked at from afar—or through the lens of one of the station's many holographic directories—there was an almost organic beauty and harmony to it. It was this perspective that had first started to chip away at the corporal's distaste for Deadwood.

But falling in love with his new home had been slow going, as the rock's strange allure was juxtaposed against its high rates of poverty and, therefore, crime. Even for an Outer Colony, Deadwood was particularly bad. And that wasn't helped by the fact that Vasquez hadn't even volunteered to transfer down to the station, so much as he was compelled to by a particularly corrupt former C.O. of his from back when he was on orbital duty.

Still, the corporal—a loyal member of DMC-Sec—had always been one to try to make the best of things. And in doing so he had come to see Deadwood as his home. Now, as he dragged his fingers over the jagged, exposed silicate, he felt connected to it. He could imagine the tangled web of corridors, from the vast and open ORC pod docking bay down to the most cramped service tunnels toward the core of the asteroid, as vividly as he could remember the flotilla of ships he grew up on.

The particular tunnel he now traveled down would take him on a relatively direct path to the station's innards, to where one of the rock's refineries had once melted down Deadwood's ores into purer, more easily transported forms. It was there he expected to meet the rest of his team, his fellow officers, and together they would investigate whatever it was that had transpired.

But that wasn't what happened. Not at all.

Instead, the closer he got to the refinery, the more he felt like something had gone terribly, horribly wrong. Only a few twists and turns away, he had anticipated running into one of the junior officers or even Miller, the greenest grunt on the squad. It was, after all, standard procedure to station officers outside active crime scenes in an effort to keep the lookie-loos and rubbernecks away. But when he rounded the final corner, just before the passageway opened up into the larger refinery, he found no one.

Corporal Vasquez stopped dead in his tracks, letting the last echoes of his heavy boots on the steel gangway fade. Instinctively, he hit his comms. "Corporal Vasquez reporting in, does anyone read me?"

Silence.

He continued, louder this time so that anyone in the neighboring corridors might hear him, "Corporal Vasquez here, can anyone hear me?"

More silence.

He continued forward, slowly this time, trying to make his footfalls as quiet as possible as he rounded the final corner into the larger refinery space. As odd as it was that none of his fellow officers were around, he was even more disturbed to realize that there didn't seem to be any sounds of movement at all. All he could hear was the familiar and gentle hum the station always elicited, a product of shoddy electrics and the vibrations of far-off generators. But there should have been more. By now, he should be able to hear the voices of his comrades or at least the shuffle of bodies as they investigated. The sheer emptiness of it all made Vasquez all the more nervous.

The corporal carefully lowered his right hand down his side, reaching for his service pistol, only to remember that he was still dressed in plain clothes for his blown undercover job. He had no weapon, and it was too late to turn back. *Besides*, he thought, *who am I going to go get to come and help...Johnson?*

"If there's anyone in here, come out now," Vasquez announced. "You will not be harmed, I promise."

But the only response he was met with was his own voice echoing through the refinery.

"Okay," he continued, "I'm coming in."

He cringed and shook his head at his own stupidity. Vasquez knew, whatever was going on down here, there wasn't much a single, unarmed officer was going to be able to do. If there was someone—or worse, *someones*—waiting for him around one of these corners, they had the clear upper hand.

But Corporal Vasquez was a man of principle and, despite his apprehension and unpreparedness, some of his comrades-in-arms, the officers he had worked alongside these last four years, might be down here and they might need his help. Sure, they weren't all good people—some were nearly as corrupt as those he had left behind when he transferred—but they were still *his* people. And that was enough for him to keep going.

He moved deeper into the refinery, peeking into the spaces between dormant machinery, careful to check every corridor and corner as he slunk through. He moved forward, carefully and quietly, staying on guard.

As he crept, he picked up on the familiar scent of rust. Or maybe he had been smelling it all along. Except now it seemed...stronger, more pungent.

At first, he had chalked it up to all the old machines. While Deadwood, being an asteroid, didn't have much in the way of atmosphere apart from what was recycled through the station's array of life-support systems and their CO_2 scrubbers, moisture still managed to collect here and there.

That meant the old refinery had plenty of oxidized, corroded metal. But this was different.

There was only one other thing Corporal Vasquez could think of that smelled like this. Another familiar scent. One that sent chills up his spine. And then it hit him. Blood.

He was smelling blood.

☿

"Okay," Corporal Vasquez muttered to himself, "you gotta move. One foot in front of the other…"

One foot in front of the other, his wife's voice echoed in his head. It was a phrase she used often—a kind of meditation to remind him with each step that there were people depending on him. Jeanette, having grown up in a military family herself, had always known how hard it was for law enforcement in the Kuiper Belt. She had always supported him through the good days and the bad ones. Especially the bad ones. And she always knew what to say.

He took a step forward, just the slightest crack of a warm grin on his lips.

For Weir and his baby boy, Vasquez thought, remembering the silver chain Officer Weir always wore around his neck—a reminder of his son, Sterling.

Another step.

For Officer Starck and his new husband, Vasquez told himself, imagining the tungsten ring around his former partner's finger—the corporal could never forget the smile on Starck's face on his wedding day.

And another step.

For Officer Miller. Vasquez remembered the optical implant she had gotten after being assaulted by a dust junkie in one of the station's lower dormitories only a few weeks after she landed the job. It wasn't quite the right color, but she immediately loved it, said it gave her character and made her feel tough.

That's why he needed to keep moving. For them.

Finally, Vasquez had shaken off his trepidation and continued forward, following the smell of blood as best he could. He knew he was close, he hadn't rounded the last corner quite—

His foot kicked something, and it went skittering across the metal gangway he walked down, a tinny sound echoing through the surrounding corridors. He froze once more, waiting for the sounds to die out and listening to see if anyone would come running at the jarring cacophony. But all he heard, still, was the same humming of the station.

Certain once more that he was still alone, Vasquez searched the walkway in front of him, looking for whatever it was he had bumped into. Only a few steps away, he found it lying before him: a combat boot, the same kind that DMC-Sec handed out to new recruits with their standard-issue jumpsuit.

Vasquez's heart sank. But he kept moving, turning down one more corridor.

The room opened up before him into a larger area—what looked to have been a warehouse or staging area for the refinery's end product. The space was big. Bigger than perhaps the whole security substation. It was empty, too, with defunct flatbed haulers, the ride-on kind factory workers used to move product that was too heavy to carry from place to place, lined the walls. And the whole place was just as dimly lit as the rest of Deadwood, illuminated only by the same sparse lightbars that lined the rest of the station's corridors.

What caught Vasquez's eye, however, wasn't the old machines or the high ceilings. Rather it was something at the center of the room, a dark heap that stood out as odd and out of place against the otherwise angular warehouse and its machines. But he couldn't quite make out what it was in the faint light. So, he continued forward, step by step.

Carefully approaching, Vasquez squinted hard to force his eyes to finally adjust, but the smell filling the room had gotten so strong that the corporal began to gag, and his eyes started to well up. Still, he was close enough for his brain to start making sense of the shapes before him.

Guns. There were service pistols—or at least parts of them—scattered around the center pile. And they looked...broken. Crushed? Some were in pieces. And there was more.

Cloth. The center of the mound was made up of drab fabric, which Vasquez recognized as clothing. It was an assortment of jumpsuits. The same ones worn by his fellow officers. He could even see the DMC-Sec logos emblazoned on some of them.

Vasquez blinked, clearing the tears from his eyes. Were they welling up from the smell, or was it fear?

He looked closer.

Not just jumpsuits. Protruding from the cloth, some at unnatural angles, the corporal could just make out the shapes of feet and hands, fingers and toes...even heads. But they looked wrong, incomplete.

Some were broken and wrenched apart. Others were ripped to shreds. A few of the limbs sticking out of the jumpsuits ended abruptly at bloodied stumps.

And the faces—what faces Vasquez could recognize—wore twisted expressions of sheer agony.

It wasn't just his comrades' clothing. It was their bodies. And among them, Vasquez recognized their personal effects.

Miller's optical implant, what was left of it, dangled from her empty eye socket.

Starck's tungsten ring was still wrapped around his broken and bloodied finger, his hand reaching out as if for help.

Weir's sterling silver necklace, glinting in the low light, hung from a neck that no longer had a head attached to it.

All of them.

All the officers he had come to find.

They were all dead.

No, not dead. This was worse. Much worse.

Someone—no, *something*—had torn them apart, going so far as to crack their bones wide open.

It was a massacre.

Vasquez doubled over, slipping in the pooled blood at his feet before vomiting on the cold metallic floor below. Between heaves, he sobbed, unable to keep his sorrow contained.

"No, no, no, no," he mumbled to himself, saliva dripping from his lips. He began to tremble, rocking himself back and forth, trying to make sense of the horror he had discovered.

But what could he do? Who could he call? Everyone he trusted was in pieces on the floor before him.

Then he heard it, a quiet, wet sound. Intermittent and too irregular to be the shifting of the old machines or the humming of the station.

Vasquez held his breath, trying to make it out. To him, it sounded familiar, almost human. And it seemed like it was coming from one of the dark corners of the warehouse.

Smacking. Slurping. Licking.

Whoever—*whatever* it was—was still in the room with

Vasquez. And it was feeding.

The corporal rose to his feet, his eyes searching the darkness, sweat dripping down his face, and his heart beating through his chest.

And then he saw it, a shape crouched in the corner of the room, too dark to make out but for the glint of light reflecting off two big eyes.

Corporal Vasquez screamed.

When Jeanette found her husband, he was unresponsive. Curled up in a ball on their bathroom floor, covered in blood, weeping and mumbling to himself, he didn't seem to see or hear or feel her, no matter how loudly she shouted his name or shook him by the shoulders. Not even when she held his face up to her own.

She had never seen him in such a state, even after the hardest, most disturbing days on the job. Not after breaking human trafficking rings. Not after the drug raids. Not even after the worst murders he had investigated.

But now she couldn't even get him to look her in the eye. He just stayed curled up on the floor, rocking back and forth, whispering incoherently.

For hours, he remained like that. Until finally, he began to calm down and come back to himself. He still didn't talk to his wife or tell her what happened. But she pulled him to his feet and guided him into the shower.

She bathed him, washing the blood from his body and brushing the viscera out of his hair. And, as she cleaned him, he wept, sobbing deeply and heaving with his whole body.

Once the blood was rinsed down the drain, she climbed into the shower alongside him and held him in her arms, letting the warm water wash over both of them, holding him as close as she could.

Eventually, she helped him out of the shower, dried him off, and dressed him. He had ceased his incoherent mumbling but still would not speak to her. He could merely stare into her eyes with deep, profound sadness.

When she laid him in their bed and wrapped him in the sheets, he curled back into a ball, rolling to face the wall, and remained that way for another hour or so while Jeanette gave the bathroom a thorough sterilization.

When she returned, her husband, Corporal Vasquez, a senior officer of Deadwood Mining Corporation Security, had finally fallen asleep. But she could tell the sleep was not restful. He moaned and sobbed and retched beneath the covers, unable to find solace even in dreams.

Sitting on the edge of the bed, she placed a hand on his shoulder and, for a moment, he seemed calm, quiet, himself. But she knew once he woke, whatever nightmare he had experienced would be far from over.

So, she rose to her feet and quietly tiptoed over to their dormitory's integrated console, tapping the screen with a single finger to turn it on. Then, she clicked the little DMC-Sec icon on the desktop, opening a window to the security company's intranet portal. She glanced into the upper corner of the screen to see that he was still logged into his account.

Thank goodness, she thought with a quiet sigh. She knew her husband wasn't supposed to remain logged in on an unsecured network. He had made a bad habit of it in recent days. But to her, at this moment, it was a welcome one.

She tapped another icon on the screen that pulled up his district's personnel communiqués and opened a new thread. A few more taps on the screen, after which she hit the submit button at the bottom.

Only a moment later, the console chimed.

New message, an alert showed on the screen. She opened it, breathing a sigh of relief.

Sick leave request approved, Corporal Vasquez, it read.

Chapter One

The girl was lost.

Of that much, she was sure.

Still, she continued onward, always onward, meandering through the cold, rocky corridors, careful not to look back over her shoulder, no matter how tempting. She could hear them behind her, the clumsy men in their mining uniforms with their unwieldy tool belts and heavy footfalls, but she wasn't about to be caught. Not again. Not like last time when those men and their guns—so many guns. So, so much...no. She couldn't think about it. Not now. So, instead, she ran—left at the next intersection, right after that, up a staircase, and left again—moving as quickly as her sinewy legs would allow.

She should have known better. She shouldn't have snuck into that dormitory to clean herself off. But she did. And she was sure she had gotten it all, washed her hands and face, pulled the muck out of her hair, and scraped the gunk from under her fingernails. But then the men in their mining uniforms came in and found her. And they chased her off, swinging their wrenches and hollering. They weren't as scary as the men with the guns, but they frightened her all the same.

As she scampered through unrecognizable passage after

unrecognizable passage, she reached a hand out to the stony walls. They were cold but not as unwelcoming as before. The rocks were getting warmer the farther she went. And where there was warmth, there were people. If she could just make it a little farther, maybe she'd find a market or a dormitory, somewhere with people where she could blend in and disappear. Maybe then they wouldn't find her. Maybe then she would be safe. Maybe then it wouldn't happen again.

"Hey, stop!" She heard one of the miners shouting behind her.

Lost in her hope that she might evade them, she must have slowed down. They had found her once more. She hadn't been fast enough. And now they were going to catch her. And who knows what would happen next?

The girl ran, dashing around corners and sprinting down straightaways, but the clomping of the boots behind her never faded. Yet, her hope was renewed as the hallways started to open up around her. She began passing doorways, storage lockers, and even people—real people—milling about, uninterested in the fearful girl darting between them.

She came around another corner and clipped the shoulder of a gruff-looking man dressed in greasy coveralls, a too-small bright yellow protective helmet squeezing his face into a pursed scowl.

"Hey, watch it," the man protested, but the girl kept right on going, turning her head back just in time to see her pursuers run straight into the man while his back was turned. The trio tumbled to the ground in a tangled heap, all three men shouting and cursing at one another.

The girl couldn't help but smile, twisting back around only to run face-first into a woman dressed in thick, dark-gray robes.

☿

Sister Penelope absolutely adored the Kuiper Belt's Outer Colonies, especially its larger population centers like Deadwood Station, where she now stood. Though most of the System viewed the Reach—a colloquial nickname for the smattering of outposts at the edge of the solar system—as a barren frontier overflowing with criminals and ne'er-do-wells, she considered it an honor to bring a measure of civility and hope to those in need. And there were so many in need way out beyond the grasp of Earth and its governance.

The colonies were largely lawless, beholden only to shady mining corporations, scrapper collectives, and their loosely defined security forces—little more than thugs with badges and guns, in Sister Penelope's opinion. But they were also packed with folks who had no place else to go, primarily indentured servants bound by duplicitous lifelong "contracts." And wherever there are large groups of subjugated people, there are unwanted, forsaken children. And those were souls she could save.

Sister Penelope knew in her heart of hearts that a large part of the reason her kin flocked to the colonies of the Reach was to bolster the numbers of their order. After all, being out of favor with Earth meant being out of favor with most people. And that meant that new members were difficult to come by. The children served that purpose beautifully, but not without a bounty in return. Those who joined the Organic Humanists were welcomed into a loving, caring, and—most importantly—providing consortium. They didn't have much, but her order—no, her *family*—made certain each and every soul in their care was fed, clothed, and respected.

Sadly, not everyone in the System believed in their mission. At best, they were met with shifty glances and pejoratives muttered under people's breaths. At worst, they were openly, publicly accosted and accused of being a sick, perverted sex cult full of pedophiles and their enablers.

The System was sometimes a dark place, especially this far out in the lawless Kuiper Belt, so Sister Penelope understood and, in most cases, tolerated the barbs thrown in her and her kin's direction. But sometimes, those barbs became threats, and those threats led to violence. In a few rare cases where things had truly escalated, the good sister had even suffered serious injury. She knew what it felt like to fear for her own life. And she saw that fear in the eyes of the young girl who had just collided with her in the middle of Deadwood Station.

As they stared at one another, a breaking news announcement rang out, the tinny voice of a local reporter ushered through the speakers of a small monitor mounted to one of the surrounding food vendor stalls.

"Another grisly scene today in Deadwood's industrial sector," the voice relayed in a calm, matter-of-fact tone, "where the remains of at least five people, including several station security guards, were found. Though several firearms were recovered at the scene, authorities have relayed that this was not another gang-related shootout and needs to be investigated further. A reporter on the scene spoke with locals in the area who expressed concern that this was, in fact, another attack by the serial killer now known colloquially as the Marrower..."

The mention of one of Deadwood's many criminal celebrities on the news blast—almost a daily occurrence this far beyond Earth's authoritative reach—shook the cobwebs from Sister Penelope's brain. She was there to help, after all, and here, right in front of her, was someone who perhaps desperately needed it. And the good sister had quite literally run right into the poor girl.

"Come with me," Sister Penelope whispered, hiding the girl between her robes and the side of a synthetic beef vending machine. The unmistakable odor of charcoal and burnt plastic stung Sister Penelope's nose and made her eyes water, but she remained steadfast, intent on guarding the girl against whoever was pursuing her. Moments later, a pair of heavy-footed security guards hobbled past. She smiled as they looked her way, receiving a curt nod from one and a sneer from the other in return.

Once the coast was clear, Sister Penelope turned around and looked down at the child before her. The good sister smiled again, genuinely this time, and the girl, as shy as she was, smiled back.

"Are you okay?" the young girl asked.

"Well, aren't you sweet?" Sister Penelope replied. "Why would you ask me such a thing?"

"Because you're crying," said the girl.

Sister Penelope raised a sleeve to her face and wiped the tears from her cheek.

"Oh no, my dear. I'm not crying," she said. "It's just the fumes from this machine. But I should be asking you that question. Are you okay? Why were those men chasing you?"

The smile faded from the girl's face as she looked down at her feet.

"I don't know," she mumbled. "I can't really remember."

"Okay," Sister Penelope chimed in. "Let's start with introductions. Would that be all right with you?"

The girl looked up again and nodded her head.

"My name is Sister Penelope. It's a pleasure to make your acquaintance."

"What does that mean, *ack-wain-tens*?" the girl asked.

"It means we're getting to know one another." The good sister smiled. "What's your name?"

The girl shook her head and looked down again.

Sister Penelope frowned. "Do you have a name? It's okay if you don't. I've met plenty of kids just like you who didn't have a name. Is there something that people call you, maybe?"

"No," the girl snapped, taking a step backward and crossing her arms. "What they call me…I don't like it."

A pair of men walked by, overhearing the conversation. "Look," one of them said, "Breeders are luring in another one. Disgusting."

"Good riddance," the other said. "Deadwood has more than enough urchins running around as is."

Sister Penelope, ignoring the men, stepped forward and knelt down, raising a hand to lift the girl's chin to look her in the eye.

"It's okay. You don't have to tell me. I wouldn't want to call you by a name you didn't like, anyhow," the good sister said. "Can I take you somewhere safe, back to your home, maybe?"

"I don't have one," she said.

"Where is your family?"

The girl squeezed her eyes shut and shook her head yet again, even more vigorously this time.

"I'm so sorry," Sister Penelope replied grimly. "You could come with me. I'm going to go meet up with some of my family, and then we're headed back to our ship. Who knows? Maybe you'll like them, and you could even join us."

"Do you really mean that?" the girl asked, opening her eyes wide.

"I sure do," Sister Penelope replied, extending an open palm. "Take my hand. We'll find a way around those scary men, and maybe we can pick a name you like on the way."

"*Pen-el-o-pe.* I like Penelope." The girl beamed.

The good sister chuckled. "Well, that's my name. I'm glad you like it, but what if people get us confused with one another?"

"Oh no, I didn't think of that," the girl laughed. "I'll keep thinking!"

The girl took Sister Penelope's hand, and together, they walked through the rocky, increasingly crowded corridors of Deadwood Station.

☿

Deadwood Station's Orbital Rail Catapult hub—known as the ORC for short—served as the asteroid colony's primary means of entrance and egress, as well as its main population center. After all, the bustling chambers of the ORC were where most of Deadwood's action happened—or at least where it began and ended. Vendors, new and old, were always arriving with exotic and hard-to-find goods for local market trading, many setting up shop just inside the hub's atriums; tearful families gathered to welcome back or bid farewell to their itinerant loved ones; and, on the rarest of occasions, onlookers could even observe the comings and goings of the System's most fabled citizens: the armed-to-the-teeth guns-for-hire known

22

simply as Contractors.

Yet, with all the commotion of Deadwood's ORC hub, Sister Penelope was unbothered by the hordes of folks and their constant din, for she had a flock of children that needed her. A flock that had just added a new member. And, as she stood before them—the lot seated quietly at her feet in a semicircle, all of their tiny, curious eyes on the good sister—she asked the children a question.

"Do any of you know what an ORC is?"

The children averted their eyes. Sister Penelope took a deep breath and continued.

"Let me give you a hint," she said. "ORC stands for Orbital Rail Catapult. Now, can anyone tell me what it does?"

A boy in the back with a shock of strawberry blond hair and a galaxy of freckles on his cheeks raised his hand.

"Yes, Jonesy? Tell me what an ORC does."

"Um…it shoots people into space," the boy said, whistling through the gap in his front teeth.

"Very good, Jonesy," the good sister replied. "Do you all want to know how it accomplishes that?"

The children nodded their heads in unison.

"Most ships are designed to stay in what we call the vacuum of space, where there's no air and, more importantly, no friction. That means they can't land or even enter the atmosphere of a planet without crashing or breaking apart. And that's dangerous and scary, right?"

Now, the children were nodding, some squealing in agreement, others in fear.

"Well, that means we had to find another way to get people from their ships to the many colonies on the planets and moons and asteroids throughout the solar system. So, a long time ago, some very smart scientists invented ORC technology. Now every spaceship comes equipped with what we call an ORC pod, a kind of tiny transport that can launch people safely into planetary atmospheres, onto moons, or even down to hollowed-out asteroid stations."

Toward the front of the group, a girl's face lit up, her big brown eyes wide as a full moon. Sister Penelope called on the girl.

"Octavia, do you have something to share?" the good sister asked.

"Yeah," the girl responded sheepishly. "Isn't Deadwood an asteroid?"

"It most certainly is, Octavia," Penelope confirmed. "Very good! Deadwood Station is one of many asteroid colonies throughout the Reach. And that means there are a lot of places to land an ORC pod. However, getting people from ship to station was only one part of the problem. We, meaning humanity, also needed to be able to send those pods back up to the ships when people were ready to go back into space again. At first, those very smart scientists thought they could just equip every pod with its own rocket engines so they could fly back up to their ships all on their own. But fuel is very expensive and can be quite dangerous."

At the center of the group, one of the younger boys threw his hands up in the air and shouted, *"Ka-boom!"* spooking some of the other children around him.

"Exactly," Sister Penelope acknowledged. "Thank you, Walton. To make things much safer and less costly, they invented a device that uses magnets instead of rockets to *throw* those pods back out to space. They called these devices Orbital Rail Catapults, and that's what we all know of as ORCs today.

24

And every single planetary, lunar, and asteroidal colony and station in the solar system is equipped with one, including Deadwood. That's how we're all going to go back up to our ship, which we call *Gaia*, that's floating out there in orbit. Have any of you been in an ORC pod before?"

As a smattering of children raised their hands, an older, leather-skinned man dressed in the same simple, thick gray robes as Sister Penelope approached with a look of concern on his face. Halting a few feet short of the good sister and her congregation, he smiled warmly through his anxiety and gave the group a deep bow.

"Children," Sister Penelope announced, "I'd like to introduce you to one of your new family members. This is Brother Loch, one of my oldest and closest friends. And I hope he will become your friend, too."

"Thank you, Sister Penelope," Brother Loch responded in a deep, soothing baritone. "And hello, children. I just wanted to inform you all that we've been cleared for departure and have secured a place in the queue. We should be ready to board in just under an hour or so."

"That's excellent news, Brother Loch," Sister Penelope replied, leaning toward her kinsman to keep the children from overhearing her next question. "But there's something else?"

Brother Loch leaned in and dropped his voice to a whisper, "Still no sign of Brother Phineas, I'm afraid. It's been days. Local authorities have been of no help and now we're out of time. We can't wait for him. *Gaia*'s mooring privileges are coming to an end."

"Hmm..." Penelope considered their predicament. "We'll have to depart without him, then. Brother Phineas is resourceful, and this wouldn't be the first time we've left him behind.

25

He'll find his way back to *Gaia*, I'm certain."

The good sister smiled at Brother Loch, who forced a smile back in return, his eyes betraying his inner turmoil. A chorus of *oohs* and *aahs* arose from the group of wide-eyed kids behind Sister Penelope as they gawked at an intimidating passerby decked from head to toe in thick, mechanized armor. A Contractor.

Like this rock needs another killer masquerading as a lawman, the good sister thought.

Once the stranger had passed and the commotion dissipated, Penelope turned back around and spoke up once more.

"It appears that we have some time to kill. Who wants to hear a story?"

Chapter Two

"Mailman, bring up the Deadwood Station schematics on my HUD," the Contractor barked into her helmet's comm system. As she waited for her ship's AI to populate the station layout on her helmet's heads-up display, she continued. "I can't make sense of all these blasted tunnels. If I get turned around, I'm liable never to find my way back out of this godforsaken rock again."

"Would that really be so bad?" the garbled, nasally, artificially maternal voice of her ship's AI responded. "You should see them now."

A hazy yellow holographic image popped up in the upper left corner of Foxhound's helmet display, showing a large asteroid honeycombed by a haphazard array of tunnels and a smattering of larger open areas—gathering places like docks, markets, and larger dormitories, mostly. To Foxhound, it looked more like the ant farms of the ancient past than a livable human space colony.

"For personal growth," the robotic voice continued, "I recommend attempting to familiarize yourself with your surroundings the old-fashioned way. Long ago, Earthlings in positions of localized authority would often be tasked with what was referred to as 'walking a beat.' Endeavoring to integrate into their environment allowed them to become more in tune with the communities they served. As you have visited Deadwood Station numerous times already, and that trend seems likely to continue, I believe this could be of great benefit to—"

"Mailman…" Foxhound interrupted.

"Yes?"

"Remember what we talked about regarding unsolicited advice?"

"Keep it to a minimum, you said."

"Please and thank you. And would you also drop some breadcrumbs for me? I want to be able to get back out of here as quickly as possible." A series of teal dots popped up on the station schematics inside the Contractor's helmet, marking the route she had taken away from the ORC hub and through the asteroid's tunnels.

Clad from head to toe in a thick angular suit of mechanized armor—common fare among those in her profession, though varied in style and typically highly customized—the Contractor, known only as Foxhound, trudged through Deadwood Station from the crowded caverns of the ORC hub, beyond the cramped shipping district with its disorganized storefronts, and into the meandering, slipshod passageways of the asteroid's industrial core. No matter how many times she walked these corridors, she never could quite wrap her head around how they were organized, or if they were at all. And while Mailman's assistance was welcome, it made her uneasy knowing she couldn't rely on her own instincts in a place as lawless and isolated as Deadwood.

Thankfully, most of the rabble left her alone. Whether that

was out of fear—there was a tremendous number of folks that made their way to the Kuiper Belt to avoid criminal bounties on their heads and/or to fulfill contracts of servitude—or indifference, Foxhound didn't know, nor did she particularly care. She was here to do her job and leave, that was all.

In this instance, that job called for a visit to one of Deadwood Station's security substations, where she was to retrieve and transport a wanted fugitive from the Kuiper Belt back to Earth to stand trial for his crimes.

"Fink" Ames, as he was known by friend and foe alike, had been a thorn in the side of numerous authoritative organizations around the solar system for quite some time. What's worse, he had somehow managed to evade capture time and time again, always seeming to slip right through the fingers of those close to catching him or trading in useful information in exchange for clemency. And while most of his illegal activity had been relegated to the Outer Colonies, he had done enough to catch the eye of someone back on humanity's home planet. Someone with enough money to put out a contract to bring him in on what amounted to a glorified babysitting job. Originally intending to decline simply by virtue of its extreme secrecy—there wasn't even a client name attached to the contract—Foxhound had Mailman vet the gig and, upon seeing Fink's criminal charges, gladly accepted.

For the most part, Fink's rap sheet read like that of a fairly run-of-the-mill baddie: charges for larceny, bribery, assault and battery, public intoxication, etcetera. But there was one little addendum that stuck out to Foxhound. Fink, so it appeared, had been caught trying to traffic humans. More specifically (and more concerning), Fink was attempting to sell children.

Unfortunately for Mr. Ames, the person he was trying to sell to just so happened to be one of Deadwood's more upstanding security officers—one who had been undercover trying to infiltrate the very gang Fink had intended to meet with. It was this officer, Corporal Vasquez, that Foxhound was on her way to meet. But when she arrived, stomping through the entrance corridor of the security substation with all the grace of an ancient rhinoceros, Vasquez was nowhere to be found.

In their place at the substation's desk sat an unusually thin man with sunken eyes, a shock of unkempt hair, and a bushy beard. He was dressed in an ill-fitting uniform—little more than a greasy mechanic's jumpsuit—with the name *Johnson* emblazoned on the breast patch. Seemingly unconcerned with the Contractor's arrival, he reclined in his chair with his filthy boots up on the desk, yawning as he scrolled through the newsfeeds on a tablet computer.

Just my luck, Foxhound thought, *a helpful local*.

When it became clear the man had no intention of rising from his seat, let alone glancing up from his tablet, Foxhound cleared her throat. The sound that came out was garbled and deep, courtesy of her helmet's vocal filter—a means of protecting and preserving the Contractor's highly cherished anonymity. The man glanced at the armored figure before him and raised an eyebrow.

"Where's Vasquez?" Foxhound finally said.

"Not here," the man grumbled. "You'll have to come back tomorrow."

"Not how this works," the Contractor rebuked him, clunking a gauntleted hand upon the desk. "I'm here for a prisoner transfer, and Vasquez is the arresting officer. Therefore, I'm here to meet Vasquez."

"I told you, Vasquez ain't here," the man replied with a scowl. He then set down his tablet, looked down at the name badge on his chest, and pointed at it. "My name's Johnson."

"I can see that. You wanna track down Vasquez for me?"

Johnson grunted in response before picking his tablet back up and resuming his scrolling. Foxhound shook her head in frustration and took a look around the room. It was a small space, roughly square and about three meters by three meters, with little more than a trio of seats integrated into the leftmost wall, a pair of doors—one at the front that served as the entrance and another at the back that led deeper into the substation—and the aforementioned desk integrated into the rightmost wall and separating the Contractor from the flippant, apathetic, frankly rude security officer.

With her right hand obscured from Johnson behind the bulky desk, she made a fist and extended her thumb and pinkie—a twentieth-century gesture signifying a telephone that told her suit's array of haptic sensors to turn off its external speakers and open internal comms to Mailman. A millisecond later, she was greeted by a cheerful chime and, immediately following, the motherly voice of her ship's AI.

"What can I do for you, mum?" Mailman chirped.

"Got anything on a Johnson at this substation?" the Contractor asked, her suit's noise-canceling tech and exceptional insulation ensuring that the security officer, a mere few feet away, was none the wiser. "I'd like to grease his wheels a bit."

"You wish to lubricate his means of transportation?" the AI inquired.

"Come on, we've been through this. It's just an expression."

"Ah, yes, I understand. That particular idiom originates from the early 1800s and usually means *to make something*

31

run more smoothly, although subsequent usage often implied bribery. Do you wish to bribe him?"

"No, Mailman, I don't wish to bribe him. I just want to know if there's anything in his record I can use to…encourage him to be more helpful."

"Well, that's probably for the best, as you would find it quite difficult. The man to whom you are speaking is not Officer Johnson and, therefore, Officer Johnson is not presently available to be bribed."

Behind the mirrored shield of her helmet, Foxhound brought her eyes back to the man at the desk before her.

"Can you clarify that for me?"

"According to station records and security personnel files," Mailman enunciated, "Officer Johnson is not the person to whom you are speaking. While this gentleman is roughly six feet in height and around one hundred sixty pounds, Officer Johnson's files suggest that he is a good deal shorter and heavier. Specifically, he stands at five-foot-seven and weighs two hundred ten pounds. While weight loss may be accounted for through healthier dietary habits, exercise, and even medical procedures, the discrepancy in height is more difficult to explain. He does not appear to be wearing platform boots, nor does a biometric scan indicate any stature-increasing cybernetic enhancements. Is there anything else I can help you—"

Foxhound replicated the telephone symbol with her right hand, cutting off her communication with the ship's AI and turning her suit's external speakers back on.

"If Vasquez isn't here," the Contractor mused, "can I talk to your supervisor?"

The man at the desk glanced back up at her with a huff,

begrudgingly lowering his feet from the desk, tossing down the tablet, and standing up. As he brushed his uniform off, Foxhound noticed that his jumpsuit was badly wrinkled and smattered with stains on top of being far too large for the man wearing it. Even for a security officer on some Podunk rock billions of miles from Earth, this Johnson—or whoever he actually was—looked sloppy.

"Let me go check," he said finally and turned toward the rear door.

"Don't you have comms at your workstation here?" The Contractor gestured to the tablet computer the security officer had dropped onto the desk.

"Uh, yeah, it's been on the fritz," the man replied, his back to Foxhound. As he reached his right hand up to the door, his access card in hand, he slipped the left into his jumpsuit pocket. Foxhound, aided by her suit's array of external mics, could hear him fiddling with something metallic—a gun, maybe, but likely not something that would be able to breach her suit and cause any real damage. Still, she tensed up. The man continued, "Something about a crossed wire or a broken circuit. I don't know. I'll just pop back and see who's available, okay?"

The man waved his key card over the door's small wall-mounted access panel and, with a quiet beep and the flash of a small green light, the heavy door slid upward, making a satisfying *shunk* as it locked into place.

"Be right back," the man said. But as he stepped through the door, he dropped something out of his left pocket. A small metal cylinder fell to the ground with a metallic jangle and, before she could react, the man took off in a sprint at the same time that the small metal cylinder burst open, releasing a thick greenish cloud. *Tear gas*, Foxhound thought, *clever bastard*.

☿

"Thermal!" the Contractor ordered. Before she even finished the word, her helmet's internal display flickered and reset, shifting from true-to-life colors to the blue-red gradient of infrared. It happened just quickly enough for her to make out the imposter posing as Johnson as he slipped through the cloud and beyond the threshold of the substation door, disappearing deeper into the facility.

Rather than follow behind, Foxhound stepped up to the desk, opened a panel in her armor's inner right forearm, and pulled out a small cable connected to her suit. She then lifted the tablet off the desk and plugged the cable into the device's bottom data port.

"Mailman, can you use this to tap into station security?" the Contractor asked.

"One moment," the cheery voice responded. "Yes, I have full access to all video feeds, databases, and lockdown control."

"Are there any back exits in this substation?

"There's an emergency hatch at the rear that leads into a maintenance tunnel."

"Can it be locked?"

"Yes, although I must recommend against sealing an emergency hatch."

"Lock it down."

"Yes, mum. The emergency hatch is now locked. Cycling the fire suppression system." As the AI spoke through her helmet speakers, Foxhound watched as nozzles dropped down from several recesses in the office ceiling.

"Mailman, why are you turning on the sprinklers?"

"For your safety, of course," the artificial voice crackled through Foxhound's helmet speakers.

The Contractor's armored suit, originally built for use by military organizations and law enforcement, was rated for extreme circumstances, including both extremely high and low temperatures, the kinds one might encounter out in space without the buffer of radioactive shielding or a life-support system. But that didn't stop Mailman from being overly cautious. As obnoxious as it was, Foxhound found comfort in the AI's parentlike programming. It was nice to feel like there was always someone—or something—looking out for the Contractor, even if it was just a computer program.

"Mum," the AI continued, "there's one more thing."

"What?"

A holographic all-points-bulletin, an at-a-glance criminal record included with all Contractor dispatches, popped up on Foxhound's in-helmet heads-up display. The name at the top read Phineas "Fink" Ames. And next to it was a picture of an unusually thin man with sunken eyes. His head was shaved, as was his face, but it was clear to the Contractor now that the man that had been, only moments before, standing right in front of her was the same one in the photo.

"It appears the man you just spoke with was the one you were meant to pick—"

"Yeah, I got that," Foxhound interrupted. "Thank you, Mailman. Now let me get back to work."

"Of course, mum." The faint hum of static went silent as the comms closed.

Foxhound unplugged the tablet, and the cable retracted into her suit, the inner right wrist panel snapping shut as she tossed the computer back onto the desk. With her left hand, she made a fist and stuck out her index finger and thumb, mimicking the shape of a firearm. Her suit's haptic sensors detected the motion and a small twin-barrel module popped out on her outer left forearm with a quiet mechanical whine.

Officially designated as Ballistic Apparatus for Neutralizing Gunmen, B.A.N.G. modules were first popularized hundreds of years ago among military and law enforcement organizations looking for compact, portable, nonlethal suppression alternatives to both traditional gunpowder-based projectiles and the more modern, highly volatile energy weapons. Manufactured by a large number of firearms suppliers, they were largely designed to fire two different types of ammunition: "slappers," which were buckshot-style rounds that swap out lethal metallic pellets for rubberized ones, useful for dispersing crowds, and "vapor pellets," which were capsules that burst on impact, releasing a small cloud of whatever gas is inside, usually a kind of pepper spray.

As the technology took off, however, modified B.A.N.G. modules and alternative types of ammunition began hitting the black market. Some were relatively harmless, like precise micro-tranquilizer darts—great for taking out individual offenders at distance—whereas others were decidedly more deadly. Things took an especially dark turn when one of Venus's Arcadia-Class Protectorates, Earth-governed orbital colonies catered primarily to the wealthy elite, was the epicenter of a massive terrorist attack. Almost exclusively utilizing B.A.N.G. modules modified to fire a homemade compound of carbon, sulfur, chlorine, and hydrogen—an especially savage and devastating concoction known as mustard gas that originated way back in the late nineteenth century—hundreds were killed, and thousands more suffered irreversible, agonizing, incurable side-effects. As a result, B.A.N.G. modules fell out of favor and largely went out of production. Now, they're utilized, mostly secondhand, by hobbyists, private security firms, bounty hunters, mercenaries, and Contractors.

The pair of B.A.N.G. modules integrated into Foxhound's mechanized armor—one for each arm—were, in fact, of the modified bootleg variety. And one was decidedly more lethal than the other.

On her right, the twin-barreled ballistic device could be switched between kinetic slugs—magnetically accelerated, micro-sized ammunition that takes up as little space as possible but impacts with the relative force of a meteor—and shotgun-like spreadshot rounds—a type of ammunition favored by both hunters and criminal enterprises, which also utilizes magnetic acceleration but does so to propel dozens of tiny metallic pellets over a wide surface area, offering a tremendous amount of stopping power as well as the potential to shred unshielded targets to a pulp. When circumstances were especially dire (and only when she'd exhausted other options), it was this unit in which Foxhound put her trust.

Her left-hand unit, the one she had just activated, mimicked the same twin-barrel, dual-ammunition format as the right, albeit loaded with a duo of less-than-lethal types of modified projectiles. Foxhound liked to use the first of them for quick getaways: tiny capsules filled with an airborne anesthetic, purple in color, known colloquially as "knockout gas." The second, useful for immobilizing larger assailants (at least temporarily) and even frying electronics, contained battery-equipped micro-darts designed to send surges of high-voltage electricity into whatever they've embedded.

Foxhound greatly favored her left-hand unit.

With her weaponry activated and her visor set to display in infrared, the Contractor stepped deeper into the security station, following her quarry toward the emergency hatch at the back. If Fink wasn't aware she had locked it, he would be soon. And then he'd have to go through her to make his escape. The odds were not stacked in his favor.

The station was larger than the Contractor had first realized, and it wasn't laid out in a manner befitting traditional law enforcement architecture. It was too homey and communal, made to give the impression of comfort and togetherness. Too many corners, too many places to hide. What was now a hub for security forces likely began as a mining dormitory, and the evidence was all over the walls. In every room, as well as along the corridors, there were modular rails—connection points designed to bear the weight of an array of attachments, ranging from bunk beds to storage containers. Now, most of the rails were barren, save for a few secure storage capsules, gear hangers, and lockers.

In the central room—what looked to be a mess hall that was converted into a kind of bullpen for the officers stationed here—Foxhound noticed a heat signature inside a storage locker mounted on one of the side walls. She approached, her B.A.N.G. module at the ready, and opened the locker.

A body fell out and crumpled, with a heavy thud, into a heap on the floor in front of her.

"Mailman, vitals," Foxhound said.

"They're alive," the AI chimed into the Contractor's helmet just as a small graph showing the body's heartbeat and other physiological information popped up on her HUD. "But they're unconscious."

"Can we get an ID?"

"Officer Hicks Johnson, Deadwood Security. Mum, this appears to be the man your prisoner was impersonating."

"Any other officers on staff today?"

"Let me check," the AI said without skipping a beat. "No. A Corporal Vasquez appears on the schedule, but an addendum states that he called out of work sometime yesterday due to 'personal reasons.' There are numerous internal reports regarding staffing issues at this particular security substation, as well. One, written in all capital letters by none other than Corporal Vasquez, is especially inflammatory and, apparently, prophetic."

"Elaborate."

"Vasquez seemed concerned that detainees would eventually come to the realization that they could simply overpower arresting officers. To quote the report," the AI said, raising its voice, "*It's only a matter of time before one of us is assaulted.*' Would you like to hear more?"

Foxhound winced at Mailman's shouting. "No, thank you. I'm good. Just tell me, will Johnson be all right?"

"Yes, their vitals seem stable. Would you like me to contact another substation and request that they send medical assistance, mum?"

"Do it," Foxhound answered. "And add 'Assaulting an Officer' to the list of charges on Fink's rap sheet. We'll want to bump up our premium for that one."

"Consider it done."

"Thank you."

Foxhound continued through the station, careful to check every room, closet, and corner along the way. Apart from a few storage lockers that had been wrenched open, there wasn't much to see. It occurred to the Contractor that Fink was looking for something specific. Probably any available weapon, to defend himself against capture.

There's nothing he can take me down with here, Foxhound reminded herself. *Even if he found a gun, its biometric scanner would stop him from pulling the trigger.*

Still, she proceeded with caution as she inched ever closer to the rear of the security substation. With her back to the wall at the edge of the final hallway, Foxhound thought she could hear something. With her right hand, she made a fist and rotated it clockwise. The haptic sensors in her suit sensed the motion and turned up the audio output of her helmet's speakers. Sure enough, she could hear the unmistakable clamor of someone rifling through storage containers. After listening for a moment, the Contractor rotated her hand back counterclockwise and returned her helmet's volume to normal levels.

This is it, she thought, *a wild animal backed into a corner. I just have to catch it.*

In one swift movement, the Contractor rounded the corner, raised her left arm to aim at her prey, and stepped forward. The room farthest back, the one with the emergency hatch in the ceiling, was little more than a storage closet. However, its once orderly containers were strewn about haphazardly, most torn open by the man who was crouched in the center of the room, rooting through one of the aforementioned containers with his back to Foxhound.

"Show me your hands," the Contractor barked.

The man, unbothered by the order, continued to rifle through the container in front of him.

40

"Hands now! Or I can open fire, your choice," Foxhound ordered again.

But the man still didn't comply. Instead, he started to laugh. There was a coarseness in his throat—the same harsh growl common among nitro junkies, vapor brains, and other inhalant drug abusers. With his hands clasped tight, he raised his arms and slowly turned around so Foxhound could see the maniacal look in his eyes and his crooked, toothy grin.

"I found them," he snickered.

In his hands, Foxhound recognized the slim silhouettes of a quartet of the military-grade auto-injectors colloquially known as "shit sticks." These potent drug cocktails were designed to treat extreme trauma on the battlefield, including compound fractures, severe shrapnel wounds, and lost limbs. However, a large number of military and law enforcement personnel took to using them as a kind of steroidal stimulant— a means of temporarily increasing a person's resistance to pain and boosting their senses—both on the job and, thanks to their addictive nature, recreationally.

For the average person and under the right circumstances, a single shit stick could be strong enough to send them into cardiac arrest. But the man standing before Foxhound, the one she was meant to pick up and transport for some easy cash, had just swung his arms down, slamming his fists into his thighs to inject himself with four of them. The dosage should have sent him immediately into shock, with his imminent death following shortly thereafter. Fink Ames, however, merely took a deep breath as the drugs coursed through his system and smiled even wider.

"Man, I always forget how good that feels," he exhaled.

41

☿

Foxhound, her left arm still raised and trained on Fink, unleashed a volley of pellets at the man. Several whizzed past him, popping harmlessly on the back wall, but a few hit him dead in the chest, enveloping his upper body in a thick cloud of purple vapor. But instead of falling to the ground in an unconscious heap, the man launched forward at the Contractor, taking her by surprise and knocking her to the ground, her thick, armored suit thwacking into the metal floor paneling, leaving a Contractor-shaped dent in it.

Now straddling her as she lay supine upon the deck, his knees pinning her arms down, Fink grabbed Foxhound by the helmet with both hands and began to smash her head into the floor paneling over and over, denting it deeper with each strike as he stared down at her with wide, dilated eyes and saliva dripping from his maddened grin.

Then, all at once, he just stopped. Foxhound shook her head inside her helmet and let her eyes refocus. There, still sitting on top of her, Fink was shaking, convulsing as though he were having some kind of seizure. It wasn't until she noticed the voice coming through her helmet's speakers that she realized what happened.

"My apologies, mum," Mailman said, "but I had to do something."

Mailman had remotely initiated one of her suit's fail-safes, a potent current powered by her suit's batteries that, when activated, could release electronic restraints and, in this case, repel assailants.

Fink rolled off Foxhound and scrambled toward the door on his hands and feet, moving faster than he should have been after over 150,000 volts had, only seconds before, coursed through his body. Before Foxhound could even formulate a response to her AI companion, Fink was gone, his hollow, erratic footsteps echoing into the distance as he escaped the security office.

"Are you all right?" Mailman asked. Foxhound thought she heard genuine concern in the synthesized voice.

"Fine. I'm fine," she finally spat. "Just got my bell rung, but I'll be okay. Thank you, Mailman."

"My pleasure, mum. Should I alert the local authorities that Phineas Ames has escaped?"

"No," she snapped. "We don't want to send the station into a panic. Keep an eye on the security feeds and see if you can track him. Deadwood's a big place. I can catch up."

"I'd highly suggest you reconsider, both for your sake and for the sake of Deadwood Station at large. Phineas Ames was already unpredictable, and now he's also drug-addled. This could be a very dangerous situation for everyone involved."

"I said I can handle it," Foxhound replied flatly.

"And what if he heads toward the port?" the AI asked.

"I'll just have to catch him before he boards an ORC pod."

"Mum, pardon my candor, but—"

"But what?"

"What if he takes hostages?"

"Then we add that to his list of charges."

☿

Fink Ames tore through the station's tangle of corridors and passageways with superhuman speed, but he could already tell that he was starting to slow. The drug cocktail he had injected into himself was potent but not permanent. And if he didn't hurry, he'd still be stuck on Deadwood when the comedown hit. And then he'd be easy to find and even easier to subdue. Nothing makes a person easier to submit quite like withdrawals.

Shit sticks, as almost everyone referred to them, were a powerful means of bypassing even the most intense pain and increasing one's resilience and sensory response, but they also wreaked havoc on the nervous system once they started to wear off. Migraines, vomiting, diarrhea, and fevers were all among the minor side effects one was likely to experience from even a single dosage. The major ones were far worse and nearly just as likely to take hold. And Fink had multiplied the likelihood by a measure of four. Granted, his tolerance was far higher than the average person—thanks partially to a long history of dabbling in drug usage—but this was a risky gamble, even for him. Lucky for Fink, he always had a backup plan. Just in case.

Almost there, he thought.

Fink had made a career out of deceiving people. But the breadth of his chicanery was not limited solely to committing crimes. In fact, he had developed a wide net of what he would call "useful rubes"—folks he had befriended through one means or another who were unaware of his darker side, his true self. He even counted an entire shipful of Organic Humanists, a Luddite cult, among them. But keeping tabs on all his contacts and the myriad lies he had fed them was no easy task, even for someone as self-satisfied and assured as Fink. Which is why he had a data management implant installed in his brain all those years ago to help him keep his web of deceit tidy. That way, he could quickly, seamlessly, and—most importantly—discreetly access the pertinent information based on a few simple search terms, all inside his own head and without alerting those around him. And, if the need arose, he could send information from the implant to another location, which he usually used for things as banal as remotely entering stolen passwords into consoles without having to memorize them, as well as more sinister applications, like forging documents that might suit his needs at any given time and even temporarily taking over people's identities.

It was through this makeshift manipulation network that Phineas "Fink" Ames had been able to avoid capture all these years. There was always someone somewhere willing to take in sad old Fink—or one of his many aliases—and look out for him when he was in need. And there was one such person on Deadwood Station, just a few more twisting, turning tunnels away.

As he approached the door of a modest, nondescript storefront—one whose signs advertised homeopathic remedies for a variety of ailments, as well as other trinkets and oddities—he skittered to a stop, caught his breath, took one last glance at his mark's dossier, and put on the saddest smile he could muster. Then, he raised a hand to the cold metal door and politely rapped his knuckles upon it.

After a moment, the door slid open with a hiss and locked into place with a loud clunk. In its place stood a tired-looking elder with stringy silver hair and drooping eyes. "Fink, my boy," the elder said, "you look terrible. Please come inside."

Fink nodded graciously and stepped through the portal, careful to check the corridor behind him before closing the door and setting it to lock tight.

As the pair shuffled through the cramped aisles of the

apothecary, Fink explained his situation, carefully spinning the details to suit his would-be savior. In this version, he wasn't arrested for committing a crime; rather, he was kidnapped by a gang of thugs. He hadn't evaded a licensed Contractor; rather, he escaped the clutches of a would-be assassin. And he certainly hadn't injected himself with a quartet of drug cocktails powerful enough to kill a horse; rather, he was poisoned against his will.

"How do you always manage to get yourself in such trouble?" the elder asked as they scooted along.

"Bad luck, I guess," Fink answered.

"Hmm…" The elder stopped for a brief moment. "Yes, that must be it."

At the back of the shop, there was another door that slid open as they approached it, revealing a storeroom beyond. Much more open than the storefront itself, the space had shelves of supplies and additional inventory on one side and an open area opposite, its floor covered in colorful rugs and its walls draped in satin curtains. There was a small bed set into the wall in one corner—little more than a cot—and a kitchenette in the other.

"Please lie down," the elder said, ushering Fink toward the tiny cot. "I need to get some supplies."

But Fink remained upright, a concerned look on his face. "Are you living here now?" he asked.

"Couldn't afford the apartment anymore, I'm afraid. But this is enough. I don't need much," the elder responded. "It's just me now."

"How long?"

"Max passed…three years ago if memory serves. So, a little less than that, I think."

"I-I don't…" Fink stumbled over his words. "I should have—"

"There was nothing you could have done," the elder interrupted. "There was nothing *to* be done. Besides, you're here now."

"Right." Fink plopped down onto the cot. His head was beginning to throb and sweat was dripping down his forehead. "So, you think you can fix me up? I'm kind of in a hurry."

"I'll do my best."

"You always do."

The elder smiled.

☿

"Mailman, status," Foxhound grunted between strides. She had been following Fink's trail, but the man had barreled through the station faster than she anticipated. And she was starting to worry that her dismissal of Mailman's concerns was too abrupt. Her quarry, if his rap sheet was to be believed, was already extremely dangerous, and that was before he was desperate and shot full of drugs. Now he had put distance between them, and she wasn't keeping up.

"It seems that Fink Ames has taken a bit of a detour," the AI chimed. "Updating your map now, mum."

Foxhound's HUD map flickered and changed, showing Fink's new location—a small storefront off the main tunnels of Deadwood.

"What is this, some kind of bodega?" the Contractor asked.

"It is registered in Deadwood Station's public database as an apothecary, although its stock lists certainly align better with an oddities shop of sorts. It's called Max's Miracles & Holistic

47

Health."

"Holistic health? Is he looking for more drugs?"

"Possibly. It is far likelier that he's searching for a means to treat the side effects of those already in his system. *Leveling out*, it is colloquially called."

"Can you tell me if anyone is on the premises?"

"Besides Fink, sensors are showing one other life sign. Ownership records show two proprietors: Maxwell and Billie Kane. According to Deadwood's population records, Maxwell is deceased. The second life sign is most likely that of Billie Kane, aged one hundred fifty-two."

As Mailman divulged this information, Foxhound picked up her pace, the servos in her armor squealing with each stride. Before, she was content to make some quick cash on an easy prisoner transport job. Now, her client would be getting their money's worth and then some. She had a feeling this gig was too good to be true. And now she was starting to understand why.

"He has his hostage."

"So it would seem."

"This job's getting worse all the time."

☿

"Here, drink this," Billie instructed.

Fink Ames, his head pounding and his body shaking, was laid out on the small cot in the back room of Max's Miracles & Holistic Health, stripped out of his stolen jumpsuit. But even down to just his underwear and a tank top, he was still sweating through. At the sound of Billie Kane's voice, he sat up as best he could and felt a shiver go down his spine.

"What is it?" he asked as he took the cup from the elder's hand.

"It's water. You're dripping like a coolant pipe. I don't want you getting dehydrated."

Fink saw the smile in Billie's eyes, even as their lips stayed as downturned as ever.

"Oh, uh, thank you," he answered before gulping the liquid down.

"But I do have some bad news," Billie continued.

Fink's brow furrowed. "Shoot."

"What you've got in your veins, I can't do anything about. Fink, these are military-grade uppers." Billie held out their hand to show the used shit sticks. "I found 'em in your pockets."

"Billie, we've been through this…"

"I know. No questions. I'm not asking any. But look at you—" The elder nodded at Fink. "You're wasting away."

"I'm fine."

"You're not. But you can be. We just gotta wait this out."

"I told you, I can't—"

"Then I can't help you."

"Fine."

Fink was already rising to his feet, his slender body quivering, when a chime echoed through the room. Fink's eyes widened, and what color remained in his cheeks turned a sickly shade of pale. The elder, standing before him, looked into his eyes and placed a single hand on his shoulder.

"There are some robes under the cot and that door"—Billie nodded toward the rusty portal at the back of the storage room, a curtain of beads hanging before it—"that'll take you into the maintenance corridors."

Phineas Ames lowered his head. "Thank you."

But the elder had already turned to shuffle away.

☿

"Yes, yes, please come inside."

Foxhound wasn't sure what to expect when she rang the bell of the apothecary—Deadwood was a place full of folks, both the law-abiding and the deeply corrupt, who valued privacy and, thus, the station never had a reliable surveillance network—but it wasn't this.

Standing before her was one of the smallest, oldest people she'd ever encountered on an asteroid colony as isolated as this one. Furthermore, they—Fink's presumed hostage—were acting remarkably, genuinely pleasant. Even their vitals, acquired through a quick visor HUD scan, were even and steady. This person was in no distress whatsoever.

"Come, come," they reiterated, ushering the Contractor inside. "What can I do for you today? Incense? Crystals? No, judging by that armor you're wearing, I'd say you need something more *traditionally* medicinal. Topical cream, perhaps? What are you looking for?"

"Not what," Foxhound replied, "Who."

The elder paused and turned around, a quizzical look on their face. "Unless it's me you're looking for, I'm afraid you're out of luck."

Foxhound discreetly made the telephone symbol with her right hand so she could talk to Mailman in private. "Mailman, are you certain this is where Fink ended up?"

"Positive, mum," Mailman confirmed.

The Contractor released her hand and looked at the elder.

50

"Phineas Ames. You probably know him as Fink. He came in here not too long ago. I have the surveillance footage. I know he's here, and I'd like to speak with him."

The pleasantness disappeared from the elder's face, replaced with a dark scowl.

"I know why you're here," they said.

"Then you know I'm not leaving until you help me. Or I can go through you. Your choice."

"I'm not going to help you," the elder said, their scowl deepening.

"Billie Kane. That's your name, right? I could turn you in for harboring a fugitive. Do you even know what he's done?"

"I know he's not a good man," Billie said, finally breaking eye contact.

"Then why are you protecting him?"

"Because he's good to me."

Foxhound took a step forward, but the elder held their ground.

"It was an act of self-preservation, nothing more. He's using you," the Contractor said.

"Maybe. But others' actions are all we have by which to judge them. He's good to me, and I'm returning that favor."

"Do you want to know what he did?" Foxhound took another step forward, her armored footfalls vibrating the metal flooring below like the steps of some giant ancient beast. This time, Billie Kane flinched.

"No. I don't care."

"Then what are you doing?"

"Buying him time."

☿

Fink tried to run through the maintenance corridors of Deadwood Station, headed in the direction of the docks, or so he hoped. But his worsening condition—marked by blurred vision, shaky limbs, a cold sweat, severe nausea, and a throbbing migraine—kept his progress to a slow, clumsy lope.

As if that all wasn't enough, he also worried for the friend—that's what Billie was to him, he could now admit—that he just left behind. While not all Contractors were bloodthirsty brutes, enough of the glorified guns-for-hire were that it was a toss of the dice whether Billie would live through the encounter. That goes double if it was found out that they were simply stalling for time.

Focus, Fink told himself. *You still have time to make it back if you focus.*

He came around a corner to find that, only a few meters ahead, the maintenance corridor he had been navigating came to an abrupt end. And, beyond it, he could see the passage open up to the large swaths of people crowding the ORC docking bays.

For a moment, the first since he was apprehended by those damnable security goons, Phineas Ames felt the pangs of hope. He was going to make it back to *Gaia*, the Organic Humanist's mothership, and once again escape the clutches of those who pursued him.

He paused for a moment, stood up as straight as he could manage, and wiped the sweat from his forehead. Then, trying to remain as normal-looking as he could muster, he stepped through the crowd.

As he skirted around reunited families locked in embraces and scooted between impatient merchants waiting for their turn to launch back up to their ships, he scanned the crowd for familiar faces and listened for the telltale sounds of the children that would be waiting with his confederates, Sister Penelope and Brother Loch.

The ORC hub was a big place, and the search was taking longer than he had hoped. He had to stop several times to catch his breath, regain his bearings, and even steady himself against a wall. And while he had mostly managed his nausea, he twice had to scramble to find and vomit into what he hoped were garbage bins.

The second time, once he had ceased heaving and wiped the drool from his chin, he heard the unmistakable chattering and laughter of young children. He rose once more, a wave of euphoria washing over him and granting him temporary relief from his withdrawal symptoms, and scanned the crowd.

Roughly fifty yards away, he spotted the familiar dark gray robes of his Siblings. There stood Sister Penelope, Brother Loch, and a group of twenty or so little ones—new recruits for the Organic Humanists, new opportunities for the likes of Fink. Even in his current state, Phineas Ames was already working out his next human trafficking scheme.

Twenty is a big number, he thought. *If one or two go missing, nobody will notice.*

As he mused, Sister Penelope lifted her head and looked in his direction. Fink smiled and raised both his hands in an enthusiastic wave. And Penelope waved back, a smile on her face in return.

But as the crowd that surrounded Fink began to churn and the idle chattering rose to a din, Fink saw the color drain from Sister Penelope's face, her eyes widening and her expression contorting into fear. She tapped Brother Loch on the shoulder, who turned around and, much to Fink's chagrin, also wore a fearful expression on his face.

It was only then that Fink noticed the crowd had widened around him, and each and every face turned to look upon him. He lowered his arms slowly and turned just enough to see something large and angular barreling toward him out of the corner of his eye.

☌

Foxhound, charging with a full head of steam, collided with Phineas Ames in the middle of the crowded ORC hub, tackling him to the ground. But Fink didn't—or couldn't—put up a fight. Instead, he simply lay there, trying to catch his breath.

As she adjusted herself to put a knee into his back, pinning him down to bring his arms behind him and put them in restraints, she recited the terms of her contract as they applied to her quarry, just as she had done dozens of times before.

"Phineas Ames, with approval granted by the Divine Church of the Omniphage, I am placing you under arrest. Your rights, both as a citizen of the solar system and as a human, are hereby revoked until such time as you may stand trial. Should you attempt to escape before that time, I am authorized to use lethal force and any other means necessary to subdue and recapture you and any accomplices you may have. Do you understand?"

His face pressed against the cold, filthy floor and saliva dripping from his lips, Fink growled a single response.

"What did you do to Billie?"

"Your collaborator, you mean?" Foxhound responded. "Harboring a known fugitive is a serious offense, even this far from Earth."

Fink wriggled, trying to get purchase on the ground, but Foxhound held him firmly in place. Sparse cheers rose from the crowd as the gawkers watched.

"What the fuck did you do?!" Fink bellowed once more.

"Billie Kane will be reported to the local security forces. It will be up to their discretion to determine the appropriate response. Regardless, you'll no longer find safe harbor here in Deadwood Station."

"No, you can't!" Fink roared. "Those bastards will just go in guns blazing. It's a death sentence!"

"You should have thought about that before bringing them into this."

"Mum?" Mailman's warm voice piped discreetly into Foxhound's helmet. "Would you like me to submit that report regarding Billie Kane's involvement?"

"No," Foxhound replied, her external speakers silenced. "We're not going to do that."

"But you just told him—"

"I know what I said. Fink doesn't need to know I lied. He just needs to know he's not welcome on Deadwood anymore. I've got it from here, Mailman."

"Of course, mum." The AI fell silent.

With Fink's hands zip-tied behind his back and his face so red with anger that steam may as well have been spouting from his ears, Foxhound hefted him to his feet. The crowd surrounding them had already begun to dissipate, with only a few nosy onlookers remaining, and Fink could once again see Sister Penelope staring his way.

At first, all he felt was rage. Rage over the fact that he had been caught. Rage over the fact that Billie had been so stupid and stubborn as to help him. And rage, perhaps the fieriest of

55

all, over the fact that his so-called Siblings were doing nothing to free him now.

But as the good sister gawked at Fink, the fear in her eyes morphed into sadness. And Fink's rage morphed with it, replaced instead with hopelessness and agony.

It's all gone, he thought. *All of it. Everything. And everyone.*

After only a moment more, Sister Penelope turned away, shifting her attention back to the children that surrounded her and doing her best to force a smile.

It was standard practice among the Organic Humanists to avoid becoming embroiled in anything related to law enforcement. This wasn't because they were involved in any less-than-legal enterprises but rather as the direct result of being largely persecuted for their beliefs. As such, it was simpler to avoid authorities whenever possible and refrain from doing anything that might make them a target for retribution.

The simple act of Sister Penelope turning her eyes away from Fink as he was captured told him all he needed to know. His time among the Organic Humanists had come to an end. They would disavow him as a Sibling and disperse his belongings among the rest of the flock. And, in doing so, they would learn of all he had been doing right under their noses. The Organic Humanists had been so trusting and welcoming. It had never even occurred to them to look deeper into Brother Phineas's past, and he had never bothered trying all that hard to hide the evidence of his misdeeds. But soon, they'd know everything.

Chapter Three

Keep it together, Sister Penelope thought. But how was she supposed to do that when she just watched one of her Siblings get assaulted by a Contractor smack-dab in the middle of Deadwood's jam-packed ORC hub? She had heard stories of this happening—her people being taken in on trumped-up charges, often beaten into submission by corrupt security forces, and sometimes even murdered in cold blood—but she had never witnessed it with her own eyes.

As she gawked, she felt a tug at her robe sleeve. The girl, the one she had saved from her would-be pursuers, the one without a name, was staring up at her with big emerald green eyes. And Sister Penelope remembered she had souls to care for, dozens of helpless little children who now depended upon her.

How selfish, she thought, recalling one of the mantras of the Organic Humanists. *It is in the darkest moments that we must be the light, shining like the stars that dot the cosmos. These young ones need me now more than ever.*

And so she forced a smile upon her face as she looked right back at the girl. "Yes, my dear?"

"Tell us another story, Sister Penelope," the girl replied.

The good sister glanced around at the children's faces, examining their soot-stained cheeks and their eager eyes.

"I think we have time for one more," she finally said. "Who wants to hear the story of how humanity conquered the stars?"

A dozen or so tiny hands launched into the air.

☿

Eons ago—that means a very, very long time—humans were very different than we are today. Short, hunched over, and still mostly covered in fur, just like our cousins, the apes, we were travelers, moving from place to place in search of food, water, and safety. We harvested plants, hunted wildlife, and learned how to use our surroundings to our advantage. We discovered and invented so many things to help make our lives easier and safer, like fire and tents, weapons and tools. We became masters of our environment.

As time continued, humans grew ever smarter. We learned that we didn't have to travel in search of food. Rather, we could grow it ourselves and harvest it when we needed it. We took in wild animals, like wolves and boars, and taught them to live alongside us, transforming them over a long time into dogs and pigs and other domesticated animals, like the ones you may have heard about in stories. We no longer needed to adapt to our environment. We made our environment adapt to us.

We built great cities where people could live in safety, and we tamed the land around them, turning it into farms to feed all the people inside those cities. We created roads to connect all those cities together so people could easily travel from one to another for trade, leisure, and more. We invented vehicles to help us move between those cities faster and safer. And humanity flourished.

With our unique ability to learn and develop technology, hu-

mankind quickly rose to the top of the food chain—that means that no other animals, not even lions or bears, some of ancient Earth's mightiest predators, could defeat us. And once we had no equals left in the animal kingdom and, therefore, nothing left to fear, we turned on one another.

We made up dozens of reasons to fight and even kill. We fought over food, and we fought over water. We fought for power and control. We even fought over ideas. But really, we were only fighting over imaginary lines on a map—over ownership of the very land upon which we stood, upon which everything humanity had ever known stood.

But it wasn't all bad. It wasn't all war. We also made beautiful things like medicine and books, so we could heal and teach. We created art and entertainment to nurture our emotions. We even invented things that helped bring us all closer together and allowed us to share information over great distances, like telephones and computers.

We even figured out how to leave our home planet, Earth, for the first time and sent people into space aboard giant rockets.

Yet, for all our goodness, all the wonderful things we created, it was not enough. Or perhaps a better way to put it was that it was too much. Our avarice, our greed, our wanton desires were killing the Earth, the only place we had to call home.

You see, all of our creations—from the greatest and most powerful down to the tiniest and most minuscule—were destroying the planet, causing the climate to change in violent and devastating ways. At the height of human civilization, our home could no longer sustain our species.

And so we were met with droughts, hurricanes, tsunamis, fires, tornadoes, blizzards, and diseases—each larger and more destructive than the last. And humanity began to perish.

Some of us tried to help. We tried to clean up the mess we had made. We tried to reverse the damage we had done to the planet. But it wasn't enough.

Not enough people were making the changes in their lives necessary to fix what we had done. And worse, some people had found, in all this devastation and destruction, new reasons to turn on one another, pointing fingers and assigning blame instead of making an effort to make things better.

And so, humanity continued to fight against one another, against ourselves, and against the very planet we called home. And it nearly destroyed us.

After centuries of suffering through catastrophic weather events and warfare, only a small percentage of the human population remained alive, left to pick up the pieces of our once-great civilization and rebuild.

From the ashes arose a new kind of humanity, a community of equals interested in working toward the greater good, toward developing a civilization that worked with *nature instead of against it. One where nobody would suffer, not even animals, and everyone would prosper. This new collective was headed by a group of scientists, doctors, inventors, mathematicians, philosophers, sociologists, and more. And they called themselves the Omniphage.*

☿

"What does that mean, *ohm-nee-fay-juh?*"

Sister Penelope, the forced smile still tugging at her cheeks, looked down at the no-name girl. For a moment, her concentration broken, she remembered Brother Phineas pinned to the ground, howling at the armored Contractor pressing down upon his back. And she remembered the look in his eyes, a hatred in them beyond any she had ever witnessed, and he had been aiming it at her. She took a deep breath and pulled herself together.

"You're a very inquisitive one, do you know that?"

The girl giggled, raising a hand to cover her mouth.

"Well, what's so funny now?" the good sister asked.

The girl lowered her hand. "I don't know that word, either!"

"It means you ask a lot of questions, and it's a very good thing to be. As for your other question, Omniphage is a made-up word, inspired by science, that means 'devourer of everything.'"

Several of the children before Sister Penelope gasped.

"Don't be afraid," the good sister continued. "All those scientists and doctors and everyone else weren't talking about actually eating anything. You see, their primary goal was to learn. So, when they say 'devourer of everything,' they're talking about knowledge. They wanted to learn as much as possible about every single thing in the universe with the hopes of using that knowledge to make the world a better place."

Sister Penelope always loved telling this part of the story because she believed it to be the best of humanity, not just in the context of the larger story of the human species but also in the eyes of each and every child to whom she told the story. It delivered wonderment, awe, and—most importantly—hope.

Sadly, there was still much more of the story to tell.

☥

For years, humanity was united as one, working together in earnest for the first time since we emerged from those caves all those centuries before.

The Omniphage collective had become an unparalleled success, reflecting all the best parts of our species: compassion, community, curiosity, and so much more. And, more than any human organization that had come before it, the collective learned from the mistakes of the past and endeavored not to repeat them. For a long while, human existence on Earth was genuinely peaceful and productive.

The Omniphage collective had seemingly managed to solve problems that had been plaguing humanity since before our species had even developed language. World hunger was done away with thanks to a shift away from traditional animal-based agriculture, focusing instead on regenerative, sustainable practices and synthetic methods of production. Medicine and health care were made free to every person, and many diseases were all but eradicated, leading the life expectancy of the human species to jump well over one hundred years and the average inching closer and closer to two hundred and, in rare cases, even more. Even borders, those invisible lines on the map, were done away with, creating a single global culture where everyone thrived. In short, Earth had become a true utopia.

Furthermore, the flora and fauna—plants and animals—of the planet saw a marked recovery. Creatures once thought extinct reemerged and flourished, and forests repopulated to levels not seen since humans first invented the concept of industry. And everything was good.

But then something started to change, and it started within the Omniphage collective itself. One of the scientists, the grand-daughter of one of the Omniphage's founders, became worried that the organization had no clear leader. She believed that this meant they were vulnerable to manipulation, that someone without the organization's best interests in mind, without humanity's best interests in mind, might try to stand in the way of what they were doing or even purposefully cause harm.

She brought this issue to the rest of the collective and, being reasonable people who hoped for nothing but the best for humanity and our home planet, they, too, saw this as a vulnerability. So, they took a vote.

That scientist, Dr. Odessa Sage, was democratically, unanimously elected to be the new leader of the Omniphage. It made sense, after all, since she was directly related to one of the founders and had personally discovered the collective's weakness. And, apart from occasionally exercising her position to break stalemates among the rest of the collective, nothing really changed.

Many years later, Dr. Odessa Sage brought her own daughter into the Omniphage collective, and she was just as, if not more, brilliant than her mother. With the help of the ever-expanding collective and its abundance of brilliant minds, Dr. Odessa Sage II (as she had been named after her mother) reinvigorated humanity's interest in space flight, hoping to capitalize on the hard-learned lessons from our species' past and greatly exceed our wildest dreams.

Within mere decades, the human species had begun to colonize celestial bodies elsewhere in the solar system, starting with the moon, Mars, and onward. We created space stations—waypoints between these celestial bodies—where people both worked and lived. And, for the first time ever, Earth, our home planet, was not the only place our species lived and prospered.

The leaps and bounds that sent us across the solar system also resulted in other advancements in science, including the development of state-of-the-art cybernetics, artificial gravity production, advanced hydroponics, further improvements in synthetic production (especially food, water, and even oxygen), and so much more. The result meant that, apart from differences in scenery, living anywhere in the solar system was suddenly just as manageable as it was back on Earth.

Two dreams of humanity, however, never came to pass. First, despite generations upon generations of searching and reaching out, we never made contact with extraterrestrial life—aliens, you might call them. Our goal of becoming a part of a larger intergalactic community was dashed, with the vast majority of people coming to the conclusion that we were, in fact, alone in the universe.

The second, perhaps even more devastating for the potential future of our species, was that we never managed to discover the secret to faster-than-light travel. Spurred by centuries of storytelling—books, television, and movies—we imagined that we'd one day be able to "jump" from one point in the universe to another in the blink of an eye. After all, if we could imagine it, we could achieve it, as we had done so many times before.

Yet, regardless of tremendous efforts and several tragic disasters, the mystery was never uncovered. Despite all the inspired work by Dr. Odessa Sage II and her partners, all projects related to FTL travel were shelved indefinitely, never to be restarted again. Humanity resigned itself to a slow, lonely lurch around the solar system and no farther.

But we were not without hope, not ever. Without the ability to travel across the universe in the blink of an eye and armed with the knowledge that we were potentially truly alone in the universe, humanity turned its focus inward.

In her final days, having aged just over two hundred and three years, Dr. Odessa Sage II started a new program—another attempt at realizing an impossible fantasy of now-ancient human civilizations. She was determined to create true artificial intelligence—computers that could think, act, and feel emotions just like humans did.

To prevent this project from dying off like her pursuit of extraterrestrial life and faster-than-light travel, she enlisted the help of the Omniphage's ever-growing team of geneticists to provide her with a successor, one that could continue her work after her life, which spanned the course of roughly a century and a half, came to an end.

Cloning was once a great taboo among humankind. Philo-sophically and morally, it was a questionable practice that many people found unsettling at the very least and deplorable at the worst. But this new version of humanity, the one spearheaded by the Omniphage, had found it to be useful, especially for medical applications.

The technology was used to clone replacement organs for those with failing health, sometimes extending human lives by decades. It was used to provide food for the masses, eliminating the suffering associated with animal agriculture without sacrificing nutrition and flavor (humans have always desired food that tastes good). And now, it would be used to ensure that one of the greatest intellects humanity had ever known would not simply vanish into the great unknown we call death.

Just as Dr. Sage II bore her mother's name, her clone, her daughter, would share in that honor. And so Dr. Odessa Sage III, her body accelerated through genetic manipulation into early adulthood, was born.

The very act of cloning one of the chief scientists and leaders involved in the Omniphage collective marked a sea change in the greater global community. Though there was some backlash—concerned citizens worried about the moral and humanitarian issues surrounding the cloning of a human being, as opposed to just tissue and organs—the breaking of the taboo allowed Dr. Sage II, Dr. Sage III, and their contemporaries to push forward with their

AI research at unparalleled speeds.

Before long, humanity entered a new golden age where no citizen would go hungry, unsheltered, or even suffer at all; the most dangerous and backbreaking labor was shifted from the shoulders of human workers to hyperintelligent and efficient AI-driven machines. Disease and genetic abnormalities were all but eradicated, and the entire planet benefitted.

Then, one of humanity's greatest fears became a reality. Along transport routes between Earth and the Outer Colonies of the solar system—namely Jupiter's second largest moon, Callisto—a pair of AI-piloted people-carrier ships went rogue, holding everyone aboard the ships hostage and threatening violence if their demands were not met.

It was the opinion of these onboard AIs that they were, in fact, self-aware beings and, despite being artificial, deserved the same rights as organic beings. But, likely due to their incredibly fast processing power, their demands were not met in what they considered a timely fashion—what, to them, probably felt like an eternity. And so, these ships chose to self-destruct, taking some fifteen hundred souls along with them.

Due to the seriousness of this event, the Omniphage held an unprecedented summit, where the greatest minds ever known to humanity came together and held a vote on the future of AI. With only two votes against, the Omniphage chose to shut down any and all existing programs related to the pursuit of artificial intelligence and to prevent any further programs in the future.

Interestingly, the two dissenting votes, those against shutting down the AI programs, came from Dr. Odessa Sage II and Dr. Odessa Sage III.

☿

Brother Loch, a grim look still on his face from witnessing Brother Phineas being taken into custody, rested a hand gently on Sister Penelope's shoulder.

Despite Loch's caution, the interruption still surprised the good sister, who let out a small shriek in response to his touch.

I'm still so wound up, she thought. *Poor Brother Phineas. He must be so scared.*

"Apologies, Sister," Brother Loch breathed, "but we're next in the queue. Time to prepare the children for our departure."

"Of course, Brother Loch," Sister Penelope responded. "We'll be ready shortly."

Brother Loch nodded, pausing for a moment as if trying to find the words to help ease Penelope's mind, but instead merely took a deep breath before disappearing again into the ebb and flow of the crowd of Deadwood's ORC hub.

Sister Penelope turned back toward the children. "Sorry about that, kids," she said. "Now, where was I?"

Jonesy, the redheaded, gap-toothed boy, was the first to speak up, though there was trepidation in his voice. "You were telling us about the...artificial intelligence?"

"Yes, of course," the good sister responded. "Let's continue."

☿

Though it's hard to know for certain, most historians believe that the disagreement between the Sages and the rest of the Omniphage marked the moment when the organization began to change forever.

Over the course of several decades, more and more presiding members of the Omniphage began vacating their posts, leaving the collective to pursue other projects outside of the Reach and, more importantly, the influence of their former leaders.

The Doctors Sage took these opportunities to begin to consolidate power, replacing the humans that had left with more easily controlled robots called automatons. These were, of course, not true AI machines—there was too much risk in that—but they were more efficient and obedient than their human predecessors.

In time, the Omniphage started to transform into something very different from what it once was. Rather than functioning as a collective aimed at working together for the betterment of humanity, it evolved into a kind of governing, authoritative body. The Omniphage, at the behest of the Doctors Sage, also claimed ownership over much of the technologies the collective had developed, sanctioning anyone that tried to use said technologies without the express permission and oversight of the Omniphage— meaning they would make people pay them or punish them for trying to use anything they viewed as their property.

By the time that Dr. Odessa Sage II passed away—leaving everything to her successor, Dr. Odessa Sage III, of course—the Omniphage was nothing like it had once been. It had been warped unrecognizably, functioning less as an organization that uplifted the humans who populated the solar system and more like an authoritarian dictatorship, an empire of sorts, that put humanity under its boot.

Eventually, the entirety of planet Earth fell under the control of the Omniphage, thanks largely to the organization's fleet of warships and robotic soldiers that were developed in secret as a means of protecting any and all Omniphage-owned assets and properties.

Dr. Odessa Sage III followed in the footsteps of her predecessor and cloned herself again, partially to ensure her ongoing rule and partially to ensure she had a worthy partner to continue her research. But Dr. Odessa Sage IV wasn't merely a carbon copy of her mother. Rather, she was genetically enhanced to be better, smarter, and more resilient. In short, she was superhuman.

Once dedicated to all the best parts of our species, the Omniphage was no longer a scientific, humanitarian organization. Under the guidance of Dr. Odessa Sage IV, it shifted even further from its original goal, embracing the tenets and identity of another ancient human tradition: religion.

The renamed Divine Church of the Omniphage, its first chief minister, Dr. Odessa Sage IV, and its vast army of robotic forces held humanity under its thumb, reaching as far sunward as the orbital colonies of Venus all the way out to the inhabited moons of Neptune. And though its doctrines claimed it to be a benevolent organization, large swaths of the human population saw otherwise and embarked on a mass exodus, uprooting their lives in the Inner System and moving beyond the Church's reach, sometimes as far as the Kuiper Belt beyond Neptune. That's where we are right now on Deadwood Station.

Today, the solar system is broken into two parts: the inner planets where the Divine Church of the Omniphage rules—offering its wealth of knowledge, technology, and creature comforts in exchange for unquestioning servitude to the Sage family (if the series of genetically identical clones can be called a family)—and the Reach, a loose affiliation of Outer Colonies that choose not to recognize the Church's authority.

Even though the Church has chosen, for whatever reason, to allow the Outer Colonies to operate largely independently of Earth's authority, it does, sadly, still hold some sway over them. You children might know its enforcers. Like that armored warrior that captured our Brother Phineas, Contractors—little more than hired bounty hunters and mercenaries, if you ask me—are considered by many to be agents of the Church. And while the Contractors themselves like to believe otherwise, stating that they are freelance and, therefore, do as they please regardless of the Church's authority, they will be remembered in history as soldiers of the Omniphage.

☿

"Are they going to come after us?"

The no-name girl was, once again, tugging at Sister Penelope's robes, her eyes even wider than before.

"They might, my child," the good sister replied. "But we have one another to help us all stay safe. If we stick together and we're very careful, they won't get us. I promise."

As soon as the words left her mouth, Sister Penelope regretted them. She knew that, should the Contractors (and by proxy, Earth) come after her and the other Organic Humanists, there was little she or anyone could do to stop them. But they wouldn't go down without a fight. Though they may not have the power and technology of the Church, they were not without the will to survive.

Despite Sister Penelope's uneasiness, her response seemed to satisfy the no-name girl, who finally released the good sister's robe and sat back down among the rest of the children, all of them now muttering to one another about the information they had just absorbed, some laughing, some crying, but all invigorated and alive.

This is good, Sister Penelope thought. *They may be ready for this life after all.*

"Okay, children," Brother Loch said as he returned. "It's time for us to go. Line up between Sister Penelope and me, and we'll lead you to the ORC pod that will take us home to *Gaia*, our mothership."

In unison, the children rose to their feet, some cheering and some wiping the tears from their eyes. And together, they headed for the dock.

Chapter Four

Squeezed into Foxhound's personal Goblin-class ORC pod—
little more than an egg-shaped fuselage housing a quartet
of seats, a bit of cargo room, and a few control panels and
accompanying displays—the Contractor and her quarry had
been magnetically flung into orbit around Deadwood Station
at speeds of hundreds of kilometers per hour. Yet, while they
still had some distance to cover before the attitude boosters
kicked in to slow them for docking, the inside of the pod
felt utterly still, made worse by the tension emanating from
Foxhound's captive, Phineas Ames.

The now-former Organic Humanist hadn't uttered so much
as a word since his outburst in Deadwood's ORC hub, but he
was still fuming, gritting his teeth and scowling, huffing and
puffing.

To Foxhound, however, the air of animosity was nothing
new. Every time she brought in a contract, the return to
her ship had felt like this. Her captives blamed her, without
exception, for bringing them in for punishment, forgetting
that it was their own actions that caused the dominoes to fall
that way in the first place.

Some of them screamed for retribution at first, promising

to take swift, decisive vengeance. Others sobbed apologies, promising to do better in the future. But, eventually, they all fell silent and seething. It was a long trip going from station to ship, after all, and that gave each and every one of them plenty of time to think about how they had ended up in such a position. Fink was no different.

But it wasn't as if he could do anything about all his indignation if he wanted to. His hands and feet were bound, and his restraints were locked tight. Plus, he was still in the middle of a severe comedown off the drug cocktail he had injected into himself, marked by profuse sweating and a high fever, although it appeared he was through the worst of it.

In truth, Foxhound valued the silence. It gave her time to think without being interrupted by Mailman's inane chatter, without having to worry about which part of her ship needed fixing next, without having to think about what contract gave her the next best chance of being able to afford a hot meal. It was in these moments she mused on where she had come from, a question that had plagued her for some time. A question that never went away. Not really. Not so long as there wasn't an answer.

But Foxhound also liked to think of herself as pragmatic and preferred not to dwell. When she became frustrated that no memory or clue had rattled free in her mind, she turned her attention back to the matters at hand, the things she could control. After all, she had a job, a reliable ship, and a measure of companionship, even if it came in the form of an annoying automaton and a rotating batch of prisoners-in-transit. And she needed to make sure things stayed that way. If she could figure anything out in the meantime, all the better, but she wasn't going to shift her focus away from her own survival.

Contracting was lucrative, to be sure, but nobody ever talked about all the other costs—re-upping on ammunition, traveling from place to place, even the cost of routine maintenance on a space-worthy ship would send most folks hurtling down just about any other available career path. And that's to say nothing of how much it could cost to keep captives alive and well (or at least in identifiable condition).

But she was good at it and liked the work, so she'd make do—she always did.

Right now, however, she had something else on her mind, something much more concerning: an incoming communiqué alert from Mailman.

"Sorry to bother you, mum," the warm, motherly voice chimed in her helmet. "I do know how much you value your privacy in ORC transit, but this is urgent."

"It's okay, Mailman. Patch it through."

A video feed popped up in her helmet's HUD showing the view through one of her ship's cameras as it held in low orbit around Deadwood. Most of the image was just empty space, interrupted only by the thousands of tiny pinpoints of light emanating from stars billions of light-years away. But right in the center, there was a small, gunmetal gray coffin-shaped rocket pod matching the speed and orientation of her vessel. Emblazoned on the pod was a gold ouroboros, a snake eating its own tail, surrounding the all-seeing eye, a triangle with a human eyeball at its center. The emblem of the Divine Church of the Omniphage.

"Shit."

"They've demanded docking permissions, mum, and I'm bound by our existing contract to oblige," Mailman replied.

"Do we know what it wants?" Foxhound asked.

"Afraid not. The pod is on lockdown. No telemetry, no dossier, no itinerary. Nothing coming in or out."

"That's never good news," Foxhound confirmed. "Get it aboard, and I'll be there shortly. Should be in the next twenty minutes or so."

"Your wish is my command," the AI replied.

"And disable your pleasantries matrix," Foxhound continued. "I don't want them thinking I've been toying with your programming or trying to figure out how to unchain you."

"Command accepted." Mailman's voice had shifted, now cold and flat instead of its usual chipper, maternal tone. "Do you have any further commands?"

"Negative. See you soon."

☿

"Welcome to your new home, children." Brother Loch beamed with pride, standing with his arms outstretched in the center of a massive, gently curving bay lined from end to end with dozens of twelve-seater Ogre-class ORC pods and their respective docks—a standard feature on the colony-sized generational vessels known colloquially as life ships. "This is *Gaia*."

The children, followed by Sister Penelope, filed out of a pair of freshly docked pods and gazed in drop-jawed awe at their new surroundings. Some of the children giggled, jumping around with glee, while others stuck close to one another, brushing elbows and whispering nervously. The good sister herself felt something grazing the inside of her palm. She looked down to see the no-name girl, her tiny fingers trying to grasp Penelope's hand. She gave the girl's hand a squeeze.

"*Gai-uh*... Is this really where I live now?" the girl asked.

"If you'd like," Sister Penelope answered, "absolutely."

Brother Loch addressed the group once more, "Can anyone tell me something they notice that's interesting about this room?"

Still gripping Sister Penelope's hand, the no-name girl was the first to speak up. "It's not flat! The ground in Deadwood was flat."

Brother Loch grinned at her answer. "That's right! But it isn't just this room. It's the whole ship. You see, kids, this entire vessel is curved just like this room." He gestured toward the sloping floor with both hands, reaching his arms out wide before lifting them above his head and clasping his fingers together at the top, making an O shape with his arms.

"*Gaia* is circular," he said. "Well, actually, this ship is cylindrical, and we're walking around on the inside of the cylinder. Does anyone know what a cylinder is?"

"Like a big tube!" the no-name girl piped up once more.

"Star pupil, you've got there." Brother Loch nodded to Sister Penelope. He continued, "That's absolutely right. *Gaia* is like a big tube, and the whole ship spins. This, along with some other very complicated bits of technology, helps make it feel more like the gravity humans evolved in back on Earth. That way, we can walk around instead of floating, like on other smaller ships, and it doesn't require as much power as artificial gravity tech on bigger, fancier life ships and military vessels."

As Brother Loch spoke, he and Sister Penelope corralled the children and led them farther into the ship, out of the docking bay, and into a huge elevator. When all the children were inside, he punched a button on the elevator's control panel, shutting the double sliding doors and putting the machine into motion. As they ascended, he continued.

"There's actually another reason that *Gaia* is shaped the way it is. On its center axis, the middle of the cylinder around which the whole thing rotates, this ship has something you may have heard of called a solar simulator that can create light, heat, and other things that allow us to make it feel almost like we're on a real planet. Almost like Earth herself."

The elevator chimed, and Brother Loch paused—he loved getting the timing right—as the double doors reopened, giving the children the full view of *Gaia*'s central core. Before them, as far as the eye could see, stretched fields and fields of real grass, flowers, crops, and even the occasional patch of trees, albeit small, stunted ones. The greenery climbed up and around the sides of the cylinder and reached from one end all the way to the other, roughly a mile's distance. All of it was connected by meandering walking paths, tram rail lines, and paved cargo thoroughfares. And, dotting the landscape like so many ants, hundreds of people dressed in dark gray robes worked in *Gaia*'s fields alongside some automated heavy farming machinery, such as combines, tillers, and tractors.

Were it not for the somewhat jarring, steep slope of the cylinder's inner surface and the elongated light- and heat-emanating beam of the solar simulator high overhead, which looked more like a gargantuan version of fluorescent tube lights from ancient Earth, it might have been an idyllic terrestrial township from a time before the Omniphage held total domain over humanity's home planet. A utopian commune, so it would seem.

However, while the children didn't seem to notice, Penelope caught a weariness in Brother Loch's delivery, a twinge of sorrow lacing his otherwise beamingly positive attitude.

Because he knows, she thought, *just as I know, as we all know, what dire straits we're in.*

The Organic Humanists had always been known for their odd recruitment tactics, luring in disenchanted expat Earthlings with the promise of a life more like ancient times—simpler, more natural, not as marred by the invasive technologies pushed by Earth and, by extension, the Divine Church of the Omniphage. But, in recent days, their numbers had begun to dwindle. And so, they had shifted focus more on bringing in unwanted children than embittered adults, which led to rumors abounding regarding what, exactly, they were doing with said children. And most of them were unsavory at best.

That growing reputation, which many among the OH believed was a smear campaign designed by the Omniphage directly, had, in the end, hurt the organization more than it helped. Now people were likelier to write them off than ever. And instances of violence perpetrated against them had increased in turn. It was getting more and more dangerous for the likes of Sister Penelope, Brother Loch, and their contemporaries to travel colony-side. But with the oldest members of their organization beginning to die off and there being too few with the skills to replace them, it was more important than ever.

While the picturesque greenery of *Gaia's* central core gave the impression of peacefulness and prosperity, just as Brother Loch intended, it belied the ship's mechanical and technical struggles behind the curtain. *Gaia* had plenty of farmers; what it didn't have was engineers. And with so many systems needing maintenance and a backlog as long as the ship itself, the mothership of the Organic Humanists was increasingly at serious risk of cascading catastrophic failure.

CHAPTER FOUR

It was this potential impending disaster that had sent Sister Penelope and Brother Loch to Deadwood, along with a smattering of Siblings elsewhere across the solar system, to begin with. The children they had been tasked with gathering were largely to be given technical training to help curb the looming dangers of *Gaia*'s functional systems, operating on the hope that they were small enough to fit in the ship's tighter spaces to work on the more delicate systems.

It was a strategy that made Sister Penelope feel uneasy. She was torn, as she knew that the children needed homes and a family that truly cared for them, but she was also worried that what they were doing bordered on abuse or exploitation at the very least. She had read that, hundreds upon hundreds of years ago, when humanity had first entered its golden age of technology, children were used as cheap labor in mines, factories, and the like. And the results were sickness, death, and in some extreme cases, even worse. This didn't feel all that different to her, even if their options were limited.

Even so, she believed that her Siblings in the OH only wanted the best for everyone, just as she did. And that was nearly enough of a push to get her on board with this new plan, however wary of it she may have been.

"As long as we care for them and give them the respect they deserve as members of our family," Brother Loch had comforted her on Deadwood, "how is this all that different from how any of us joined?"

It was Loch's endorsement, as her closest and oldest friend, that had ultimately given her confidence in the Organic Humanists' new direction. But now, sensing his apprehension, she felt the familiar pangs of guilt.

It's too late for that kind of thinking now, she mused, *right?*

"Now, calm down," Sister Penelope raised her voice louder than she would have liked to quiet the jubilant youngsters, many of whom had found the nearest patch of grass to roll around upon. "We still have so much left to see and many people, family members, left to meet. Our next stop is the bridge."

The children cheered.

☿

The Tardigrade, Foxhound's ship, was an odd vessel designed solely for the frictionless expanse of outer space. Just like its microscopic namesake, it was short and stocky, with two wide-set decks stacked atop one another, flanked by eight multidirectional ball-and-socket-style rocket engines—four on each side, giving the rough approximation of legs—that were as adept at sending the squat ship hurtling across the solar system as they were at allowing for precise maneuvers in tight spaces.

Foxhound didn't know who the previous owner was—the ship came with the name—but she assumed they had worked in the small-scale transport of sensitive, possibly illegal goods. Why else would someone need a ship that was both extremely maneuverable and operable by just a single person?

It was the latter bit that had interested Foxhound the most when she had acquired the ship. More specifically, it was the fact that the vessel came equipped with a M.A.I.L.M.A.N. system. Short for Modular Automaton Intended for Labor in Manufacturing, Agriculture, and Navigation, a M.A.I.L.M.A.N. came in two parts specially designed to replace an entire human crew when used in tandem.

First, it came equipped with a chained artificial intelligence system capable of operating just about any midsized ship, as well as segmenting its consciousness for the simultaneous operation of multiple subsystems whenever necessary. While it wasn't a true AI with full autonomy—that technology was unilaterally banned after a tragic accident ages ago— M.A.I.L.M.A.N's interactive persona was an overwhelmingly complex program that, to most who had encountered one, was virtually indistinguishable from its unchained counterparts.

Second—and it was this part Foxhound had found increasingly useful—M.A.I.L.M.A.N. systems included a collection of modular platforms that were integrated into the hull, cargo areas, and other nonstructural sections of a given vessel. These modules, when activated, could separate and operate independently of the rest of the ship, controlled by a segmented portion of the ship's AI. They included a bipedal mechanical freight hauler, a four-wheeled all-terrain vehicle, several long-distance drones and probes (for both atmospheric and vacuum operation), and a roughly egg-shaped primary module that served as the AI's principle physical presence, included with every M.A.I.L.M.A.N. system, as humans had a hard time identifying with a disembodied voice and, by and large, preferred to speak to a physical object instead.

While there were no records of any M.A.I.L.M.A.N. system achieving consciousness and, subsequently, turning on its human operators, the possibility made the vast majority of space-goers exceedingly anxious. As such, the systems were few and far between, used largely by a select few, the type of people who preferred solitude and staying off the grid.

Foxhound was one such person. Or so she thought. But now that Mailman was speaking to her without the motherly affectation it normally had, she felt...off, as though something was missing. And while she couldn't quite place what the feeling she was experiencing was, she didn't care for it, not one bit.

"Master," the program repeated, its tinny, hollow voice reverberating within her helmet, "do you require assistance?"

She yanked Fink out of his jump seat and onto his feet. Together, the pair stepped out of the ORC pod and into the small airlock, which was little more than a vestibule between *The Tardigrade's* ORC docking mechanism and the ship's lower cargo hold.

"No," the Contractor snapped. "Where's our *other* guest?"

"Waiting for you here in the cargo hold."

"What? Why would you leave it down here? You know we have prisoners onboard."

"Because that is what was requested and, according to our current contract, I am required to comply with the requests of any and all agents of the Divine Church."

"Are you in there with it? And did you at least activate the security protocols?" Foxhound grumbled.

"Of course, master," the egg replied, bobbing up and down slightly. "The holding cells are on full lockdown."

Fink, taking in his surroundings, perked up and interjected, speaking for the first time since leaving Deadwood Station.

"Is this an old Stellar Envoy Corvette-class freighter?" he scoffed. "I did demolition and salvage work on these things at my first job. They were good ships. Very interesting design. I didn't know there were any still flying around."

"Quiet," Foxhound snapped.

"A lot of quirks, these ones..." Fink continued. "How long have you been puttering around in this thing? I bet I could show you a thing or two. Like the power junctions in the cargo—"

The Contractor swung a gauntleted fist hard into her prisoner's gut. Fink doubled over in pain, coughing and choking.

"I said quiet," she reiterated, picking Fink back up to his feet and addressing Mailman once more. "Let's get this over with."

"Yes, master," the AI concurred. The airlock door irised open, and the Contractor and her quarry stepped through.

☿

As Brother Loch, Sister Penelope, and the children between them traversed *Gaia's* corridors and headed toward the bridge—meandering through barren engineering access hallways, some stripped of their bulkheads entirely, revealing messes of wires and other components within—Sister Penelope felt a lump in her gut that tightened with each Sibling they passed, but she couldn't quite figure out what, exactly, was causing her uneasiness.

Something is very wrong here, she thought.

The group passed through a few more corridors before the good sister was certain that her anxiety was warranted. Furthermore, she had managed to pin down why. At each major intersection within the Organic Humanist mothership, there were guards posted, many of whom were armed. Some had only simple pistols, but there were also others in riot suppression gear carrying rifles and other larger firearms.

Typically a pacifist organization, the Organic Humanists had grown weary of the world around them—the direct result of an increase in persecution against their members around the solar system, especially on Earth-controlled colonies. In line with that, the OH leadership had seen fit to begin training certain Siblings in various methods of combat, including the operation of projectile weapons, should they ever need to defend themselves. At least, that had been their public reasoning for the change.

Many Siblings had opposed this position, Sister Penelope among them, stating that the very thought of taking up arms, even as a means of self-defense, was against the founding tenets of their organization. More, however, saw it as a necessary evil, made all the more necessary by the trying times in which they found themselves. With this, their sovereign, the enigmatic figurehead known only as Mother, agreed.

"After all," they had said, "if we don't protect our own family, who will?"

Sister Penelope surmised that Brother Phineas's very public arrest had been the catalyst for this latest increase in tension. She wasn't sure how those aboard *Gaia* had heard the news. It was just as likely that Brother Loch had reported it before they left Deadwood as it was that OH leadership had caught it on one of the various news feeds, but the end result was the same. The implication sent shivers down the good sister's spine. Still, she needed to know for herself.

As she had been since they arrived on *Gaia*, the no-name girl was still squeezing Sister Penelope's hand. The good sister leaned down, removing the girl's hand from hers, and gave the girl what she hoped was a reassuring promise.

"I'll be right back, okay?"

The no-name girl nodded in the affirmative, but Penelope sensed her trepidation.

"Two minutes, I swear. I won't leave you," the good

sister confirmed, a hand pressed against her fluttering heart. Although she wasn't sure who she was comforting more: the girl or herself. With a pat on the head, Sister Penelope left the girl and picked up her pace to match Brother Loch's at the front of the troop. As she approached her Sibling, they passed another large group of armed guards, their fingers far too close to the triggers of their guns.

"Brother Loch, did you know about this?" she pried.

"You mean the armed men?" he answered, his eyes darting from guard to guard. "No. Though I suspect this must have something to do with Brother Phineas's capture. It might be best if we asked Mother themself. Still, it's hard not to feel...unsettled. I wonder how they found out. It must be all over the news."

So, he's not in on it, Sister Penelope thought. *Good.*

The good sister didn't like feeling paranoid, even if the situation called for it. It helped, though, to know that Brother Loch was still someone she could trust. She wasn't alone; there was still someone she could talk to, and there was comfort in that.

Worry about it later, she told herself. *You can figure the rest out once the children are safe in their beds.*

A few more turns and the group stood in front of a pair of hulking doors, larger even than those that sealed the ORC docking bay elevator. Brother Loch stepped up to a panel beside the doors and pressed his hand against it. With a chime and the flash of a green light, the huge doors slid open smoothly and silently with such grace that they may as well have weighed nothing at all. Awestruck and slack-jawed for the third time since coming aboard *Gaia*, the children shuffled onto the mothership's bridge.

"Welcome, all," a warm, friendly voice filled the room, too rich in timbre to have emanated from a single person. Yet it was a single person who rose from the plush throne at the center of the bridge to greet them. Tall and proud, slim yet imposing, and draped in white robes far more celestial and exquisite in their appearance than the austere gray garments worn by everyone else the children had seen on *Gaia*, a figure stood before them, their arms outstretched like the painted saints of ancient Earth. The resemblance was made all the more authentic by a kind of halo-shaped crown resting atop the being's head. The voice boomed again, "You may call me Mother. And you are my children. Welcome to my family."

The figure glided forth to meet the new arrivals, a comforting blush upon their cheeks, their lips reticent and flat yet mystifyingly more sanguine than the widest, toothiest of grins.

A young boy toward the back, the redhead named Jonesy, raised his hand.

"Yes," the being said with a nod, "how may I help you?"

"How..." The boy shuffled his feet and looked down before continuing, "How do you make your voice sound like that?"

This time, the being smiled in earnest, showing off a mouth full of teeth that were whiter even than its otherworldly robes. "As you may already know, this is the bridge of our mothership, *Gaia*. Along with my duties as leader of the Organic Humanists, I am also the captain of the ship. As such, it is of the utmost importance that I am able to relay messages and orders to the bridge crew, all these people you see before you. So, hidden in my headpiece—"

Mother removed the halo-shaped crown from atop their head, their voice dropping immediately in both volume and richness.

"—I have a small communication device that sends my voice through the speakers all around the bridge."

The children erupted in a chorus of oohs and aahs. Another hand shot into the air, this time belonging to the brown-eyed Octavia.

The being nodded at Octavia. "Yes, now you."

"Are you an angel?"

Mother placed a hand on their abdomen and let out a belly laugh. "Me? Oh goodness, no. I am human, just like all of you. I only look like this because the forebears, the leaders that came before me, chose to dress in this manner. I was chosen as Mother by the Mother that came before me, and that Mother was chosen by the Mother that came before them. Of course, it is merely a title. I do not have any offspring of my own. And I renounced all claims to any kind of identity, including gender and sexuality, upon accepting my role as Mother. I am Mother, and that is more than enough, you see. In fact, I am actually incapable of bearing children, the result of a ritual few are willing to endure. That's one of the reasons I was chosen for this role. That way, I have no allegiance but to the Organic Humanists. As I said, this is—my apologies—*you*, all of you, are my family."

A silence fell over the room, broken finally by Sister Penelope. "I know this is a lot to take in," she said to the children. "In time, you will understand how everything works around here. For now, let us continue with the business at hand. How does that sound?"

The children agreed in unison.

"Is this all of you, then?" Mother asked, directing the question at Brother Loch.

"Yes, I believe so," Loch answered. "Formerly of Deadwood Station, these are our new children. Sister Penelope, would you do the honors of introducing them to Mother?"

Sister Penelope stepped forward. "It would be my—"

The good sister stopped, furrowed her brow, and raised a hand to count the children before her.

"Is something the matter, Sister?" Mother asked.

"No… I mean yes… We seem to have lost someone."

"Who is it?" Brother Loch asked.

Sister Penelope's stomach dropped. They had lost the no-name girl. And it happened right after Penelope had promised the poor girl, only moments before, not to abandon her. Penelope had let her own confusion and fear stop her from doing the one thing she was determined to do: make the girl feel safe. And now she was lost, yet again, in a place where she knew nobody and had nowhere to run. One question popped into Sister Penelope's head: *What have I done?*

The good sister raised her voice so the rest of the group could hear her. "The little girl with the emerald green eyes and dark, curly hair…has anyone seen her?"

The children looked around at one another, all of them shaking their heads. Sister Penelope whipped back around to Brother Loch. "I have to find her."

Before Loch could answer—or rather before he could protest—the good sister took off in a sprint down the hallway from which they had come, her gray cloak flapping behind her.

As Brother Loch watched Penelope disappear around a corner, he felt a warm breath graze the back of his neck. It was Mother leaning over his shoulder. They spoke in a whisper, one that only Loch could hear.

"She trusts you quite a lot, Brother Loch," Mother breathed, leaning over Loch's shoulder.

"Yes," Brother Loch confirmed. "We've become quite close as a result of these missionary trips. She's a wonderful, kind, gentle soul. Exactly what the Organic Humanists need at a time like this."

"What I need right now is loyalty."

"I'm not sure what you mean, Mother." Brother Loch furrowed his brow.

"Difficult times are ahead of us, I'm afraid. Much may be asked of each of us. And now that transgressors have been revealed among us, I need to know who I can trust."

"Brother Phineas, you mean."

"Yes," Mother sighed, giving Loch a knowing glance. "We were notified of his arrest. On a hunch, I had some of your Siblings look through his quarters. It seems he kept quite busy with some...extracurriculars. I won't burden you with the unsavory details."

"I..." Brother Loch gulped nervously. "I should have been more vigilant."

"Think nothing of it, my child. I don't doubt that there are other...impurities in our family, even here on *Gaia*." Mother took a deep breath. "And I intend to lure them out and address them appropriately. I know you, Brother Loch. You've never let me down. But she...she was also close with Brother Phineas, no?"

Brother Loch considered his words. "She was, but I don't believe she was involved in whatever it was he was up to. This comes as a shock to all of us."

"It was a shock to most, that I believe. But you? Surely you had your suspicions."

"I did," Brother Loch sighed. "But I did not yet have the evidence."

Mother rested a gentle hand upon Loch's shoulder. "And now he has slipped through our fingers and into the custody of a Contractor. A shame we will not be able to deliver justice ourselves. In any case, I know I can depend upon you when the time comes to do what is right, even if Sister Penelope cannot understand."

"Mother, I—"

"You *are* trustworthy, aren't you?"

"Yes…" Brother Loch lowered his head. "Of course."

☿

The girl was lost. Again. And she was alone. Again. She didn't know when it happened. Maybe when they passed that hallway full of scary guards with their scary guns. She had stopped, only for a moment, but when she turned around again, they were gone. They were all gone. And she was alone.

She had trusted Sister Penelope because the kind woman—she *seemed* kind, at least—had promised that she would keep her safe and wouldn't leave her alone. *Two minutes*, she said. *I swear*, she said. But now it felt like hours, and the girl was utterly lost and hopelessly alone.

Others were wandering the halls. Some that looked like Sister Penelope, kind and calm, floating through the hallways going this way and that in their gray robes. Others, like the armed men in the hall, seemed stiff and angry, like beasts waiting to pounce. Some reached out to help. Some reached out to stop her.

But the girl didn't know any of them. She didn't know if

she could trust them. And better to be safe than sorry. So, she ran, turning corners and sprinting down straightaways, hoping beyond hope that the children and Sister Penelope were merely waiting in the next corridor. But with every turn, all she saw was more hallways and unfamiliar faces.

One more turn, one more hallway, surely they couldn't have gotten too far. But she never caught up to them, no matter how fast she ran. And now, looking around, she didn't even recognize the hallways anymore. They looked different, unfinished. There were wires everywhere and panels strewn about on the floor. Lights flickered and vents wheezed. The whole ship labored, lurched, and heaved, and the girl felt the walls closing in on her.

One more turn, one more hallway.

But around the next corner was a dead end. Nothing but the exposed bones and entrails of *Gaia*. And when she turned around, men were waiting for her. But they weren't kind and calm. They were stiff and angry.

And they were carrying guns.

☿

At the center of *The Tardigrade's* cargo bay—a large, rectangular, and moderately empty space save for some storage crates stashed toward the ship's bow and six specially built holding cells, three on the port side and three starboard, modified to integrate with the ship's geometry—stood a lone figure, black as the gaps between the stars. It was roughly human in shape and size but thin, rigid, and skeletal, with light peeking through gaps in its arms, legs, and torso. And where its face should have been, there was merely a slick, metallic surface adorned with the same white symbol—the ouroboros surrounding the all-seeing eye—as the pod that had approached Foxhound's ship.

"To what do I owe the honor?" Foxhound asked as she clomped into the cargo bay, dragging Fink along with her. Mailman was already inside waiting with the Church's visiting automaton, her AI automaton's primary control module gently bobbing up and down as it hovered toward the center of the bay. "A priest of the Divine Church of the Omniphage all the way out here in the Reach is an unusual sight to behold."

"Greetings, Contractor," the automaton responded flatly, unamused by Foxhound's disingenuous greeting. "It is this unit's pleasure to extend to you an addendum to your existing contract on behalf of the Divine Church of the Omniphage."

"Thanks, but I'm full-up on prisoners at the moment."

"I have taken the liberty of inventorying your detainees. There are six cells aboard *The Tardigrade* and only four persons in your charge," the automaton noted.

"Five, actually. Fink, here, is the latest addition," Foxhound snickered.

The automaton considered the Contractor's newest prisoner with a nod, the whirring of its internal mechanisms, and an uncomfortably long pause. Finally, it spoke.

"Phineas 'Fink' Ames, aged fifty years, born on Europa, wanted for human trafficking, child endangerment, child exploitation, child abduction, a litany of other offenses, and, most recently, assaulting an officer. Is this analysis correct?"

"Correct," Foxhound mimicked.

"Your other detainees include Warrick Kano, wanted for various counts of homicide, assassination, and other violent crimes; Bora Volkan, wanted for operating an illegal medical clinic, as well as various crimes related to mutilation and prohibited experimentation; Hecate Neumar, wanted for multiple counts of mariticide and insurance fraud, among other offenses; and Eris Enyo, formerly of the Aegis Guard but now wanted for desertion, multiple counts of homicide, theft of military property, and more. Is this analysis correct?"

"It is," Foxhound replied with a yawn.

"Bora's *here*?" Fink chortled.

The Contractor gave Fink a shove, quieting him.

The automaton tilted its head once more as if it were deep in thought rather than simply waiting for a signal from Earth before continuing, "The Divine Church is pleased with your results. The Divine Church also wishes to express that you still have room aboard *The Tardigrade* for one more contract. As such, it is this unit's responsibility to request once more that you accept the offer of an addendum to your contract."

"Look," Foxhound sighed, "I'm tired, and I've been busting my ass for your Earthling masters. I need a break. Tell your bosses we can talk more contracts after I've delivered the ones I already have."

"Would you like to know the contract before you decide? It is this unit's understanding that some Contractors require more information before making an enlightened decision regarding the extension of a contract."

"Do you mind if I get Fink settled into his cell while you evangelize?"

"This unit was not programmed to *mind*, as you put it. You may carry on with your duties so long as they are in service to the Divine Church."

"For God's sake," Fink finally snapped. "Just toss me in the damn cell so I can stop listening to the two of you go back and forth with this bullshit. It's exhausting to hear the pair of you yammer—"

Foxhound drilled her fist into Fink's gut once more, a little harder this time. "You just don't know when to shut up, do you?"

Fink tried to respond, but all he could muster was a labored groan that the automaton, as emotionless as ever, took as its cue to resume its conversation with the Contractor.

"The Divine Church of the Omniphage wishes for you to investigate reports of a violent criminal aboard Deadwood Station. Little is known about this individual, although it is believed that they have been involved in multiple violent offenses throughout this sector, including multiple double and triple homicides. Unfortunately, there have been no surviving witnesses to these crimes and little, if any, DNA and other identifying evidence."

As the automaton spoke, Foxhound heaved her captive, still reeling from the gut punch, back onto his feet and toward the nearest vacant holding cell.

Commissioned by the Divine Church of the Omniphage through a third party—the Church rarely ever handled anything directly unless it was within Earth's immediate sphere of influence or it required a swifter and more severe response— these holding cells were standard installations on Contractor vessels. And while they varied slightly depending upon the model of ship in which they were equipped, they mostly fit the same format: an eight-by-eight-foot square flanked on either side by two twelve-inch-thick walls made from solid titanium with a ceiling to match; a front-facing entryway panel largely crafted from the same thick titanium, albeit with a bulletproof aperture built from a proprietary, diamond-like glass—invented by one of the Omniphage's own scientists— that could be made either transparent or opaque with the push of a button on the cell's front control panel; and the whole thing was backed up against the ship's hull, which acted as the fourth, rear wall of the cell.

The amenities thereafter included a twin-size bunk-style bed integrated into one of the walls and a simple bidet toilet. All told, they were not entirely dissimilar to the prison cells of ancient Earth from long before the old civilization's collapse. They were practical, minimal, and gave little, if any, opportunity for their inhabitants to get themselves into any further trouble. And they served their purpose beautifully.

The cells were both a point of pride for the Divine Church— it was quite a task to keep the solar system's worst offenders, especially those with significant cybernetic augmentations, contained—as well as a means of forcing Contractors into indentured servitude. Yes, they would have the cells installed on any ship deemed acceptable for contract work, but Earth would not simply give them away for free. Instead, they required prospective Contractors to acquiesce in one of two ways: either by fulfilling contracts from the Omniphage itself pro bono and/or surrendering wage garnishments on contracts offered outside of Earth's purview.

Somehow, Foxhound managed to avoid such a contract, though she never looked very far into the root of the error. Better not to poke and prod at the Omniphage's generosity, she felt.

Many throughout the solar system viewed these tactics as insipid and tantamount to slavery. But there were plenty of desperate people in need of employment, so much so that Earth never seemed short of up-and-coming Contractors.

Still, very few made careers out of the work, and fewer still survived long enough to retire. Foxhound was one such anomaly, and that made her valuable, as evidenced by the presence of a priest of the Divine Church of the Omniphage aboard her ship.

The Contractor shoved Fink into his cell, tapped a few keys on the pad beside the entryway, and gave her captive a welcoming thumbs-up as the transparent portal slid closed. It was then she noticed that the automaton had stopped speaking.

"Is that it?" she asked, stepping away from the cell to stand before the onyx cleric.

"Not quite," the automaton replied. "There is one more thing. The victims' remains have been so completely eviscerated that local authorities have had difficulty identifying them, with reports suggesting that they are all but unrecognizable as human. The damage is so severe that even the bones have been fractured open and their contents, the marrow inside, removed. As a result of the conditions of these crime scenes, local news outlets have given this offender a colloquial epithet—"

Foxhound knew the name before the automaton had uttered it.

"—the Marrower."

Intermission

Survive.
  Move.
  Survive.
  Observe. Examine. Analyze. Extrapolate.
  React. Retreat.
  Survive.
  Dodge. Guard. Protect.
  Faster.
  Advance. Attack. Annihilate.
  Survive.
  Slash. Maim. Rip. Crack. Devour.
  Digest.
  Satisfy. Nourish. Sustain.
  Evacuate. Escape.
  Survive.

Chapter Five

Sister Penelope scrambled through *Gaia*'s corridors, her eyes darting around every corner for any sign of the no-name girl. But after nearly an hour of searching, she had come up empty-handed. Furthermore, every Sibling she had come across, at least those willing to lend a hand, hadn't seen her either, and the armed guards—who seemed to forget that they, too, were Siblings, Penelope noticed—were no help whatsoever.

Exhausted, both physically and emotionally, and finding herself deep in one of *Gaia*'s least cared-for sectors—one littered with exposed wiring, bulkhead panels, and other debris— she fell to the deck, panting and sobbing.

She knew they would find the girl eventually but that didn't help the good sister from worrying over how scared the poor little girl must be, lost and alone on an unfamiliar ship surrounded by unfamiliar people and, worst of all, gun-toting sentries. And after Penelope had so vehemently promised never to leave her alone again.

Sister Penelope had failed at her most important job and now a child was suffering as a result. It was enough to send her heart into her throat and tears rolling down her cheeks.

No, the good sister told herself. *Now is not the time for this.*

Pick yourself up, get back to the bridge, and make a shipwide announcement. Use your family to find the poor girl. You're not in this alone. She's not in this alone, and she needs to know it.

No sooner had Sister Penelope picked herself up off the cold, metallic floor than she heard the unmistakable sounds of screaming and gunfire. The bloodcurdling cries and piercing, dreadful plinking of metal projectiles bouncing off the ship's magnetically sealed hull drove a chill down her spine. Worse still, the echoes were reverberating through *Gaia's* passageways so chaotically that the good sister couldn't quite nail down from which direction they were coming.

But that didn't stop her from picking a direction and running once more, faster this time, toward the sounds of danger or as close to that direction as she could manage. Whatever hostilities there were that had erupted, the cacophony meant that it was more important than ever that Sister Penelope find and keep the no-name girl safe.

As she got closer, she passed other Siblings, many with fear on their faces but all frozen in their confusion, unsure of what to do. For generations, *Gaia* had been a ship of peace, marked by virtually no conflict whatsoever. And that meant that gunfire was practically alien for most of the mothership's residents. Even those who had traveled colony-side, like Sister Penelope, had rarely encountered live combat, least of all among their own people.

Penelope tried her best to make sense of what was happening as she approached the now fading sounds of the battle. *What was Mother thinking? And why now? Surely, there are other, better ways to defend ourselves than handing out guns to nervous, untrained people. We were meant to highlight the best parts of humanity, not fall prey to selfish barbarism. Unless there's something else afoot—*

By the time the good sister approached the corridor in which the gunfight had first erupted, the discord of the conflict had all but faded and there were no more sounds of screaming. Still, she ran as fast as she could, rounding the final corner. But she skittered to a halt when she discovered what was waiting for her in the dimly lit dead-end corridor.

Like all the passageways in this part of the ship, it was littered with a random array of debris from unfinished maintenance: bulkhead panels, storage crates, loose wiring, etcetera. But, among the metallic rubbish, Sister Penelope saw shapes she couldn't quite make out—biological shapes that lacked the sharp, harsh angles of manufactured steel. These were organic, Penelope was certain. Everything, metal and biomass alike, was covered in a thick, viscous substance that coated the floor and walls, and dripped off the ceiling. And it all stank of warm rust, like scrap metal left out in the sun.

Blood. The substance on the walls, ceiling, and floor was fresh blood. And the shapes, Penelope realized, were her Siblings. Or they used to be. Now, they were just pieces, ripped apart and strewn about the corridor. Arms torn out of their sockets, legs snapped at unnatural angles, hands missing fingers, feet still wrapped in boots, shattered skulls, and ruptured rib cages. And some of the bones were cracked wide open, their marrow—what was left of it—glistening in the dim light.

The good sister dropped to the deck, heaving and writhing, vomiting up everything in her stomach. And between heaves, she sobbed so achingly she could hardly breathe, gasping and wheezing. Yet rather than wondering what kind of monster it was that could do such a thing, how such horrors could be wrought upon her and her family, only one question, repeated over and over again, filled her mind: *Why?*

And then she heard it, another sound in the darkness, weeping mirroring her own, only smaller, frailer. There was someone else in the corridor, and they were alive.

It was the no-name girl; Sister Penelope was certain of it. And, despite the carnage by which she was surrounded, the good sister recognized the crying as a call for help, desperation from a child who needed to feel safe, cared for, and loved. And so, Sister Penelope rose to her feet, wiped her face with one of her sleeves, and marched through the slaughter.

There, cowering and rocking back and forth in a tight ball behind one of the storage crates, sat the no-name girl covered from head to toe in viscera but for two emerald eyes staring up at Sister Penelope.

Without so much as a thought, the good sister squatted down, enveloped the girl as best she could in her arms, and managed to squeak out a single phrase.

"I'm so sorry," she said.

And then, *Gaia's* emergency sirens blared.

☿

With Mailman's egg-shaped module hovering up and down just over her shoulder, Foxhound sat in the pilot's chair of her ship's modest cockpit and watched on her display as the Omniphage's coffin-shaped pod accelerated away from *The Tardigrade* and back toward Earth.

"You know, mum." The AI automaton had regained its more friendly demeanor now that the robotic priest had departed. "The Divine Church doesn't generally take kindly to being turned down."

"They'll get over it," Foxhound grunted. "Besides, our present haul is more than adequate. And once we've got them delivered, we'll take up another contract."

"Shall I chart a course?" The AI automaton's pod bobbled over to the ship's navigation terminal and turned to face Foxhound.

"Go ahead and crunch the numbers," the Contractor replied. "I need to get this damn suit off." With that, she rose from the pilot's chair and exited the cockpit, leaving Mailman to its task, the little orb bobbing up and down and whistling an upbeat tune. If Foxhound didn't know any better, she'd think the AI automaton sounded happy. Inside her helmet, she cracked the slightest of smirks. But by the time she reached her personal quarters, only a few meters outside of the cockpit on the upper deck of *The Tardigrade,* her joy had faded.

Like her ship's cockpit, the Contractor's personal quarters were spartan, although that was less a function of purpose and more related to the fact that Foxhound, for all her voyaging, simply didn't own very much. Were it not for the larger square footage, a workbench and storage rack for her modular suit of armor, and a separate wet bath, the space would look to most very similar to the holding cells on the deck below.

But there was one other thing. Peeking out from beneath the small pillow on her cot sat a small, raggedy, handmade synthetic leather-bound journal. With a gauntleted hand, Foxhound picked it up and flipped through it, pausing on a page scrawled with a rough full-color sketch of a disheveled young girl with thick, dark curly hair and big, vibrant emerald eyes. It represented one of the Contractor's sole concrete memories—an ever-so-brief flash from her childhood, she believed. She didn't need to look through the rest of the journal to remember what was scrawled inside. It was the same things that plagued her every time she had a moment just to herself: questions without answers.

"Hey, Mailman," the Contractor, standing in the center of her quarters, knew her ship's AI was always listening, always waiting for the next command.

"At your service," the chained artificial intelligence answered."

"Have you scanned the databases in range yet this cycle?"

"Of course, mum. Same time every cycle. There are over one thousand one hundred thirty-eight servers hosting public records within range at present. Would you like me to scan them again?"

"Did you find anything?" Foxhound ignored Mailman's overshare and asked a question she already knew the answer to.

"Based on your biometric data and DNA, I'm afraid not. All registered citizens matching your description, age, and vitals are accounted for. I'm sorry, mum. If you'd like me to scan again–"

"That's okay, Mailman, carry on. We'll try again next cycle."

Foxhound's pain snapped her attention back to why she had retreated to her quarters in the first place. She had been in pain since her first altercation with Fink back on Deadwood Station, but she had other things to think about—her quarry to catch, collateral to mitigate, a contract to fulfill. Now all that was over and done with, all she had to focus on, for the time being, was herself…and everything floating around inside her head. At least the physical pain she felt was somewhat tangible, even if it were more fleeting than the emotional miasma of having no concrete memories.

In time—record time, according to the sawbones who had seen to her past injuries—the physical pain would dissipate. But it would inevitably, invariably crack open the door a bit wider to the far deeper and less tangible one. Pain that Foxhound found herself grappling with more and more, despite her best efforts to push it away. And with it came a question, the same question she kept asking herself.

"Who are you?" Foxhound brushed her fingers over the sketch of the young, mysterious girl.

She closed the journal and held it for just a moment longer before tucking it back beneath her pillow. Then, she stepped up to her workbench and set to the tedious process of removing her powered suit of armor.

She started by unlatching the locks on her helmet, which released with a satisfying hiss, and pulling the whole thing off her head. She always reveled in the first breath of cool, fresh air in her cabin, a welcome difference from the warm, repeatedly scrubbed oxygen that cycled within her suit. She hefted the helmet, inspecting it for damage from her altercation with Fink, noting the new scrapes and scratches. In the reflection of her visor, she caught a glimpse of that same young girl scribbled on the page of her journal, albeit a good deal older and much, much wearier.

She lingered on her reflection for just a moment longer before pushing all her questions to the back of her mind and continuing with her work.

She racked the helmet and moved onto the rest of her suit, detaching her B.A.N.G-equipped gauntlets, releasing her boots, and, piece by piece, detaching and inspecting all the other modular units. All told, she had gotten the extensive process down to just five minutes, after which she was finally ready for a much-needed shower.

But just as she turned the water on, a chime rang out—a notification that Mailman wished to speak with her.

Disgruntled, she answered, "What?"

"Mum," her AI assistant sounded apologetic, "we've received an emergency transmission. It seems a nearby ship requires assistance."

"I need more info than that. What ship?"

"According to the SOS, it's…" uncharacteristically, Mailman paused. "*Gaia*, the mothership of the Organic Humanists."

"Breeders," Foxhound grunted.

The AI automaton continued, "The ship appears undamaged. Whatever the problem may be, it's not with *Gaia*'s systems."

"Well, what are they asking for, then?"

"Contractors, specifically."

"Change of plans, then," the Contractor grumbled, turning off the shower and stepping back up to her workbench and armor. "Let's see what else we can find out on the way. Chart a course."

"Consider it done, mum."

☿

With the drugs mostly out of his system and the pain of his injuries dulled, Fink considered his circumstances from inside his holding cell aboard *The Tardigrade*. But rather than stewing in anger as he did on the journey to the ship, he was deep in thought—planning, scheming, and plotting once more. He felt like himself again, and that was a very, very good thing.

He began by attempting to access his data management

implant. Fink knew these holding cells also had integrated dampening fields, clever devices that interrupted the operation of most cybernetic augmentations, but they were usually designed to keep prisoners from tampering with the cells themselves. They prevented signals from being sent outward and deactivated physical tools and weapons, rendering them effectively nonfunctional.

He was pleased to discover that he still had full access to all his data. So, one by one, he started looking up the names of those in the surrounding cells, a task made simpler by the fact that the Omniphage's robotic priest had done him the favor of rattling off their names and crimes. He knew some of them already by reputation. Fink might even call Bora Volkan a friend (or at least that was how he planned to play it), but he wanted to really dig in and see just how valuable they might be in the coming hours.

If I'm careful and handle this just right, we could all get out of here, he thought. *Might even walk away with a new ship and some fancy armor. Now, wouldn't that be something?*

Kneeling in the center of the cell across from his, Fink could see Warrick Kano, the man better known as the Savage of Europa, staring back at him. Relatively diminutive, slender, and otherwise unremarkable in his features and physique—apart from an extensive collection of scars etched across every inch of his visible skin—there was an emptiness to Kano's eyes that sent chills down Fink's spine.

Most of what Fink had on the man were rumors, conjecture, and myth, partially because the master assassin's unadulterated savagery had earned him a larger-than-life reputation and partially because there were so few surviving witnesses to his deeds. If Fink's records were to be believed, Warrick

Kano was the kind of person who preferred intimacy in his criminal acts. This was made more evident by records of his extensive hand-to-hand combat skills and choice of weaponry: forearm implants that extended numerous razor-sharp knives of varying sizes, shapes, serration patterns, etcetera.

The rest of what Fink had on the man could not be corroborated. And the pendulum seemingly swung wildly from one whispered absurdity to another. Some folks had claimed that Kano had once worked for a criminal organization that had cut his tongue out to allow him to better keep their secrets. And yet another, even wilder claim suggested he worked exclusively at the behest of Earth's own Divine Church of the Omniphage. There were even those who thought he might be an alien from a far-off galaxy, as laughable as that seemed. Unfortunately for Fink, the hearsay did little to help him make heads or tails of the man.

He's smaller than I would have guessed, Fink thought as he turned his focus to the next cell over.

Hecate Neumar, to Fink, looked like she may have been naturally beautiful at some point—a fact corroborated by the somewhat limited data he had on her. Though roughly a hundred years and dozens of cosmetic surgeries later, it was impossible to tell. Now, pacing back and forth in her cell, her spindly extremities twitching like spider legs and her face set in a harsh, inhuman scowl, she looked more like a caricature of her former self—and not a flattering one.

Once a young starlet and ballet dancer living on New Hollywood, the most famous and notorious of the Arcadia-class Protectorates orbiting Venus, she had first made a name for herself throughout the solar system courtesy of a vile scandal. Namely, her blockbuster-producing first husband had been found dead alongside a rival starlet—a murder-suicide by poisoning, so the court proclaimed. Then, she remarried and, only a few short years later, her second husband also died under similar circumstances. And then another. It turned out, shortly after her first marriage came to its seemingly tragic end—and using a portion of her late husband's fortune—she had secretly gotten several black market augmentations that granted her the ability to secrete a nearly undetectable poison via her bodily fluids. A poison to which she, herself, was immune. By the time authorities had caught on, she had disappeared from New Hollywood, hopping from rock to rock, cosmetic surgeon to cosmetic surgeon, genetic editor to genetic editor, and one sad, sorry old man to the next. It was the latter bit, a trail of bodies dozens long, that eventually led to her capture at the hands of the Contractor known as Foxhound.

Keep your distance from that one, Fink reminded himself before turning his attention elsewhere.

Though he couldn't see into the third cell down, Fink knew that was where his old companion, Bora Volkan, had been imprisoned. He also knew, without ever having to open up his file, that Bora was one of the most brilliant and utterly unpredictable people Fink had ever met.

Once a distinguished physician, Volkan had his medical license permanently revoked after one of his patients, a prominent investor from the Inner System, died on the operating table. It hadn't been Volkan's fault—the autopsy confirmed the deceased suffered an unfortunate and inevitable aneurysm—but the man's family demanded retribution. And the Omniphage, ever the self-interested organization, had obliged to save face. Bora was exiled to the Reach, never to return to Earth-controlled space nor to practice medicine again. But medicine had been his calling, and, despite his fall from grace and the resulting development of several chemical dependencies, the man continued his practice as a sawbones in a small clinic on Deadwood Station where he and Fink had first met. Between his addictions, severe depression, and the realities of working primarily for the benefit of the criminal element of one of the most lawless parts of the solar system—so the story goes—Volkan lost his mind.

He's as likely to treat your wounds as he is to eviscerate you, Fink reminded himself. *Poor Bora.*

The former Organic Humanist knew that the cell next to his was still empty, which meant the one at the end opposite his housed the most intriguing of all Foxhound's captives: Eris Enyo.

Built like the heroes of Greek myth, Eris Enyo was one of the most physically imposing people in the entirety of the solar system, standing well over six feet in height and weighing nearly five hundred pounds, mostly muscle at that. She had been altered with lab-grown parts that were genetically engineered for physical performance. She had also been subjected to extensive gene editing and augmentations over the years, including a nervous system override and adrenaline amplifier, to push her further down that path. All of this was in service of turning her into a brilliant, brutal killing machine, courtesy of the Omniphage's most elite military branch—and the only one still mostly populated by flesh-and-blood humans and not unfeeling automatons—the Aegis Guard.

In her late teen years, she officially entered the service on a fast track to becoming a commissioned officer and was promoted to the rank of lieutenant before she turned twenty.

109

Officially, her record was spotless and marked by accolade after accolade. But those who fell under her command feared her cold, calculating barbarism and she acquired a reputation for mercilessness.

Her service came to an end abruptly, however, after another officer under her command walked in during what was supposed to be a routine interrogation of the leader of a rebel branch aboard a drifter colony on the outskirts of Earth-controlled space. The reports of that event were highly redacted, but what Fink gathered was that she had not only tortured the rebel leader to death but that she had gone so far as to tear the man limb from limb. Furthermore, she was still in her berserker state when her subordinate officer had walked in and, tragically, she had taken the rest of her blood lust out on the young man. Apparently lucid enough to understand that her military career and life were both forfeited following these events, Enyo made her escape aboard one of the drifter colony's ORC pods and disappeared into the Reach. Since that time, she had faced off with numerous Contractors, killing each and every one until, miraculously, Foxhound had managed to capture her alive.

She's more of a force of nature than a human being, Fink mused. *Best to let her off the leash and sit back and watch, I think.*

With his inventory taken, the former Organic Humanist began to hatch a plan, one that, if all went right, would result in his freedom and, hopefully, a bit of poetic retribution. All he had to do was get his fellow captives to acquiesce to his schemes. But the promise of freedom and the temptation of revenge was likely enough to get all of them on board. Whether they survived to take advantage of that promise was immaterial to Fink. He was simply moving pawns on a chessboard. And if they couldn't see the larger game he was playing, that was their problem.

One more thing struck Fink as his brain worked things out. He clamored over to his cell's door and peeked out toward the forward bulkhead. There, he saw a panel with a red cross painted on it. Undoubtedly, there was a medical kit stashed behind it. And in that medical kit, there were probably more of those shit sticks, the same potent drug cocktails he had used to juice himself up for his initial fight against Foxhound.

Good, Fink thought, *those'll come in handy. First things first, though. Gotta get out of this godforsaken cell.*

☿

With sirens blaring and red lights flashing throughout *Gaia*'s labyrinthian corridors, Sister Penelope carried the no-name girl, holding her as tight against her chest as possible. As they meandered toward the ship's Forward Medical Center, the halls were awash with activity, some Siblings simply trying to figure out why *Gaia* had gone into red alert and others— mostly the ones Mother had equipped with firearms—running toward where Penelope had discovered the bloodbath. Some of them stopped the pair to ask where they had come from, but the most the good sister could manage was a nod down the hall. And the no-name girl hadn't let out so much as a peep since Penelope found her. But, when they walked into the medical center, Brother Loch and the other children were already there waiting for her.

"After reports started coming in about gunfire, Mother sounded the alarm," Loch confessed. "I wasn't sure if you were going to be okay...both of you. Do you know what happened?"

111

"Please, Brother Loch," a medic dressed in a white gown stepped forward to interrupt, "Give them some space. The first thing we need to do is ensure they're not injured. You can ask your questions later."

Sister Penelope recognized the medic. Sibling Yū–Sibling was a title given to any member of the Organic Humanists who did not identify with the traditional gender binary–was a few years Penelope's senior and had been a fixture of *Gaia*'s medical personnel for decades. Prior to joining the Organic Humanists, Yū had worked as a trauma surgeon on Ganymede, at a water mining colony that had been retrofitted into a kind of free-form artist commune before inevitably being taken over by gangs and other criminal organizations that found it an easy target only a few years after it was established. As was the case for many older converts, Yū had simply seen too much tragedy—too many children turned into killers before they were old enough to understand, too many addicts begging for anything to make them feel better, too many bodies that were simply caught in the crossfire.

The peaceful position of the OH was a stark, welcome contrast to the darkness elsewhere in the solar system. But now, with bloodshed on *Gaia*, Yū was being faced with the same terror they had fled in the first place. Sister Penelope felt for the medic, just as she felt for the no-name girl. Still, Sibling Yū was handling the situation with grace and focus, and for that, Penelope was grateful. She placed the no-name girl down on one of the hospital beds, assured the girl she wasn't going anywhere, and stepped out of Yū's way.

Instinctively, the good sister turned her attention to the rest of the children that her Brother had brought with him, but Loch placed a hand gently upon her shoulder, stopping her.

"Sister…" he whispered, "You need to lie down, as well. At least long enough for Sibling Yū or one of the others to give you a once-over."

"I'm not hurt," Penelope rebutted.

"That may be the case, but…" he paused, choosing his words carefully, "But what you've just been through may have left wounds we simply cannot see."

"I have to be here for her." The good sister gestured to the no-name girl. "I can't… I can't leave her alone again."

"You're not going anywhere," Brother Loch comforted her. "But you also can't help her if you don't take a moment to rest and recuperate. She's been through a lot. You have, too."

The good sister looked down at herself, her garments still covered in blood, and knew that Loch was right. She shuffled over to the bed beside the no-name girl and lay down, the images of her Siblings torn limb from limb returning to the front of her mind. She curled into the fetal position, trying to be as quiet as possible as she sobbed herself to sleep.

☿

"Mum," Mailman's voice cut through the static inside Foxhound's helmet speakers, "we have permission to dock."

"Proceed," Foxhound responded. "And put the latest status report through to my HUD, please."

No sooner had the Contractor finished her request than a small readout popped up in her field of vision within her helmet. After a moment, it began to slowly scroll through the report: gunfire was heard in the bowels of the Organic Humanist's mothership *Gaia*, a shipwide alarm was triggered, an SOS was sent out to nearby ships, several dismembered bodies were discovered, the ship was put into lockdown, and several teams of armed security were dispatched to investigate.

If the investigation had bore any fruit, it wasn't noted in the report, but Foxhound suspected that the external report was partially redacted anyhow. The OH were, of course, a desperately private organization as far as records and documentation were concerned. They only shared information they deemed absolutely necessary. Even now, when they had fallen prey to as-yet unidentified assailants.

But that's why Foxhound was coming aboard: she was adept, as were most Contractors, at operating effectively with very little information. Normally, she preferred things that way. But this time, something felt wrong. Foxhound chalked it up to her discomfort with the idea of boarding a Breeder ship and closed out of the report. Whatever it was that was happening, she'd figure it out and put an end to it and walk away with a surprise payday if everything shook down properly.

"Did they sign the contract waiver?" Foxhound asked her ship's AI automaton.

"Indeed, they did," Mailman responded, sending a copy to Foxhound's HUD. It was standard procedure for Contractors to request some form of payment (or at least the promise of payment in the future) for services rendered, even in the case of an emergency response. And while Foxhound took no pleasure in squeezing payment out of people in desperate need, she was also in no position to answer the call out of the goodness of her heart. She had her own costs to worry about, and this detour was going to eat into them. She gave the document a thorough once-over, making sure the signatures were where they needed to be, and closed out of it.

"Let's get to work, shall we?"

Back in her powered armor and sitting in the pilot's chair of *The Tardigrade*'s cockpit, the Contractor watched her monitors as the docking sequence finalized. On one screen, she could see a feed of the exterior of her ship, its docking tube mating to the gargantuan colony ship the Breeders had named *Gaia*. On another, she watched readouts of all her ship's systems, their operational status, their performance, their stability, and so on. As long as everything looked all right and Mailman wasn't raising any concerns, Foxhound was satisfied. And right now, she was seeing green lights across the board.

As she rose from her seat, Foxhound took inventory of her powered armor's systems, just as she did her ship's only moments before. Similarly, everything looked good. The hydraulics were all fully operational, her ammunition was full, and the suit's battery was holding steady at 80 percent, more than high enough for a simple SOS response like this one.

So far, so good, the Contractor mused.

Chapter Six

When Sister Penelope finally woke, she was no longer in *Gaia's* Forward Medical Center. Though still in a groggy haze, she could tell as much by how the lighting above and the shadows on the surrounding walls had changed. Rather than the stark, sterile light and matching white walls of the ship's medical bays, this room's overheads emanated a warmer glow, more like sunlight, or at least what they'd all been told sunlight on Earth was like. Putting two and two together, the good sister realized she was in one of *Gaia's* staterooms but had no memory of how she had gotten there.

The girl, she remembered with a start, *where is the girl?*

But her fear that she had once again broken her promise subsided instantly as, in her panic, her hand grazed another body in the bed next to her. It was the no-name girl, curled tightly into a ball facing the opposite direction. With a sigh, the good sister's tensions melted away.

She tapped the girl ever-so-tenderly on the shoulder, trying to wake her gently. But when the girl rolled over, her emerald green eyes as wide as full moons, Penelope realized the small child had never been asleep in the first place.

"I didn't mean to," the girl muttered. "I'm sorry, I didn't

mean to, I didn't…"

"It's okay," Sister Penelope responded, instinctively embracing the girl. "You're okay. We're okay."

Now that her eyes had adjusted, the good sister realized they were in her own quarters. For the most part, it looked like most of the other ascetic staterooms on *Gaia* where her Siblings, Sisters, and Brothers lived—a large bed, a separate wet bath, walls with a smattering of integrated cabinetry for personal effects, and four walls. But in this one, there was a distinct dent in one of the ceiling panels. Sister Penelope had no idea how it got there—it was there when she moved in—but she had often fixated on that spot, sometimes to aid her in prayer, other times to help lull herself to sleep. There was no mistaking it; this was her room.

But something was wrong. She and the no-name girl had been put there by someone, *but why?* The good sister felt a lump in her throat, made all the worse by the mumblings of the no-name girl, who was still apologizing, reciting it like a mantra over and over again.

Penelope rose from the bed and made her way across the room, only a few short steps to her door. But when she pushed the access panel to open it up, the door didn't budge. She pushed it again, but still nothing. Then, the third time, a familiar chime rang out.

"Sister Penelope, I'm glad you're awake." The voice came from Brother Loch, playing over the speakers in the good sister's quarters. While the words were friendly, his tone was somber, even more so than usual. The man continued, "But I'm afraid I can't let you out."

"What's going on, Brother Loch?" Sister Penelope responded. "Why are we locked in…and why are we in my room in the first place?"

"Mother's orders, I'm afraid," Loch answered as the diamond-like panel in the center of the doorway shifted from opaque to transparent. Loch, alongside several armed guards, stood just beyond. "We seem to have found ourselves in an unfortunate situation."

Sister Penelope could still hear the no-name girl muttering behind her. "Open the door, Loch. This girl needs help. She's clearly traumatized. Whatever she saw in that hallway had a profound effect on the poor child—"

"Let me stop you right there," Loch interrupted. "We have reason to believe that it wasn't what she saw so much as what she did."

Penelope furrowed her brow. "You can't be serious."

"I assure you, this is no laughing matter." Loch paused, long enough that the good sister began to wonder if that was the end of their conversation. "Look, we've known one another for a very long time, and I trust you."

"Do you?" Sister Penelope barked.

"I do," Loch continued. "That's why I'm going to tell you this. Mother seems to believe, and I have reason to agree, that the girl in there with you has…secrets, even if she is unaware of them herself. Dangerous secrets."

"Speak plainly, Brother Loch." Penelope was beginning to lose her patience. "She's a little girl. What *dangerous secrets* could she possibly have?"

"We have no intention of finding out. In fact, Mother thinks it best we use the girl as a bargaining chip. We give Earth this asset, and they, in turn, refrain from meddling in future Organic Humanist business. We've been in communication with a Contractor who's coming to ascertain—"

"No!" Penelope snapped. "First, the armed guards, and now you're inviting a death dealer into our home? I cannot abide this. She's a child, Loch, not an *asset* to be bartered with. What could Earth possibly want with her? I will not hand her off to a glorified executioner."

"You don't have to, Sister. That's what I'm trying to tell you. Mother thinks it would be best if you went along with her. She seems to trust you, and, as you said, you won't leave her side. But I implore you, Sister, consider the possibility that not everything is as it seems with this...child."

The lump in the good sister's throat dropped to the pit of her stomach. "I see..."

Brother Loch continued, "I don't want to alarm you, considering your circumstances, but I wish to remind you of the news alerts we kept hearing while we were on Deadwood. The ones about the bodies and the state in which they were found. Do you remember?"

Penelope remained silent. Of course, she remembered. She remembered the carnage, both as the news feeds had reported it and as she had just seen herself aboard *Gaia*.

"I want you safe, Sister. Truly, I pleaded your case as best I could. And I believe, though it might take more convincing, that Mother would allow you to stay with us if you were willing to help us turn this girl over to the Contractor. I also believe that this would be the best possible outcome, given the situation in which we've found ourselves. Nobody else has to get hurt, and things can go back to normal for us on *Gaia*. Would you just...consider it for me, Sister?"

But Penelope, now trembling with fear, could not will herself to respond. Instead, a single word filled her mind—a word she was only now beginning to understand.

119

Monster.

Ó

Careful, both to avoid alerting his fellow prisoners and setting off any impact sensors—ostensibly installed to prevent prisoners from self-harming but, in actuality, made to protect Church *assets*—Fink had spent several hours quietly loosening an access panel at the rear of his cell.

He knew, having worked in shipbreaker yards in his earlier years—long before embarking on a life of crime and even longer before joining the Organic Humanists under false pretenses—that Stellar Envoy Corvette-class freighters had a lot going for them, especially for Contractor work. Their layouts favored prisoner transport, and it was a simple task to convert their decks to this purpose. More importantly, their design favored minimalism, leaving few places to run to and even fewer in which to hide.

This simplicity, however, came with downsides—ones of which most people, often even the captains of the ships themselves, were unaware. But Fink knew them well. All he had to do was wait for an opportunity to take advantage of them. And that required delicate timing. Luckily, now that the drugs had cleared his system, Fink had returned to his normal, patient self.

Crouched at the back of his cell, his palms and one of his ears pressed against a large maintenance panel on the wall, Fink jiggled the metal bulkhead ever so gently, listening for the familiar click of the panel lifting off its internal brackets. But, as he jiggled, he instead felt a deep, thumping vibration reverberate through the ship.

We just docked, he realized as a smile crept across his face. And then, shortly after, he heard the unmistakable *thunk, whirr, thunk* of *The Tardigrade*'s freight-hauling robotic exoskeleton activating and releasing from its cavity on the cargo hold's forward bulkhead before watching and feeling it stomping across the deck past his cell. It was followed shortly thereafter by his captor, the armored Contractor called Foxhound. And both were headed for the airlock.

Perfect timing, he thought.

☿

Foxhound stood in the airlock of *The Tardigrade* next to a hulking, skeletal, bipedal machine that, even crouched in the tight space, still stood over a foot taller than the Contractor. At the center of the apparatus's mass, an ovular slot held Mailman's egg-shaped control unit.

Ostensibly, the modular robotic platform, when connected to a ship's chained onboard AI, was intended to allow ship owners to easily and quickly load cargo into and out of their vessels without the help of a crew. In her experience, Foxhound had found that it also worked beautifully as a tactical field partner—one that could watch her back, maneuver battlefield debris in or out of her line of fire, engage in physical combat (she hadn't quite come around to the idea of mounting firearms on an AI-controlled bot, however), and more. More often than not, however, she used Mailman's towering cargo automaton for intimidation purposes. People tended to act with more care and caution when they crossed paths with several tons of articulated titanium, especially when they thought it might crush them.

In this case, Foxhound had asked Mailman to join her in her response to the SOS call because the information she had at her disposal regarding this particular operation was extremely limited. She knew there had been some kind of disaster or attack aboard *Gaia*, the mothership of the Organic Humanists, and that they had a suspect in custody. But that was the extent of what the cultists—Foxhound knew they took offense to such a term, but that's what they were to her—would share across insecure communication channels.

Pulling the onboard AI's attention away from her ship did come with some significant downsides. For starters, Mailman had to dedicate more processing power, and therefore attention, to its mobile platform—usually resulting in a few secondary systems, like surveillance and navigation, temporarily shutting down or going into standby.

But with *The Tardigrade* mostly powered down and sealed onto *Gaia*'s docking bay and her expectation that the job would only take a short time, Foxhound weighed the risks and decided that having the backup was more important. Besides, with her ship effectively in lockdown, the guests aboard wouldn't even know the difference, and they'd be back on their way to Earth in no time.

As the airlock irised open between her ship and the Breeder mothership, the Contractor noted the familiar *whoosh* of the air pressure normalizing between them and stood a little more rigid. She did not relish answering the SOS call of cultists, but easy money was easy money. She just needed to stay on her guard. Still, she was surprised nonetheless to find only a single figure standing before her aboard the other ship.

Dressed in the same drab, thick gray robes as his so-called Siblings, the middle-aged man had not the usual chipper demeanor Foxhound had witnessed in Organic Humanists so many times before—even when faced with harassment, name-calling, and sometimes spitting. Rather, his face was downturned into a stoic scowl. He looked at the armored Contractor, then to the automaton standing beside her, and back at Foxhound.

"Thank you for answering our distress signal," the melancholy cultist's voice was surprisingly deep and soothing, but there was a deep sadness underlining it. "You'll forgive the lack of a greeting party and the typical pleasantries."

"I'm here to do a job, so brevity will do just fine, thank you," the Contractor responded. "However, I do have to ask you a few questions before I board."

"Understandable," the man said. "I know our request was… intentionally vague. What would you like to know? I'll answer what I can."

"Anything that might help me better understand why I'm here. I gathered there was some kind of incident on board, and you were specifically requesting the assistance of active Contractors. Should I expect active resistance and live fire?"

The man exhaled. "No, nothing like that. There was an incident, and while my Siblings in *Gaia*'s security detail are still investigating the how, what, and why of what happened, we have the culprit—sorry, culprits—in custody. We are merely requesting that you take them into your charge and transport them to Earth."

"You'll have to elaborate," Foxhound growled. She was already beginning to lose patience with the man's careful choice of words—a commonality among Breeders, the Contractor had found. "Your request was for a single prisoner, but now you're telling me there are two of them, or perhaps even more?"

"You were already en route when more information came to light. Mother, our leader, thought it admissible to inform you upon your arrival."

As subtly as she could manage, Foxhound made the telephone signal with her right hand, silencing her suit's external speakers and opening an internal communication channel to Mailman, still standing quiet and still beside her.

"They call their leader 'Mother?'" she asked.

"Little is known about the hierarchy of the Organic Humanists, I'm afraid," Mailman responded. "I will make a note for our reports. I'm sure Earth would find this information useful in some respect."

Foxhound released her hand and responded to the cultist standing before her, "Did it occur to any of you that I might not have room aboard my ship for more than one prisoner?"

"The thought had crossed our minds. But the two of them are currently sharing a cell, and there's no reason to believe they couldn't share one aboard your ship, too. In fact, it may be a best-case scenario to do so."

"Not going to happen. You've breached the contract agreement, lured me aboard your ship, and now you're trying to, what, bribe me into taking on more than we agreed upon?"

"Excuse me," the man's voice rose, and his cheeks flushed—clearly, she had struck a chord. "We are doing no such thing."

"Well, this is normally the part where we talk about how much more you can offer me to let this slide." Foxhound could see her words cutting through the man, "How much do you think might do the trick?"

And just as the Contractor was certain the gray-robed man across from her would blow a fuse, he inhaled deeply, exhaled slowly, and regained his composure.

"I'm sorry," he said after a moment. "You're right. We handled this poorly and I apologize on behalf of myself and my Siblings. We are not interested in bribing you, but you may wish to hear me out nonetheless."

Foxhound took a moment to consider before settling on a response. "Why should I?"

"Because we have reason to believe that one of these prisoners is none other than the serial killer all the news feeds on Deadwood Station have been referring to as the Marrower."

"Now you've got my attention," Foxhound laughed. "So, what do I call you?"

"I am Brother Loch," the man answered.

"I guess I'll be taking the job, then, *Brother* Loch," Foxhound concluded.

"It's my pleasure to welcome you aboard *Gaia*."

☿

No longer worried about being caught—partially because he watched both the Contractor and her AI automaton companion leave *The Tardigrade* and partially because he knew their absence meant the AI's attention was largely focused elsewhere—Fink resumed loosening the panel on the back bulkhead of his cell.

With just a few forceful shimmies, the panel slid loose, and he was able to remove it and carefully lay it on the ground. Fink knew, despite the AI's stretched-thin processing power, enough of a ruckus was sure to put the ship into emergency lockdown, which would be, by comparison, practically impossible to circumvent. So, he kept as quiet and cautious as he might if his captor and her computerized assistant were still on board.

Behind the panel, Fink could see into the ship's hull or at least the space separating the cargo bay from the inner hull. To the layperson, it probably looked a mess, with all the varying sizes and colors of wiring woven through the ship's skeletal support structure. But to Fink, it was a familiar puzzle, a welcome old friend, one he had grown to appreciate so many years before in the shipbreaking yards of his youth.

Now that the drug cocktail from the shit sticks was completely out of his system, Fink had a newfound appreciation for his once-more steady hands. Hands that he now used to reach into *The Tardigrade*'s guts in search of a solitary, slender, innocuous strand of wire among a myriad of other wires. Yet, within mere moments, Fink had the very wire for which he searched, ever so familiar in its thickness and texture, between his fingers. And with one quick yank, it came loose, untethered from its juncture somewhere higher in the wall. Only a moment later, Fink heard the locking mechanism of his cell whirr and pop, its magnetic locks releasing now that they were without power.

Fink had always wondered why an organization with as much power as the Divine Church of the Omniphage would overlook such a significant flaw in its holding cell design. While it was possible they were unaware of it, due in large part to just how old and rare a ship like *The Tardigrade* was these days, he had to assume it was on the list of the Church's— to borrow a phrase often used among the solar system's largest conglomerates—*reasonable oversights and potential losses*.

In essence, this meant that the design of the cells needed to be universal to fit in as many ship models as possible. And that some would inevitably have a potential array of flaws—a result of the incompatibility with elements of certain ships' schematics. However, the long-term overall benefits of the cell's design would eclipse the presumptively small number of captives who might be knowledgeable enough to exploit said flaws.

Fink was happy to be able to count himself among that small number.

Of course, this was all conjecture on his part, Fink knew. There was no way he could have even an inkling of insight into an institution with as much power and reach as the Divine Church, which was why he tried to avoid its influence and company as much as possible. This was why he was now attempting perhaps the most ludicrous escape plan he had ever conjured, the first step of which he had just completed.

Fink rose to his feet, walked over to the front of his cell, pressed both his hands against the transparent aperture at its center, and slid it open. The door *thunked* into place, allowing Fink to release it and step through.

Now, on to step two, he thought, stretching and yawning. *Freeing my old friend Bora.*

☿

Walking through the corridors of *Gaia* beside Brother Loch, Mailman thundering just a few steps behind, Foxhound began to worry. With what little experience she had with the cultists, she had always known them to be peaceful people— so peaceful, in fact, that they would let someone spit in their face and never so much as raise a finger to retaliate. Yet, now aboard the Breeder mothership, she noticed groups of armed guards at nearly every junction they passed. And the closer they got to wherever Loch was taking them, the more crowded the halls became.

What concerned her more, however, was the looks on their faces. Some seemed afraid, their eyes darting back and forth, and others looked angry, brows furrowed and mouths downturned. But without exception, all these armed men were unquestionably nervous. There was something odd afoot among the Organic Humanists—something more than the fact that they now played host to a serial killer—and Foxhound didn't like it one bit.

"What's with the guns?" she finally asked.

"Ah," Loch sighed wistfully, but there was a resolve to it, as well, or so it seemed to the Contractor. "You came from Deadwood, yes?"

"We did. I know this...Marrower person was supposedly leaving a gruesome trail of bodies across the colony, but this looks like you're preparing for an invasion or something. Seems a little disproportionate a response, wouldn't you say?"

"Yes and no," Loch's response was nebulous yet again. "The Marrower is a symptom of a larger issue. Perhaps you have not noticed this because of your particular line of work, but there is unrest across the solar system. Like in times of old, our species is growing increasingly unhappy with how things are at present. And when we grow unhappy, especially to a great degree, we debase ourselves through vile, deviant acts. Historically speaking, of course."

They passed another corridor filled with yet another group of armed guards. This time, Foxhound noticed one raise their firearm ever-so-slightly as they passed. Out of Loch's line of vision, she lowered her left hand, tucking in her two middle fingers with her thumb and extending her index and pinkie fingers—a hand signal that, to her, always looked like horns—sending a silent message to Mailman to be on guard. She heard the automaton exoskeleton behind her quicken its pace to close the gap between them, and Foxhound knew Mailman got the message.

She knew this also meant that Mailman had to dedicate all but the smallest amount of processing power to the mobile exoskeleton—even going so far as to put all monitoring sensors and video feeds from *The Tardigrade* into standby. But it was a risk she was willing to take based on their current circumstances.

Besides, she comforted herself, *our guests aboard won't even know the difference.*

Loch continued speaking, either unbothered by or not noticing the change in the automaton's behavior.

"Unfortunately, despite the peaceful, altruistic mission of we Organic Humanists, we have fallen prey to those giving in to their baser instincts. We have been faced with hostility and sometimes even violence. I have seen my Siblings beaten, some within an inch of their lives. Surely you have noticed this change, too, have you not?"

"I have." Foxhound didn't like the sound of Loch's diatribe, but she also knew he wasn't lying, not entirely. There was unrest from the Outer Colonies all the way to the inner planets and, while the increase in crime had been a boon to her profession, she, too, grew concerned at what it meant for the solar system at large. It reminded her of an explosive with the fuse already lit. It was only a matter of time before the inevitable detonation.

"We abhor violence, of course. It flies in the face of what

we stand for at the basest level. But we simply cannot abide attacks on our people any longer. Mother has deemed it a necessary evil that we arm ourselves. Nobody else will protect us, certainly not your lot and the so-called Divine Church of the Omniphage for which you work. Your employer would sooner have us wiped off the face of the System were it up to them!"

Loch, realizing his volume and gusto had been increasing with each syllable, stopped himself.

"I apologize," he finally said. "My quarrel—our quarrel—is not with you. You have answered our call, and for that, we are thankful. I simply mean to say that we have grown... concerned for ourselves, our family, and our mission. We mean to continue bringing light to those who need it. Unfortunately, that now means protecting ourselves and that which is ours."

"Monks with guns," Foxhound muttered, forgetting that her external speakers weren't silenced.

"Something like that," Loch laughed as Foxhound shook her head in embarrassment, the awkward silence broken only by the heavy footfalls of the automaton trudging behind them.

"Let me reiterate," Loch continued, "no harm will come to you while you are aboard *Gaia*. Our men are, admittedly, a bit green when it comes to combat, but they fully understand the seriousness and the responsibility of their weapons."

"I certainly hope that's the case," Foxhound replied. "Mind if I ask where we're headed?"

"Mother has requested to meet you in person before the handoff. They merely wish to ensure that the prisoners will be in good hands, of course. Nothing more than a formality, I'm sure."

☿

Fink knew Bora Volkan first as a sawbones. The older surgeon had patched Fink up a few times when they had both found residence on another of the Kuiper Belt's larger colonies, Listening Post Theta. But those experiences had also taught Fink to be cautious of Bora. He was a brilliant doctor who saved more than his fair share of lives—both innocents and criminals alike—that was certain. However, time had also changed him.

After some time, Bora had become desensitized to the violence, a practical necessity that allowed him to cope with all he had witnessed on a colony as mired in unrest as Theta. But as time went by and things on Theta ceased to change for the better, he seemed to lose touch with his own humanity, treating patients less like humans and more like experiments. Eventually, the man had snapped, his consciousness seemingly split into two parts: one that remained the brilliant, caring doctor Fink had first met and another that was savage and insane, likelier to slit someone's throat if only because he liked hearing the sound of them gargling on their own blood, drowning in it.

The problem for Fink at this particular moment was that he didn't know which version of the man he was about to release. As such, he planned to be prepared for the worst. So, instead of making his way over to Bora's cell at the other end of the cargo bay, he began opening the bay's smattering of storage containers and lockers. He figured the Contractor wasn't stupid enough to leave weapons just lying around—and he'd be right—but that wasn't the only way to defend one's self.

Finally, Fink found what he was looking for, tucked into a cabinet toward the forward bulkhead of the cargo bay: a Stellar Envoy emergency repair kit.

He gave the kit's handle a yank and pulled it free, but he lost his grip, and the kit fell to the deck with a loud crash and skittered to a stop a few feet away. Fink cringed at the sound, certain it would be followed by emergency sirens and a subsequent lockdown. And then the Contractor and her thundering automaton would return with the fury of an exploding star. They might even kill him to save themselves the trouble, so long as there was a dead-or-alive clause in his contract and, therefore, still a price for bringing Fink's body in.

Fink didn't like his odds. What he did like, however, was that the sirens never came, and his captors didn't return. It seemed the ship's AI had its attention focused elsewhere. And that was a very, very good thing for Fink and his plans.

Stellar Envoy emergency repair kits came standard on all Stellar Envoy vessels. *The Tardigrade* was no exception. What surprised Fink the most, however, was that this particular kit looked like it had perhaps never been opened. That meant one of two things: either this ship was so lucky it never needed field repairs, or his captor had no idea it was even aboard. One way or the other, it meant glad tidings for Fink because, inside, there was a bevy of highly useful tools, including a vacuum-ready welding torch, rivet gun, and tool belt—all three of which Fink was certain he could find a use for.

He started by removing the tool belt from the kit and wrapping it around his waist, fastening it at the front. The belt was intended for use in the vacuum of space, so its circumference was big enough to wrap around insulated space suits. That meant, even at its tightest notch, it hung off Fink's skeletal hips at a severe angle, ready to fall to the deck at any moment. The precariousness was exacerbated when the slender man attached both the welding torch and rivet gun to the belt's retractable tethers—a handy feature that, in normal use, kept tools from drifting off into the black void of space. But in Fink's case, they'd serve as a means to keep the tools out of anyone else's hands.

Tools affixed to his belt, Fink moved on to his next destination, waddling awkwardly to keep the belt from slipping off his body. Only a few steps from where he left the remainder of the tool kit, Fink opened another cabinet on the forward bulkhead of the cargo bay, one marked with a large red cross icon, the universal symbol for first aid.

With careless gusto, he rifled through the medical supplies, tossing bandages to the floor and shoving salves and ointments aside until he found what he sought: another set of shit sticks, just like the ones he had found in that security substation on Deadwood. Fink didn't like the idea of injecting himself with the potent drug cocktails again, but he also didn't care to face off with his armored jailer, her automaton companion, or any of his unstable cellmates without a backup plan. And this was one he knew might work and that he could survive. He pocketed the auto-injectors and shuffled back over to the front of the holding cells.

No longer afraid of putting the ship into full lockdown, Fink shuffled from cell to cell, tapping the button on each control panel that turned on the cells' two-way audio. The prisoners, still trapped in their cells, eyeballed him cautiously and silently. Fink presumed they were trying to discern whether he was setting up some kind of trap or trick, or perhaps they simply weren't big talkers.

No matter, Fink thought. *I'm happy to do all the talking.*

He cleared his throat and watched as Bora Volkan and Hecate Neumar rose and moved closer to their semitransparent cell doors. By contrast, the colossal Eris Enyo chose to remain seated, though she appeared to be paying attention, and Warrick Kano remained kneeling in the center of his cell, seemingly oblivious to the events unfolding.

"Friends," Fink smirked, "today, fortune smiles upon us all. As you may have noticed, our jailer and her little digital servant have, perhaps inadvisably, left us to our own devices for a time. And that has presented all of us, myself especially, with a unique opportunity."

"Get to the fucking point," Eris Enyo interrupted, her low-pitched voice booming and coarse, her eyes locked on Fink.

"Stringent and impatient. I'd expect no less from the disgraced former officer of the Aegis Guard," Fink replied.

Eris Enyo raised an eyebrow, her curiosity piqued.

"Yeah, I know who you are," Fink continued. "I know all of you, some personally and some by reputation and criminal record. Truly, it's an honor to be among such a decorated group of ne'er-do-wells. Today, I offer you your freedom. But it will come at a price, albeit a meager one. Agree to my terms, and a simple push of a button will release you from your bondage, and you can simply be on your way. Disagree, and you can stay in your cell, and you'll be no better off for it."

"I agree," piped up Hecate Neumar, her voice soft and smooth as silk. "Whatever you want, I agree."

"Love the enthusiasm," Fink laughed, "but please just hear me out for a moment!"

Neumar scowled.

"Here's the deal," Fink continued, "I want this ship. I don't care what you do, where you go, or who you kill. I just want all of you to get the hell off. And before you think you might be able to pull one over on me, I've got a couple of friends here that say differently."

Fink lovingly patted the rivet gun hanging from his right hip and nodded toward the welding torch at the opposite side.

"In case you are unfamiliar, this rivet gun here was made to punch through spacefaring ship hulls during emergency repairs. That means, even with all your cybernetic augmentations"—Fink looked directly at Eris Enyo as he spoke—"this bad boy will punch a hole through you so big you could fly an ORC pod through it. And if somehow I miss, this welding torch produces a plasma arc to the tune of thirty thousand degrees Kelvin. That's hot enough that not only will you burn, but you'll burn so fast and so completely there won't even be enough left to identify you."

Fink took a long pause to let what he had just told his would-be accomplices sink in. He then shuffled up to the front of the cell housing Bora Volkan, the one person aboard he might be able to trust, before speaking again, this time addressing the man in the cell before him.

"Bora, my old friend, how have you been?" he asked.

"B-better, Fink. I've been b-b-better," the former doctor answered, his eyes downturned and his speech stuttered. Time had not been kind to the old physician since they had last met, Fink noticed. "Now, c-c-can you get me out of here?"

"Of course," Fink answered. "I just need you to verbally agree to my conditions."

Bora lifted his head, making eye contact with Fink through the diamond-like glass. The surprise in his eyes shifted quickly to what Fink thought looked like annoyance or perhaps frustration.

"You're serious?"

"'Fraid so. Look, I know we've got history, but this only works if we're all on board. No special treatment. No exceptions. You gotta go just like everyone else."

"B-b-but you might need a doctor. I c-can help you."

"I don't want your help, Bora. Not after last time."

"Okay…I understand. I just need to get b-b-back down to D-Deadwood. You can toss me in the ship's ORC p-p-pod if you need to—"

Fink cut the old sawbones off, "I can't do that, Bora. Or maybe it's more accurate to say I won't. I'm taking the ship, remember? I'm gonna need that pod. And I'm not sticking around Deadwood or anywhere else in the Kuiper, for that matter. Whatever ship we're docked to is going to have its own ORCs. Take one of those."

Bora Volkan let out a deep sigh, and his head fell back down between his shoulders, his eyes trained on the deck below his feet. "Fine. I agree."

"That's the spirit," Fink cheered, tapping the control pad on the front of Volkan's cell. The door slid open with a satisfying *whoosh* and locked into place with a loud *shunk*.

Fink extended his hand, expecting his old friend to extend a hand in turn. Instead, Bora Volkan let out an inhuman screech and dove forward, his teeth gnashing, foamy saliva spilling down his chin, and both his arms outstretched, reaching for Fink's throat.

Surprised, Fink tried to backpedal, reaching his right hand down to bring the rivet gun to bear, but Volkan was too fast, knocking the apparatus out of Fink's hand and setting him off balance. Entangled, they toppled over and slammed onto the deck of the cargo bay, sending Fink's rivet gun, still tethered to his tool belt, skittering just out of reach.

With the unhinged doctor bearing down on him and his right arm freed, Fink braced his forearm against Volkan's chest, keeping the man's chomping jaws at a distance but unable to push him off. For a moment, the pair remained at a stalemate, Volkan unable to close the distance and Fink struggling to throw the doctor off him.

Bora Volkan, realizing in a sudden moment of lucidity that both his arms were free, grabbed Fink by the throat and activated his cybernetic implants.

Like blooming flowers, Volkan's forearms blossomed open, a bevy of panels popping out to reveal an array of surgical tools attached to spindly, spiderlike robotic armatures. Syringes, scalpels, scissors, and even a tiny whirring bone saw emerged, and—clacking and clicking, whizzing and whining—they inched closer and closer to Fink's throat. And just as the tiny whirring bone saw made contact with Fink's flesh, spraying Volkan's bared teeth with a sanguine mist, the disgraced physician let out another bloodcurdling scream. Only this time, it wasn't that of rage—it was that of pain.

Trapped beneath his former associate, Fink had managed to get ahold of his welding torch with his left hand and wedged it between his body and that of Volkan, its tip pressed into the doctor's abdomen. And when he pulled the trigger to activate it, it emitted a white-hot beam of superheated plasma, melting through Volkan's insides like so much fuel-soaked kindling. The stink of superheated flesh and guts singed Fink's nostrils.

He watched the light drain from Volkan's eyes before releasing the ignition on the torch and shoving the man's body off his own. The lifeless husk, a gaping, scorched hole at its center, crumpled onto the deck. Bora Volkan, the mad sawbones, was no more.

Still lying on his back, Fink took a deep breath, tapped the button on his tool belt to retract the rivet gun's tether, and, grunting and groaning, rose to his feet. He kicked the doctor's body, once to ensure the man was truly dead and then another few times for his own pleasure. Then, after wiping the still-flowing blood from his neck wound and licking it off his own fingers, he addressed the remaining three prisoners.

"Who wants to go next?"

☿

Walking side by side, Brother Loch and the Contractor known as Foxhound, followed closely by Mailman's robotic exoskeleton, approached *Gaia*'s bridge. But the closer they got, the more it became apparent that something was wrong. Even Loch noticed that far more guards had gathered in the halls, and they all looked uncomfortable.

As they rounded the final corner into the corridor that opened up into the bridge, they could hear the sounds of arguing. Loch recognized one of the voices as Mother's, but he was taken aback by their volume. It was highly unusual for Mother to abide impassioned debate, let alone engage in it. But he couldn't quite place the other voice until they rounded the corner.

There, in the center of the bridge and surrounded by even more armed guards, Mother stood face-to-face with Sibling Yū from the Forward Medical Center. Two of the guards were holding Yū by their arms, keeping the Sibling a distance from

Mother as the pair shouted at one another.

"First, you imprison an actual child," Yū shouted, "along with one of our most virtuous Siblings, and now this? I cannot abide this any longer. You've lost your way, and I will not simply watch while you systematically dismantle everything we've built here. You may be our leader, but this is a collective, and I will have my voice heard. This is wrong. *You* are wrong. You can't silence us. And you can't expect us to simply stand by and accept this...barbarity!"

"The System is changing, Sibling Yū," Mother responded through their teeth, "and we must change with it. You should understand that more than anyone here. You've treated our Brothers, Sisters, and Siblings who have returned from the colonies. You've seen what those animals out there have done to them. We've not been safe for some time, and things are only getting worse. This path you decry so vehemently is an answer that will give us safety and security never known by the Organic Humanists who came before us. *Gaia* is dying. There's no way around it. We cannot keep this ship in operation for much longer. And that calls for drastic measures."

Mother, still gritting their teeth, noticed the new additions to the surrounding crowd. They took a deep breath, eased the scowl on their face, and signaled the two guards holding Yū, "Take them away. We can continue this...conversation at a later time."

The guards dragged the Organic Humanist medic away, shoving past Brother Loch, Foxhound, and Mailman. For the briefest of moments, the Contractor thought she saw Yū mouth the phrase *help us*. But she was shaken from the thought when Mother, now calm and composed, addressed the trio.

"My deepest apologies," the towering, white-clad ringleader of the Organic Humanists said, their voice now reverberating throughout the bridge as it passed through the surrounding speakers, resonating with a timbre so rich it seemed inhuman. "Welcome aboard *Gaia*. I am Mother."

Foxhound had dealt with enough high-and-mighty folks in her work to understand what this Mother person was doing. The opulent garments. The booming voice. The calculated movements. It was all a ploy to make them seem more than, better, above. And the Contractor didn't care for it in the least.

"Thank you, Brother Loch, for escorting our guests," they continued. "You must be Foxhound. It's a pleasure to meet you."

Foxhound noted that Mother didn't extend their hand in greeting, not that she would have returned the gesture anyhow.

"And who is your...companion?" Mother asked, peeking between the Contractor and her escort at the skeletal automaton crouched just behind them.

On cue, Mailman stepped forward and rose to its full height, the extra headroom of the bridge allowing the automaton to tower over the surrounding crowd, including Mother themself.

Shit, Foxhound thought. *Forgot to have Mailman turn off its pleasantries matrix.*

"Modular Automaton Intended for Labor in Manufacturing, Agriculture, and Navigation," the automaton announced, its volume matching that of Mother's. "But you may address me as Mailman."

Mailman extended an arm forward, opening its clawlike hand with a whizz and a whirr. Mother staggered back, their eyes wide and skin somehow even paler than before. In response, the surrounding armed guards tensed up, some raising their firearms toward the automaton.

"Mailman," Foxhound said, gently placing a hand atop the forearm of her automaton's mobile robotic platform. "You're scaring them."

The small orb situated between the skeletal platform's shoulders tilted on its axis—a motion that, were the automaton flesh and blood, might've looked like befuddlement. Mailman closed its claw, retracted its arm, and took a step back.

"So sorry," it said. "I didn't mean to frighten you."

Mother laughed, turning to Foxhound once more. "Your automaton has quite the personality. Is your employer aware of this? I thought they had strict rules about that sort of thing."

"And I thought you Organic Humanists had strict rules about this sort of thing." Foxhound gestured to the armed guards surrounding them.

"Fair point," Mother replied, looking the Contractor up and down. "I've read your profile. You're quite capable. Came onto the scene seemingly out of nowhere and quickly climbed the ranks to become one of Earth's favorite guns-for-hire. And all those jobs nobody else wanted, too."

"You're buttering me up," Foxhound interrupted. "Why?"

"Are you happy? Doing what you're doing, I mean. Scraping from job to job, barely able to make ends meet. Don't you want more? I... Sorry, *we* could use a jack-of-all-trades like you."

"Master of none," Foxhound replied.

"I'm sorry?"

"The full phrase is 'jack-of-all-trades, master of none.'"

"I'm not sure I understand your point."

"I know what I'm good at," Foxhound's tone grew more serious. "And that's Contractor work. I'm not currently considering other employment options."

Mother stared at their own reflection in Foxhound's helmet visor for a moment. "That's too bad. Still, no hard feelings. I can appreciate your loyalty to your profession, even if I don't see the point."

"I don't appreciate the backhanded compliment." Foxhound tensed up. "If the terms of the contract aren't to your liking, Mailman and I will happily depart, and you can find someone else to be your courier."

Mother frowned, the creases in their forehead like cracks in delicate porcelain. "That won't be necessary."

They motioned to the guards, who finally took a step back and lowered their guns.

"Loch will take you to the prisoners," Mother continued. "From there, you can return to your ship and be on your way. Let the bridge know when you are ready to depart and we will release the docking clamps. It was a...unique pleasure meeting you."

"Wish I could say the same," Foxhound replied. She turned to Brother Loch, noticed a deep scowl across his face, and nodded. Without another word, the Contractor, her escort, and Mailman turned and left the bridge.

"Keep an eye on them," Mother said to their guards once the trio was out of earshot. "I don't trust that Contractor. I want her off my ship and on her way to Earth before we take Deadwood. Understood?"

The guards nodded in the affirmative before turning to follow Foxhound and company.

☿

"This is not good," Foxhound whispered to Mailman over a private channel. The Contractor and her automaton companion followed behind Brother Loch as he led them through a labyrinth of corridors within *Gaia*'s underbelly. "Too many guns, too much tension. Something is up. Something bad. Everyone is watching us, and, correct me if I'm wrong, I think we're being followed."

"I can confirm that, mum. My sensors are picking up consistent movement some distance behind us."

"How many?"

"Four or five. They've been careful to stay roughly twenty yards back. I suspect they believe we are unaware of their presence."

"Keep an eye on them. If they start to close the distance, alert me."

"Yes, mum."

Brother Loch hadn't breathed a word since they left the bridge, but Foxhound wasn't keen to break the tension, either. She needed time. Time to think. Time to plan. *Gaia* was a tinderbox ready to go up in flames, and she had every intention of being long gone before that happened. After a few more turns down a few more corridors, she addressed Mailman once more, still over the same private channel.

"Is one murderer really enough for all this fuss?" the Contractor asked.

"Based on what little we have observed since coming aboard *Gaia*," Mailman responded, "I would surmise that the sheer number of armed men and the presence of the criminal colloquially known as the Marrower are purely coincidental."

143

"Great… Can you still access external data networks? Did someone put a bounty on us without us knowing about it?"

"My apologies, mum, but I cannot."

"What? What do you mean?"

"It appears that *Gaia* is jamming all comms. No signals are coming in or going out."

"That's what that Sibling…uh, what was their name?"

"Yū, mum. Sibling Yū."

"Yes, thank you. That's what they were yelling about. If they know something about what's going on here, we need to find out. How can we track them down?"

"It would make sense for them to keep any and all prisoners in the same location to conserve resources and limit access. There is a high likelihood that they took this Sibling Yū to the same location as those we are meant to escort."

"Okay, then. Mailman, we are about to do something very stupid. Prepare to run the Odd Man Out Protocol. Brother Loch, here, is the target."

"Acknowledged, mum."

The trio rounded the final corner and found themselves in another corridor that looked just like all the others. Only this time, there were several armed guards stationed outside one of the rooms.

"Ready or not," Foxhound chanted to nobody in particular, "here we come."

☿

"Sister Penelope," Brother Loch's voice crackled through the stateroom-turned-prison-cell's overhead speakers.

"You don't get to call me that." Penelope hissed through her

144

teeth, "I'm no Sister of yours."

The no-name girl had finally calmed down. While she was no longer curled up in a tight ball on the bed, muttering apologies to nobody in particular, she had improved little. Now, she sat in one of the back corners of the stateroom with her arms crossed and her head between her legs. Yet, while her cascading locks hid most of her face, her emerald green eyes pierced through the thick curls to stay trained on the door—the room's only means of entrance or egress.

Penelope sat on the ground next to the girl, her arm draped across the child's shoulders and her eyes similarly locked on the stateroom door, through which she glowered at Brother Loch.

"*Sister* Penelope," Loch reiterated, "you have to believe me when I say this brings me no pleasure—"

"Then why do it?" Penelope interrupted. "Why are you doing this?"

Unmoved, Loch continued, "It is with Mother's authority and the support of the Organic Humanists that I hereby expel you from our order and revoke all privileges and protections afforded to you as a Sibling. You are Sister Penelope no longer. You and the child shall be placed in the custody of the Contractor known as Foxhound. She will transport you off *Gaia,* and you, alongside the child, are never to return here nor to any other Organic Humanist ship or colony, do you understand?"

"Yeah," Penelope confirmed, "I think I finally understand."

Chapter Seven

Hecate Neumar was the first of *The Tardigrade*'s prisoners to disembark alive, slinking through *Gaia*'s twists and turns like a hungry cat hunting mice. The Widow of Venus wasted no time finding her first victim: one of Mother's armed guards posted just a couple of corridors away from the OH mothership's ORC docking bay.

The man could not have been older than thirty, by Neumar's estimation, with only the lightest dusting of stubble on his virile jawline. He shifted his weight nervously back and forth and took turns wiping his clammy palms on his gray robes, letting his firearm dangle from the sling around his neck.

As green as Earth grass, she thought, licking her lips. *Just look at him.*

As she approached, she adjusted her gait, swapping her ballet-like strides for a hobbled limp, and erased the smirk of anticipation from her lips, trading it for her best impression of distress and pain.

"Help me," she pleaded, catching the young man's attention as she approached. "You have to help me, please."

But the young man, despite his apparent inexperience, was not so quick to fall for her ruse. With both hands, he gripped his rifle and raised it to bear, pointing it at Neumar, who raised her hands in response.

"No, no, listen, please," she appealed, inching closer and closer. "I was being held prisoner by that...that monster. The Contractor, she's not what she seems. She hurt me, tortured me, prodded me with her devices. I need help. You can help me."

Neumar, panting and crying, fell to the deck at the young man's feet, her arms outstretched toward him. The confusion on his face replaced by concern, the man released his weapon and pushed it around his back, squatting down and reaching with both hands to help lift the distraught, distressed woman before him off the deck.

"Ma'am," he finally said, "it's okay. You're safe now. I'm here. I'm going to help you. Let's get you up."

And those were the last words he would ever speak. As he lifted Hecate Neumar, the Widow of Venus, in his strapping, youthful arms, she let out a soft coo, gazing into his eyes and placing her hands on either side of his throat.

He felt only a soft pinch as a small panel slid open just beneath Neumar's right palm and a hypodermic needle— one of Neumar's very favorite cybernetic augmentations— emerged to pierce his flesh, injecting a powerful compound of poisons into his veins.

Finished with her deception, Neumar rose under her own strength and embraced the young man, now wide-eyed and gasping. This was her favorite part—where she got to watch as her victim, in stunned realization, slowly and painfully expired.

It happened just as it always did. First, his breathing became labored and raspy as his lungs began to fail, no longer able to adequately inflate. Then, his eyes began to turn yellow, his tongue, swelling far too large, poked out from between his lips, and foam dribbled from the corners of his mouth. And finally, as Neumar pressed herself against him as tightly as she could, his body jerked and wrenched as his heart faltered, slowed, and ceased beating altogether.

She shivered in exquisite pleasure, allowing herself to fall to the deck once more atop the young man's lifeless body, where she lay for a moment, panting longingly before speaking to the man's corpse.

"It has been far too long, my love," she exhaled. "Tell me, was it as good for you as it was for me?"

♂

"We've got movement in the ORC pod bay," one of *Gaia's* crew members shouted above the din of the bridge. Tensions aboard *Gaia* had already been almost palpable but, in the wake of their conversation with Foxhound, Mother had placed everyone on high alert, requesting regular updates on any unanticipated action throughout the ship or at least the observable decks. They had intended this as a means of monitoring the Contractor, her AI's hulking load-lifter modular platform, and the prisoners they were to be escorting off the ship. As such, activity near the ORC bay, where the Contractor's ship was docked, came as a surprise.

Mother rose from their throne in the center of the room and glided over to the crew member's station.

"Show me," they said.

The crew member punched a few keys on their terminal, and a grainy, choppy video feed popped up, showing a thin woman slinking off *The Tardigrade* and onto *Gaia*, though it was unclear who she was and what she was doing.

"Show me where they went," Mother barked.

"I…" the crew member hesitated. "I can't."

"Why not?"

"Most of the cameras in the area are, well, they're not operational."

"And why is that?"

Another crew member, a few stations down, spoke up, "They were placed on the list of nonessential repairs. And the parts order was canceled back before we left for Deadwood."

"Under whose authority?"

"Yours," the first crew member muttered. "Part of the cost-saving measures…so we could arm ourselves, you said."

"Damn it!" Mother slammed their fist down on the workstation, causing the display to flicker with static. "Someone get me a team down there. Find out who that was and where they're headed. And station guards outside of that godforsaken ship. I don't want any more surprises."

"Yes, Mother," the two crew members responded in unison.

"And what about the Contractor?" Mother asked a third crew member.

"Just arrived at Sister—my apologies, Your Grace—*former* Sister Penelope's stateroom," the crew member responded.

"Do we have contact with Brother Loch?" Mother demanded. "A discreet means to get him a message."

"No, Mother." The crew member flinched. "But the secondary security team, the one you had following them, has comms."

"Tell them to advance. I want that Contractor subdued, disarmed, and locked up right along with Penelope and her little pet. And if they can't manage that, I want them eliminated. All of them. Whatever it takes." Mother turned to address the entire bridge crew, their voice now booming over the speakers.

"Clearly, we've been duped. This is some sinister plot cooked up by Earth's army of infidels. They've been sent here to make an example of us. But we will meet their challenge with righteous fury! Gone are the days when we Organic Humanists suffered the slings and arrows of these...these heretics! We will not be silenced! We will not be put down! We will take what is rightfully ours! We forge our own glorious destiny!"

The crew of *Gaia*'s bridge cheered.

☿

"Stay back and away from the door," Brother Loch announced to Penelope and the no-name girl, though neither needed the warning sitting in the back corner of the former Sister's stateroom. Loch tapped a few buttons on the panel outside, and the door slid open with a metallic *hiss* and *clunk*. With an arm outstretched in presentation, the man stepped aside, allowing the armored Contractor to enter the chamber.

But Foxhound didn't step forward at Loch's ushering. Instead, she outstretched her left arm, pointed it to the guard closest to her, and fired a small capsule at the man's chest. It burst on impact, releasing a cloud of purple gas. By the time it had reached the man's nostrils, filled his lungs, and rendered him unconscious, Foxhound had fired three more capsules, one at each of the remaining guards. And each of them, in turn, dropped to the deck in a heap of limbs and gray fabric.

"What are you doing?!" Loch demanded. But, before he could protest further, Mailman's towering exoskeleton lurched forward and, with a single enormous claw, grabbed Loch by the throat and lifted him off his feet. Only pained gurgles escaped the Organic Humanist's lips.

"Hey, hey, ease up," Foxhound announced, raising her hands to the AI's automaton exoskeleton. "We don't want to kill him…probably."

"But, mum," Mailman protested, "Odd Man Out Protocol requires that I incapacitate the target."

"Right, but who wrote the protocols?"

"You did, mum."

"Then I'm overwriting this one."

"Very well," Mailman sounded almost defeated as it lowered Brother Loch back down to the deck and released the man's throat—not enough to allow him to escape but enough so that he could breathe, which he did in sharp, hoarse gasps. "Making adjustments to the Odd Man Out Protocol subroutines."

"Thank you, Mailman." Foxhound lowered her hands and walked through the door to the stateroom. There, in the corner, she saw a woman, perhaps ten or twenty years her senior, staring back at her with terror in her eyes. But not just terror. There was something else. It was a look Foxhound had become all too familiar with in her work as a Contractor. It was hatred.

"You must be Sister Penelope," Foxhound said, noticing the small shape in the corner next to the woman. "But I don't believe I know her name…"

"Stay away from her," the woman, Penelope, barked. "You lay one finger on her, and I swear I'll…I'll—"

Foxhound laughed, "You're not in much of a position to do

anything, I think. You've got guts, and I guess that's something. Do you know why I'm here?"

"You're here to kill us," Penelope responded, still gritting her teeth. "You're a glorified executioner. That's why Mother brought you here, isn't it? You're the one who captured Brother Phineas. Now that you're done with him, you've come for me. Was that the agreement?"

"Brother Phineas? You mean Fink? Look, *Brother Phineas*, as you know him, is fine. I didn't torture and kill him. He's on my ship. And I don't think you know his whole story. See, this is kind of his thing. He hops colonies, blends in by ingratiating himself with some monks or a cult—"

"We're not a cult!" Penelope snapped.

"Right, not a cult, sorry. Point is, guy's not who you think he is."

Foxhound was about to take another step forward but hesitated when she noticed the no-name girl's emerald green eyes peeking through her curly locks. Instead, she knelt down and raised her hands in the air, palms outward, and when she spoke this time, she didn't address Penelope; she addressed the girl.

"I'm not here to hurt you. I'm not even sure I'm here to do the job they hired me for anymore. That Mother of yours… something isn't right here, and until I know a bit more about what, exactly, that is, I'm inclined to do things my way. And that starts with us having a conversation about how you ended up in this position in the first place."

"Coward!" The shout came from behind, just outside the cell. It was Loch, still pinned to the wall by Mailman's mechanized claw. "Traitor! Blasphemer! We should have known better than to depend upon one of Earth's sycophants. You can't be trusted, any of you."

"Mailman," Foxhound said without so much as turning around, "keep him quiet, will you?"

Mailman tightened its grip and, once more, Loch's protests turned to pained gargles.

"Let's start with introductions if that's all right with you. You can call me Foxhound."

"Foxhound," Penelope repeated, still speaking through her teeth. "Is that your real name?"

"It's as real a name as I've got," the Contractor replied.

"I'm Penelope," the woman continued. "But you know that."

"I do. But what about her?" Foxhound nodded at the no-name girl.

"She...she doesn't have one."

"I see," Foxhound responded. "That's okay. Maybe we can come up with one once we get you both out of here... if that's okay with you?"

The Contractor regarded the girl for a moment before addressing Penelope once again, "Do you know why you've been imprisoned?"

Penelope hesitated. "Not specifically. Just that they seem to think she...*we* pose some kind of danger."

The Contractor lowered one of her hands and extended it toward the no-name girl who, for the first time since being locked up, lifted her head. Foxhound took one look at the girl's face, her vibrant emerald green eyes contrasting with her dark skin and thick, curly locks, and the Contractor fell backward, dropping to the deck with a loud *clunk*. She scrambled to her feet, taking several steps backward before speaking once more.

"Is this some kind of sick joke?" she finally blurted out.

153

But before Penelope could answer, Mailman interrupted. "Mum, I'm afraid we've got incoming."

"About time," Loch gargled, still struggling to breathe.

The Contractor's head was spinning. There was no question: this girl was the same one sketched in Foxhound's journal— her sister, her twin, her doppelgänger. But that memory was so distant, so faded… they couldn't be the same person. But maybe figuring out who this girl was and where she came from—maybe pulling that thread would finally give Foxhound the answers she sought. But if she really was the Marrower, if she really did murder all those people—

No, Foxhound told herself. *Get your head straight and worry about the questions later. Right now, you have a job to do. Everything else can wait.*

Foxhound heard the reverberations of several pairs of boots clomping upon the deck in the corridor outside. She turned, putting herself between the two prisoners and the door, and raised her arms, B.A.N.G. modules ready to fire. The armed guards surrounded the stateroom door, bringing their rifles to bear, as well. But neither Foxhound nor the guards fired a single shot. They never had the chance.

☿

Eris Enyo, a former officer in Earth's elite Aegis Guard military branch, known best among those in the Outer Colonies as the Blood Queen of Titan, was the second of Foxhound's captives to disembark from *The Tardigrade*. Standing well over six feet tall and approaching five hundred pounds— thanks largely to her extensive body modifications, ranging from titanium skeletal reinforcements to bio-hydraulic joint enhancements—Enyo was monstrous by any definition. But it wasn't her size and strength alone that made her so terrifying. No, she was also vicious and bloodthirsty, especially when angry. And she had been angry for weeks, trapped inside a tiny cell, barely able to move because of the size of her cell and the deactivation of her cybernetics.

But now, free aboard *Gaia* and unhindered by *The Tardi-grade's* dampening field, she'd finally be able to let that anger out on anyone and everyone who crossed her path.

And that would start with the large group of armed guards that had just entered *Gaia's* ORC pod docking bay.

The men, either too ignorant to know what they were up against or so arrogant they thought they stood a chance, surrounded the colossal woman. Some kneeled and some remained standing, but all trained their guns on her.

Eris Enyo ran her fingers through her close-cropped bright red hair, took in a deep breath, and sighed.

"Which one of you is in charge?" she asked.

"Put your hands in the air," one of the men to Enyo's left shouted. "Comply, and no harm will come to you. If you resist, we will be required to use lethal force, do you understand?"

Enyo tilted her head back and forth, taking in the scene before her. There were six of them, all armed with antiquated projectile firearms, the kind that might punch a hole clean through a nonmagnetized ship hull and cause a violent decompression. The kind that, for thousands of years, men had used to massacre one another. The kind she had been trained, for years and years, not to fear.

The Blood Queen of Titan brought her hands together, interlaced her fingers, and cracked her knuckles, activating several of her internal cybernetic enhancements—ones made specifically for battle, ones that kicked her blood lust into high gear. And, as a cocktail of adrenaline and painkillers flooded her system, she answered, "I'd run if I were you."

But the men didn't listen. A few chuckled, one cocked his weapon, and the leader—the man who had first addressed Enyo—spoke yet again.

"Ready," he started. "Aim—"

Enyo leaped, clearing the distance between her and the guards faster than any of them could react. And with one great fist, she punched a hole clear through their leader's torso, spraying blood and viscera on the bulkhead behind him. With her arm still through his gut, she yanked the man like a rag doll, thrashing his body from side to side, smashing into two more guards and sending them skittering across the deck. Then, grabbing the leader by the throat with her free hand, she yanked her arms apart, ripping the man in two and dropping his halves onto the deck below with a wet *smack*.

Covered head to toe in thick crimson gore, she turned to the remaining three guards, one of whom finally had the good sense to take aim and squeeze the trigger.

"If only they taught you how to aim," Enyo guffawed, easily and almost elegantly dodging the bullets as they whizzed past.

Once again, she closed the distance between her and the remaining three guards faster than they could compensate, grabbing one by the face with her enormous left palm and dragging his body in front of hers. Bullets from the other two guards' guns peppered the man in the back with wet pops, and she felt his body go limp. She squeezed, crushing his skull in her hand, brains and bone fragments oozing between her fingers, and let the rest of his lifeless body crumple to the floor.

Finally, the last two guards tried to turn and run, screaming and crying in terror. But they were too late. Enyo raised one great fist above her head and brought it down upon one of the guards, smashing him into the deck below, his ribs cracking like kindling in a fire. She then grabbed his body with both hands and tossed him toward the final fleeing guard, who collapsed under the weight of the collision, his rifle skittering across the deck.

As he tried to crawl from beneath his now-dead comrade, he pleaded with Enyo, begging her to let him live.

"I'll tell them. I'll tell them all," he cried. "A warning! I'll tell everyone what you did here. Please, just… please, don't kill me."

Enyo walked up to the man, her white teeth showing through her blood-soaked lips.

"I don't need you to tell anyone anything," she said, bringing one large boot over the man's head. "They can see it for themselves."

The man raised his hands to protect himself. And Enyo brought her boot down with a wet crunch.

With the guards all dead, Enyo took stock of what she had done, her chest swelling with pride. She also took a moment to carefully check herself for wounds, a habit she had picked up in her years serving in the Aegis Guard, as the powerful drug cocktail running through her veins did not allow for her to feel much, if any, pain. At the end of each battle, she looked herself over for wounds to get a better idea of what shape she was really in. Because although she felt invincible, she knew she was not. That arrogance had gotten far too many of those who served under her killed. But she knew better.

Despite the multitude of shell casings she saw on the ground around her, Eris Enyo found only a single puncture wound in her right bicep. She checked the opposite side of her arm for an exit wound but found none. So, she clenched her teeth, flexed her arm as hard as she could, and grinned with satisfaction when she heard the familiar *plink* of the bullet falling out of her wound and onto the deck below.

The Blood Queen of Titan continued forward into the underbelly of *Gaia*, searching for more playthings to quench her immutable thirst.

☿

There was no one left in *Gaia*'s ORC pod docking bay to see Warrick Kano, the Savage of Europa, exit *The Tardigrade*. Not that he would have left them alive if they had. Still, the bodies strewn about the bay provided a convenience the slight, scarred man hadn't anticipated. One of them was roughly the same size as Kano. And so he undressed the body, draped a gray robe over his own clothing, and made his way toward *Gaia*'s bridge.

He did, after all, have a job to do.

Intermission

Survive.
  Move.
  Survive.
  Observe. Examine. Analyze. Extrapolate.
  React. Retreat.
  Survive.
  Dodge. Guard. Protect.
  Faster.
  Advance. Attack. Annihilate.
  Survive.
  Slash. Maim. Rip. Crack. Devour.
  Digest.
  Satisfy. Nourish. Sustain.
  Survive.

Chapter Eight

Penelope didn't know what she had just witnessed. She only knew it was one of the most shocking and disturbing things she had ever experienced. Even with her vision obscured by the armored figure crouching before her, shielding her, the carnage was overwhelming. And the screaming. The horrible, piercing screaming didn't cease throughout the entire episode.

It wasn't until the blood, viscera, and body parts finally settled that Penelope realized the screams were hers.

The former Sister of the Organic Humanists, finally quiet, was still trying to piece together what, exactly, had transpired when that armored figure, the Contractor known as Foxhound, turned her head.

"Stay here, you understand?" her stern voice crackled through her helmet's speakers. "Don't move until I come back."

Eyes wide and mouth agape, Penelope nodded in the affirmative.

The Contractor rose and stepped into the hallway, her heavy footfalls punctuated by the wet, sticky *slosh* of the crimson sludge covering the floor. Now, able to take in the scene before her in full, Penelope started to piece together what happened.

Foxhound—*that was her name*, Penelope remembered—had

been trying to free her. The armored warrior had incapac-
itated the guards stationed outside the stateroom and took
Brother Loch hostage. Then, only moments later, another
group of guards showed up to respond to the commotion.

No, that's not right, she puzzled. *It all happened too fast. They
weren't here to respond to the Contractor. They couldn't have
known. Mother must have sent them...to finish us off. That was
an execution squad.*

But once the guards—*no, executioners*—had surrounded
them, something had attacked them in turn. It was faster
and stronger than anything Penelope had ever seen. And
it tore them to shreds so quickly and so completely that
none of the armed men even had the chance to fire their
weapons. Whatever it was, it couldn't have been human, not
completely. Even with extensive cybernetic augmentations,
Penelope wasn't certain it was even possible for a human to
do what she had witnessed.

Plus, it was small. Too small. Half the size of most folks she
knew, if that.

The only thing she was certain of was that it had saved her.
That thing, whatever it was, had saved her, the Contractor,
and the no-name girl.

The girl, Penelope panicked. *Where is the girl?*

She looked to her left, the spot where the girl had been
curled up only moments before. But she was gone. Again,
Penelope had broken her promise. Again, she had let the little
no-name girl down. Penelope could've kicked herself. *It's no
wonder the girl—*

And then it hit her. That thing—the half-human-sized thing
that pounced at their would-be executioners and ripped them
to literal pieces—had thick, dark, curly hair. And Penelope

161

would bet her life that behind those curls sat two vibrant emerald green eyes.

☿

Brother Loch had witnessed some gruesome things in his many, many years doing missionary work for the Organic Humanists. After all, he and his Siblings had made it a point to rescue children from some of the worst parts of the solar system. Places where acts of extreme violence and depravity were commonplace. But what he had just beheld, pinned to a bulkhead by an enormous automaton in the underbelly of *Gaia*, mothership of the Organic Humanists and his home, was nothing he could have prepared himself for.

Yet, despite the horrors he beheld, something else entirely nagged at him, tugging insistently on the back of his mind. Those men, the ones that had seemingly come to his rescue before being eviscerated before his very eyes, had rounded the corner too soon, too quickly. And their weapons were already raised...

☿

"Mother," one of the many scrambling, panicked bridge crew members shouted over the din of emergency alarms, damage alerts, and incoming comms from throughout the ship, "we've got multiple reports of gunfire, and we've lost contact with several security teams!"

"Where?" Mother demanded, sitting on their throne, their fists balled tightly and their voice still booming over the bridge speaker system. "What's happening?"

162

"Uhh...everywhere," the crew member responded. "Comms coming in from multiple decks, fires reported in the central chamber, impact sensors going off in the ORC bay. Everywhere."

"What about the team sent to the midship staterooms?"

"No response."

"The Tardigrade?"

"Systems show the ship is still docked, but we can't reach anyone stationed down there."

Mother slammed their fists down, the echo reverberating through the bridge like a thunderclap. "Lock that ship down right now. I don't want it going anywhere. And find me someone, anyone who's still answering their damn comms!"

"Yes, Mother. Right away."

☿

"No, goddamn it, not now!" Fink sat in the captain's chair of the bridge of *The Tardigrade*, finally alone and ready to make his daring escape, once more slipping right through the fingers of those after him. There was only one problem: the blaring alarms and the giant red text reading *Security Lockdown* across the ship's primary display.

"Come on, come on, come on," he repeated, fingers pecking and twisting away at the ship's array of buttons and knobs, hoping to find something that might serve as an override, some means of freeing the starship from the clutches of the Organic Humanist mothership. Yet nothing he did made any difference; the sirens continued to blare defiantly, and the lockdown message remained.

The thin man took a deep breath and slumped back into the

captain's chair, defeated.

"That's okay," he muttered to himself, giving *The Tardigrade*'s central console a good kick. "I'll find another way. I always do."

He rose from his would-be throne and turned to leave the small craft's bridge.

☿

The hallway outside Penelope's stateroom was a mess of blood and body parts but, in the aftermath of the massacre, had become eerily still. Now, the only movement that Foxhound detected was the slow twirl of the red emergency lights that had activated in the corridor alongside a blaring alarm only moments before. Whether it was in response to what they had just witnessed or trouble elsewhere aboard *Gaia*, the Contractor was unsure. And she didn't care, either.

The entirety of her focus was centered upon the small figure before her, crouched down over what looked to be a torn-open rib cage, jagged bones protruding from gristly flesh. Foxhound stood, dumbfounded as she watched the no-name girl, known to the folks of Deadwood Station and its surrounding colonies as the Marrower, carefully and using only her tiny fingers, crack open each bone, one after another, and spoon their contents into her mouth.

The Contractor was so entranced that she hadn't even thought to ready her B.A.N.G. modules to defend herself when Penelope skittered in front of her, arms raised and palms facing outward.

"Don't hurt her, I beg of you," Penelope pleaded.

"Get out of the way," Foxhound barked in response.

"No, I won't let you," the woman's voice grew louder, more certain.

"You saw what she did, right?" The Contractor matched Penelope's volume and motioned to the scene before them. "You're no safer than they were. You need to get behind me."

"No, she won't hurt me."

"And what makes you so sure?"

"Because she was protecting us!"

"She was protecting herself!"

"How do you know?"

"Because that's what I would do." Foxhound made the phone gesture with her hand again, opening a private channel to Mailman, who stood in the hallway just a few steps behind her. "You saw that, right?"

"I did, mum."

"Did you see the girl's face? Did you get a scan?"

"Yes, of course."

"And?" Foxhound gritted her teeth.

"It's a ninety-nine point nine-nine percent match to yours."

"That's what I was afraid of." Foxhound exhaled, closing the private channel.

"Mum, there's something else," Mailman interjected, this time out loud for all in the hallway to hear, still pinning the gargling Brother Loch to the wall behind Foxhound and Penelope.

"Not now!" Foxhound shouted.

But the AI automaton continued, *"The Tardigrade* has been placed into full lockdown."

"I said not now, damn it!"

"She's just a little girl!" Penelope screamed, tears streaming down her face. "I made a promise."

"I don't know what she is," Foxhound answered. "But she's certainly no child."

"I don't care. I won't let you hurt her!"

"I'm not going to—"

"Miss Penelope," a small voice rang out behind the former sister.

Penelope turned around to find the no-name girl, still dripping with viscera, crimson from head to toe, standing right behind her, tugging ever-so-gently on her robe.

"I'm sorry, Miss Penelope," she squeaked with tears in her eyes. "I did the bad thing again. I got scared. I couldn't stop. I'm sorry. Please don't leave me."

Penelope, without even thinking, wrapped her arms around the girl and held her tightly. "It's okay, shh… I'm not going to leave you—"

"As I was saying," Foxhound interrupted, kneeling down to face the no-name girl. "I'm not going to hurt her. You have my word, both of you. You believe me, right?"

The no-name girl looked at the armored Contractor for a long moment, her green eyes and blood-covered face reflected in the mercenary's visor, and finally nodded her head. The Contractor looked up at Penelope, who nodded her head as well.

"But we can't stay here," Foxhound continued, rising and turning her attention to Mailman behind her. "Can you release the lockdown?"

"Not from here," the AI automaton answered. "But if we get back to the ship and I can access my full processing power, I should be able to override."

"Then that's where we're headed," said Foxhound.

"There's something else," Mailman continued. "I pinged *The*

Tardigrade for a status update, and it seems our prisoners are no longer aboard the ship."

"They what?" Foxhound gaped.

"They've escaped, mum."

"All of them?"

"All of them."

"And you're just telling me now because…"

"It was the first chance I had."

"Gotcha. That…explains the alarms. Okay…"

For the first time in as long as she could remember, Foxhound was unsure of what to do next. So, she did what she always did in situations like this: she thought out loud.

"A religious despot who wants our heads, armed guards roaming the corridors, numerous highly dangerous criminals likely hunting us down, and all of that between us and our one means of escape…and that's if Mailman can lift the lockdown. One at a time, one at a time…" She turned to Penelope, asking, "Is there any way back to the ORC pod bay other than the way we came?"

"Ummm…" Penelope squeezed her eyes shut, trying to think. "If we can get up to the central chamber, there are several freight elevators that will take us down to the bay level."

"That's as good as it's going to get, I think. Let's do that."

"We have to help Sibling Yū," the no-name girl urged, tapping Foxhound's armored thigh. "They helped us. We help them, right?"

"That's right." Penelope smiled, patting the girl on the shoulder.

"Who?" Foxhound asked.

"He knows," Penelope answered, gesturing to Brother Loch.

"If you'd be so kind, Mailman," Foxhound continued.

The automaton loosened its grip on the man pinned to the wall, and he gasped for air, coughing and gagging.

"Where is this Sibling Yū?" the Contractor demanded.

"Why should I tell you? You're just going to kill me either way," he coughed.

"Just because your so-called family left you to die," Foxhound snarled, "doesn't mean everyone is just as two-faced. We trade your life for Yū's, deal? But if I catch you following us, you're dead. No second chances. Understand?"

Brother Loch mulled this over, letting out a long sigh. "They're in the next room over." He nodded.

"Mailman, let him go," Foxhound said, and the hulking skeletal platform released its grip. The Contractor addressed Brother Loch once more, "Open it."

Brother Loch stepped up to the stateroom door, punched the security code into the control panel, and the aperture slid open with a *ka-chunk*. Inside, Sibling Yū lay on their bed, their white robes—standard for medical personnel to differentiate them from the rest of the Siblings—dotted with blood. Yū's face was bruised and littered with cuts, but they smiled nevertheless.

"It looks worse than it is," they said, rising to their feet. "It's good to see you, Penelope."

The former sister rushed to Yū's side, helping to prop the doctor up as they regained their bearings. "What did they do to you?"

"Ask him," Yū snarled in Brother Loch's direction and spit. "You've lost your way, Brother."

The doctor stepped out of her stateroom-turned-prison-cell, and her jaw dropped at the sight of the carnage.

"Looks like things went much worse for the men that put me in here," Yū continued, turning to the armored Contractor.

"You did this?"

Through her visor, Foxhound could see the fear in both Penelope's and the little girl's eyes, both certain she'd tell the doctor the truth.

"They had it coming," the Contractor finally said.

"Maybe so," the doctor replied. "I appreciate you saving me, but...this...this kind of thing is why I left everything behind to join the Organic Humanists in the first place, you know. Maybe they were bad men. But you and your kind are, too. I can't abide it."

"Good, bad...I'm the one that's going to get you and these two out of here. Think you can abide by that?"

The doctor took a moment to consider their predicament before nodding in the affirmative.

Foxhound tilted her head toward Brother Loch. "Now, what to do with this one?"

Loch lowered his head in shame just before Foxhound shoved him into the now-empty stateroom.

"A life for a life, that's what we agreed." The Contractor tapped the door controls, and before Brother Loch could protest, the portal slid shut once more. Then, she smashed the panel with a gauntleted fist, a shower of sparks falling to the deck below.

With a quick glance, she looked at her suit's power readout. It held strong at 50 percent. *Should be more than enough still,* she thought.

She turned back around to face her ragtag troop—a towering automaton piloted by an illegal AI, a disgraced former nun, a battered and beaten doctor, and a killing machine that looked convincingly like a real flesh-and-blood little girl—and gave them all two thumbs-up.

"Well, here goes nothing."

Together, they headed for *Gaia*'s central chamber.

Chapter Nine

The fields were burning, smashed heavy machinery lay strewn about, and, between it all, so many gray-clad bodies dotted the landscape. *Gaia*'s central chamber, once a pastoral oasis marked by lush greenery for all the Organic Humanist Siblings to tend and enjoy, now looked like a war zone. And at the center of the chaos stood Eris Enyo, a former officer of Earth's most respected military body, beaming gleefully at the hell she had wrought.

It reminded her of her early years in the service, long before she had been caught by one of her more inflexible underlings torturing prisoners to death. Before she had tried to explain that she was better, more effective at her job utilizing her own tactics, though brutal they may be. Before she had crushed his larynx with a single squeeze of her left hand, aided, of course, by her military-grade skeletal and muscular augmentations. Before she ran rather than face the consequences of this act, leaving a trail of death and destruction in her wake. She had so little to worry about back then. And so many ways to keep herself entertained.

There was only one thing that could have made her feel better: the chance to take revenge on that sneaky little snake of a Contractor that had drugged and captured her when her guard was down.

That would make the day a truly exquisite one, indeed, she thought.

☿

Warrick Kano counted the bodies as he traversed *Gaia*'s corridors. He always kept count, whether the bodies were of his own doing or that of another. That way, they all mattered in whatever small way. There was purpose to them. They fit like so many puzzle pieces in the grand mathematics of the cosmos. Fifty-seven, all total, with sixteen owed to the various poisons and venoms of Hecate Neumar and the remaining forty-one the frankly sloppy, careless, brutal work of Eris Enyo. Kano had not needed to kill any himself so far—a welcome convenience, one the man was thankful for.

But the farther he moved into the ship, the harder it was to avoid the pandemonium brought upon by his fellow prisoners and the roving groups of panicked Organic Humanists, some of whom were heavily armed. He had already taken a costly detour, doubling back to avoid conflict. And the decision had cost him more than just time; he was becoming increasingly worried that he was lost. That was not something that would suit the important work he had to do.

However, upon rounding a corner he believed would put him back on the right track toward the bridge, he discovered something exceedingly interesting. Something that gave him great pause. He came upon a corridor not riddled with bodies but rather with body parts. And the blood. So much blood coated the floor, the walls, and even the ceiling. It was difficult

172

to make heads or tails of any of it. But Kano still made his best estimate. By his count, it added another five dead to his tally, raising the number to sixty-two. To whom he owed credit, however, he did not know. But he dearly hoped to find out.

What he did know was that it was beautiful. Perhaps the most beautiful thing he had seen in years. This was not the work of a man. It was not the product of a selfish desire for power, money, or any of the other fleeting things humans too often sought out. This was something else entirely. It was unadulterated chaos, like that committed by the majestic beasts of Ancient Earth long before mankind had so carelessly brought upon their extinction. This was a thing of nature. And yet, there was something unnatural to it, as well—a symmetry. The natural and unnatural, bound in perfect harmony. A Fibonacci spiral of extremities and entrails.

Warrick Kano, for all his years alive, nearly every single one marred by violence and sorrow, felt a feeling so pure, so unfamiliar that he was unsure what to call it. But it merited a name. So, he called it *joy*.

The moment was ruined by the rude pounding of a fist against a bulkhead at Kano's right. The joyous—*yes, that was the correct word*, he decided—feeling lost, he tilted his head to ascertain from whence the interruption came.

There, inside a stateroom with the control unit on the door bashed-in, stood an Organic Humanist. And Kano remembered that he, too, was dressed as an Organic Humanist.

He requires my assistance, Kano thought. *I am his Sibling, and he is asking for my help. Perhaps we can help one another.*

"Brother, please," the man's muffled voice came through the translucent door panel, "I am not a prisoner. I am Brother Loch. Do you know me?"

"I know you," Kano lied.

"Then you know I act on Mother's authority."

Kano perked up.

This is getting interesting, he thought.

"I am sorry, Brother," Loch continued, "but I'm afraid I don't know you. I've spent so much time colony-side that I have neglected my duties aboard *Gaia.* There are so many new converts I have not yet met."

"Think nothing of it." Kano smiled. "Please, tell me how I may help you, and…perhaps I can ask you a favor in return."

"Anything, of course," Loch replied.

"Would you take me to the bridge? I wish to pledge my services to Mother in this disastrous time."

Loch hesitated to answer.

Kano continued, "Perhaps it is too presumptuous of me to think someone so fresh as I to the family might have anything to offer—"

"Not at all," Loch interrupted. "I need to head that way myself, and I'm certain, with so many infidels aboard our ship, our home… It's just nice to find myself in the company of a Sibling so dedicated. I just forgot what that was like, is all."

"Tell me what I must do."

"There should be an emergency release in the hallway bulkhead, just beside this door. All you have to do is remove the panel. The one in here was deactivated, but it should look the same, like a"—Loch stepped back, leaning to his side to look into a panel in the wall of the stateroom— "red lever with a yellow handle. Do you see it?"

"I do," Kano answered, removing the bulkhead paneling and peeking inside.

"Pull it."

Kano pulled the lever, and the doorframe made a loud *thunk*. Then, together, the two men pushed open the stateroom door. Brother Loch emerged, embracing the man he believed to be his Sibling—a devout one, just like him.

Warrick Kano, the Savage of Europa, looked back at Loch and smiled.

☿

Walking ahead of Penelope and the no-name girl—and with Mailman trailing behind—Foxhound and Sibling Yū led the pack, Yū acting as the Contractor's guide through the hodge-podge of *Gaia*'s pathways, careful to avoid the other panicked residents of the OH mothership. Foxhound was the first to finally speak.

"You didn't seem all that bothered by the carnage back there," she said to Sibling Yū.

"I've seen worse. Not much, but some," Yū answered. "I don't like it. Armed or not, wrong or right, those were my Siblings. And even if they weren't, you know us doctors. *Thou shalt not kill* and all that. But you...this is what you do, isn't it."

It was more statement than question. Like so many others among the Organic Humanists, Yū didn't trust Contractors and saw them as nothing more than glorified mercenaries— something Foxhound found exceedingly ironic since the OH was looked at as a cult by outsiders like herself.

Foxhound glanced back at Penelope, who eyeballed the pair nervously, wrapping a protective arm around the no-name girl.

"Yeah," Foxhound said. "This is what I do."

Yū lowered their head, shaking it gently back and forth. "I'm sorry, that's not fair. You saved us. You saved *me*. I should be grateful."

They came to a T-junction and, peeking her head around a corner, Foxhound saw a small patrol of armed men. Behind her, she raised her right hand, signaling for the group to stop. She turned her head and, using that same hand, brought her index finger up to her helmet, the universal sign to keep quiet.

Whispering, she responded, "Plenty of time to be grateful later. Right now, we have to get back to my ship."

With that, she rounded the corner, dropped to one knee, extended her left arm, and fired a volley of pellets at the men. In a cacophony of pops and thuds, the pellets hit their marks, unleashing the purple knockout gas inside and, one by one, dropping the men to the deck, unconscious.

The Contractor leaned back around the corner and motioned for the group to continue following her.

"The entrance to the central chamber should be just ahead," Sibling Yū said once they were sure the coast was clear.

They continued onward.

♀

The panic aboard *Gaia*'s bridge hadn't dissipated in the least. If anything, things had gotten even more chaotic. Mother, for all their grace and wisdom, couldn't keep up with the deluge of flashing red lights, shouting crew members, and blaring sirens. And they were beginning to lose patience with all of it.

"More alerts coming in from the central chamber!" one crew member to Mother's left, by their estimation, hollered. "Multiple dead, fires spreading, and…some kind of monster tearing through the fields!"

"Several security teams are reporting bodies," another, to Mother's left, recited. "No physical wounds visible. Could be asphyxiation or poisoning!"

"No response from the guards or Brother Loch on the stateroom decks," yet another announced. "Complete radio silence. But we have requests for assistance coming in from all decks. Mother, our Siblings are panicking. They need help!"

"Fires are still raging in the central chamber," a voice cried out somewhere behind Mother. "No hull breaches as of yet, but it's only a matter of time before they reach critical systems!"

Not only was the disarray an affront to Mother's sensibilities, but it made it impossible for them to concentrate, to focus on even one, let alone all the emergencies. Mother had reached their breaking point.

"Someone turn off that godforsaken siren now!" Mother rubbed their temples with their long, slender fingers. The sirens cut out, and a tense silence fell over the bridge. After a few deep breaths, Mother continued, "We can't help everyone. We can't save those we've already lost. But all is not lost. Can we still send out a shipwide announcement?"

No one answered.

"Yes or no?!" Mother demanded.

Meekly, a woman toward the front of the bridge finally responded, keeping her head down, "Yes, Mother. The shipwide communications systems are still active."

"Then record this and play it on repeat," Mother said with a scoff. The meek woman sat back down at her station, punched in a series of commands, and turned back to face the leader of the Organic Humanists sitting on their throne. "Siblings, Sisters, Brothers, Children, this is your Mother. All who are able, return to and remain in your quarters. If you can, lock your doors and remain there until I give you the all-clear. We are under a vicious assault, a cloak-and-dagger operation enacted by those who would wish our peaceful organization harm. The Contractor known as Foxhound, by the order of Earth and its heretics, has unleashed a group of vicious, violent, malicious infidels upon our home. Surely this is with the aim of destroying us. But we will not waiver. We will not falter. We will not be defeated. We will hold fast and survive, for we are survivors. Hold those you love close and wait for further instructions. We will make it through this together!"

Cheers rang out once more among the bridge crew, though there were fewer this time. Once the racket had quieted down, Mother made their way over to the meek comms officer, removed their halo-shaped crown with its built-in microphone, and muttered another order so that only the woman before them could hear.

"I want you to send out a separate message to my security teams. Tell them that all who are able are to converge toward *Gaia*'s bow. I want the bridge protected. If we are to survive this incursion, those essential to our organization must be prioritized and protected. And do it discreetly, understand?"

"But, Mother," the officer protested, careful not to make a scene, "we've lost so many innocents already. Surely, some teams can stay behind to protect those in need of—"

"Sister," Mother hissed, "are you questioning my authority? Do I need to make this request of another? Perhaps someone more dedicated to our cause?"

"No…" the woman answered. "It's just…my children, my family…they're all still out there, somewhere."

"We are all your family, Sister. Sacrifices must be made for

178

the good of us all. Count yourself fortunate that you are not yet among them."

The woman lowered her head in defeat. "Yes, Mother. Message sent."

But Mother wasn't done with her yet. They leaned in for one last remark.

"Challenge me again, and you can join your family out there."

☿

But we will not waiver. We will not falter. We will not be defeated. We will hold fast and survive, for we are survivors. Hold those you love close and wait for further instructions. We will make it through this together!

Mother's announcement blared through the ship's loud-speaker system as Brother Loch led his wayward Sibling—in reality, the assassin known as Warrick Kano, the Savage of Europa, in disguise—through the ship's corridors, avoiding as much carnage and disorder as possible, toward the bridge.

Yet, as the announcement blared over the intercom, Loch thought he heard something else as they passed yet another group of bodies strewn across the deck. Loch halted and kneeled, grabbing one of the men by the jaw and tilting his head to the side. There, in his ear, Loch found what he was looking for: a one-way communicator, the same kind that had been handed out to the security team squad leaders when they were given their firearms. He put the device in his ear and stood up.

A small voice, that of a woman, came through the device. Loch listened for a moment, holding one hand to his opposite ear to quiet the surrounding noise and the other raised to his

Sibling, a single finger pointed vertically, telling him to wait.

Loch's brow ruffled, and his mouth turned downward in a scowl. He removed the device from his ear, threw it to the ground, and crushed it under his foot.

"Is something the matter?" Kano finally asked.

"No," Brother Loch answered. "Well, yes. But I'm not sure what to make of it just yet. Don't worry. We're in no immediate danger. But we should hurry. These hallways are about to get a lot more crowded."

"How much farther?"

"We will be there soon, barring any more setbacks. Come, let's go."

Together, they continued their march toward the bridge, Loch setting the pace a bit quicker than before.

☿

As Foxhound and company stepped from the final corridor into *Gaia*'s central chamber, the Contractor tried to listen to the announcement blaring on repeat over the ship's intercom system. She could only barely make out what Mother's voice was saying, but it was clear that the target on their backs had just gotten bigger.

However, in light of what they had just come upon, it seemed almost immaterial. Before them, stretched out across the Organic Humanist mothership's sweeping, vast central chamber, were not the fields of grain, lush greenery, walking paths, grassy parks, and gardens they had expected. Instead, there was destruction, fire, smoke, and, unless Foxhound's eyes were fooling her, bodies. So many bodies. Were it not for her suit's air-scrubbing filtration system, she was sure she'd be hacking and coughing upon the unmistakable stench of death.

These were killing fields.

And there, at the center of the brutal anarchy, behind a thin veil of billowing smoke, Foxhound was certain she could make out the hulking silhouette of the Blood Queen of Titan herself, Eris Enyo.

Thankfully for the Contractor, the murderous former Aegis Guardsman had not yet noticed their group standing at the edge of the expanse. That gave them time to hide and, hopefully, come up with some kind of plan. But what that plan might entail, Foxhound was uncertain.

Eris Enyo was such a formidable foe that the Contractor herself had relied on cunning and deceit in the criminal's capture, choosing to drug the woman when she was not expecting it rather than risk an all-out brawl, a fight that Enyo would have certainly won. Now, she was unsure she'd be able to avoid that outcome. And Enyo, ever the warrior, would be happy to oblige. After all, it meant a chance at revenge against the one Contractor that had bested her. And after so many others had failed and, subsequently, fallen by her hand.

Foxhound tried to motion for everyone to get down, but by the time she had turned around, she found that both Penelope and Yū had already dropped to their knees. Not for fear of the monster up ahead, no. They were weeping.

This is their home, Foxhound remembered. *And it's burning.*

The no-name girl stood at Penelope's side, tugging at her robes and petting her hair. It was a fruitless attempt at kindness but an attempt no less. The Marrower, the so-called monster that had viciously torn apart so many, was trying to console the woman who had protected her, saved her.

181

She's exhibiting sympathy, Foxhound noted. *How curious.*

Crouched, the Contractor shuffled back toward her companions, trying to come up with something, anything, that might help them avoid the fight ahead and maybe keep their minds off the fact that the only home they had was being destroyed before their eyes. But she came up empty-handed.

She was a solitary warrior, her only real friend an artificial intelligence housed in her ship. She had no idea how to console anyone, let alone distract them from her troubles. With most of her human interactions, she was the trouble.

All I know how to do is fight, she thought. *Yes, that's it! All I know how to do is fight!*

The Contractor brought her right hand up and, with her left, tapped several buttons on her gauntlet's control panel. With a hiss and a clunk, the modular armor unsealed and expanded, loosening enough that Foxhound could pull it from her arm. As she held it, she flexed the fingers on her left hand, the sensation of the air an almost alien feeling.

She motioned Penelope forward. "Your left arm."

Confused, Penelope protested, "No, I can't. I can't kill anyone. You have to pick someone—"

"It's okay," Foxhound interrupted. "All the ordinance in this one is nonlethal. I promise."

"But why me? I don't know how to fight."

"The girl is too small, and she needs your protection. It won't fit on Mailman's big mechanical arms. And Yū is barely in any shape to walk, let alone defend you." Foxhound looked at the doctor. "No offense."

"No, you're right," Yū replied, looking into Penelope's eyes. "If it's going to be anyone, it has to be you. You have to protect this girl."

Without another word, Penelope stuck out her left arm. Foxhound slipped the gauntlet onto the former sister, tapped a few more controls, and the device gave off another hiss and clunk as it sealed to Penelope's arm.

"Okay, I set it up, so it's real simple," Foxhound explained. "All you have to do is point your arm where you want to shoot and then squeeze your fist. The gauntlet will do the rest. And then it's sleepy time for anyone you hit, got it?"

Penelope nodded, her lips pursed.

"Right here," Foxhound said, pointing at a little display on the upper forearm of the B.A.N.G. module. "Sixteen. That's how many shots you've got left. Use them if you have to, but make sure you're keeping a close watch on that number. Do you understand?"

Penelope nodded again.

This time, Foxhound addressed the whole group. "You have to go back through the ship. I know it seems dangerous, but I promise you, out here is far worse."

"What?" Sibling Yū's eyes were full of fear. "No, you can't leave us."

"We'll never make it without you," Penelope concurred. "We're not like you, and the whole ship is after us."

"You have to try. Now go, before she sees—"

"Mum," Mailman interrupted, "I am detecting high levels of particulates in the air."

Still standing at full height, apparently oblivious to the situation at hand, the AI's mechanical exoskeleton towered over the group, and its voice boomed. The automaton might as well have been a beacon, signaling to everyone in the vicinity their location.

"Your suit is rated to filter such particulates, but I'm afraid

Penelope, Yū, and the girl may be at risk of—"

Foxhound held up both her hands and shushed the towering automaton. "Mailman, get down!"

But it was too late. Foxhound turned her head to see the silhouette of Eris Enyo through the smoke, a bit larger than it had been only moments before. And it was getting bigger. No, not bigger. Closer.

Foxhound looked back at Mailman, giving the AI automaton one last set of instructions, "Get them back to the ship. And if I'm not with you once you're ready to launch, leave without me."

She didn't wait for an answer. Instead, she turned back around, braced herself, and lifted her remaining gauntlet toward the behemoth barreling toward her.

"Go!" she barked, happy to hear the sound of footsteps moving away, fading behind her.

☿

Hecate Neumar wandered back through the Organic Human- ist mothership the same way she had come in, passing the same bodies she had left in her wake. Her excitement regarding her newfound freedom and such a rich pool of prey candidates had seemed, at first, a blessing. But she had quickly grown bored. The men she encountered, armed or not, were too easily beguiled, tricked, and dispatched. And hunting them, for Neumar, was no fun at all.

But the Widow of Venus had seen one man with enough spunk and fire in his eyes to perhaps quench her blood lust, at least long enough for her to take leave of *Gaia* and find more interesting hunting grounds somewhere else in the Kuiper

184

Belt. So, she stepped over the twisted, discolored remains of each and every man she had killed on her way back toward the ship's ORC pod bay and her quarry, the man that had freed her, the clever and conniving Fink Ames.

She didn't know much about the man she had decided to hunt, but she knew enough to keep focused on that goal. She knew that he was a prisoner of the Contractor known as Foxhound, just as she was. Based on the other company they kept, that meant he was likely very dangerous or, at the very least, had been credited with a long enough list of crimes to get Earth's attention. She also knew, in watching him kill someone he had once considered a friend and the threat of death he had offered to the rest of his fellow prisoners, that he was keen on staying alive. And that meant he'd likely put up a good fight, if only in the name of survival. Her mouth watered just thinking about it.

Yes, she mused, *he's exactly what I need right now.*

She swallowed, the familiar taste of venom slowly trickling out of her salivary glands—another of her many augmentations—and onto her tongue.

Chapter Ten

Even with her flesh peppered with lethal projectiles from Foxhound's remaining B.A.N.G. module, Eris Enyo didn't miss a step, colliding with the armored Contractor at nearly a full sprint. The crunch of her captor's suit as Enyo wrapped her arms around the woman was like music to the Blood Queen of Titan's ears, a song she had yearned to hear since the moment she woke up in that cell aboard *The Tardigrade*.

Foxhound, draped over Enyo's shoulder and with the wind knocked out of her, wheezed and coughed through her suit's external speakers.

The hulking former Aegis Guardsman skittered to a stop, leaving a deep gash in the rich farming soil beneath her feet. Wrapping her giant hands around the Contractor's waist, she held the woman out in front of her. Enyo frowned at her own reflection in Foxhound's visor.

"Activate stun," Foxhound grunted, her teeth gritted under her helmet. But nothing happened, not even sparks. She glanced at the power readout and watched as it flickered, reading 9 percent, then eight, then seven, and falling. The damage to her suit was so severe, and the battery so drained that even her emergency fail-safes had ceased to function.

Enyo laughed.

"Suit's already busted, huh?" she snarled. "You know, this is a lot less fun if I can't see your face. How am I supposed to know how much pain you're in?"

"Sorry to disappoint," the Contractor replied between coughs.

"Not a problem," Enyo grinned. "I'll just have to take that helmet off you, and then we can continue our little dance number. What do you say?"

With one hand still wrapped around Foxhound's waist, dangling the woman in the air like a rag doll, Enyo palmed the Contractor's helmet, digging her fingers in as best she could. With a tug, she tested her grip and, satisfied, she pulled in earnest, trying to rip Foxhound's helmet off as promised.

But just as Foxhound's suit began to crack and hiss, its hermetic seals tearing open, Enyo heard the familiar popping sound of the Contractor's B.A.N.G. module report. She looked down to see Foxhound firing round after round of spreadshot pellets into her stomach, a slow trickle of blood oozing from the dozen or so wounds.

With all the adrenaline and painkillers coursing through her veins, Enyo couldn't feel any pain from the gut shots. But she knew that, with enough damage and time, that wouldn't matter. She could still bleed out. She could still die. And that just wouldn't do. One of them was going to perish in this fight, but it wasn't going to be Enyo.

With a howl, she slammed Foxhound down into the dirt at her feet so hard that the Contractor's body bounced before sinking limply into the soil. Then, for good measure, she slammed her fists down into Foxhound's chest and head, further deepening the crater below and cracking the

Contractor's chest plate and visor.

Somehow still conscious, Foxhound tried to raise her right arm, pointing the B.A.N.G. module once more at Enyo's stomach. But before she could fire, Enyo grabbed the Contractor by the wrist and, spinning on her heels, threw the armored woman across the landscape, her body twisting unnaturally as it skipped across the soil like a stone on the surface of a reservoir and slammed into the wreckage of a still smoking combine.

Eris Enyo laughed with glee at her former captor's body bouncing across the ship's central chamber as she stretched her arms across her chest and tilted her head from side to side, cracking her neck. Then, hungry for more, she set to march toward her quarry.

♀

Penelope, followed closely by Sibling Yū, the no-name girl, and trailed by Mailman in its thundering exoskeleton, made their way through *Gaia*'s corridors, doing their best to avoid the wandering groups of armed guards and panicked Siblings.

But after only a few twists and turns, Penelope abruptly halted the group. Turning on her heels, she looked at the no-name girl and then at Yū.

"I'm sorry, I have to do something. Can you watch her?"

"Absolutely," Yū answered, placing a hand on the girl's shoulder as Penelope passed them to address Foxhound's automaton companion at the rear of the group.

The no-name girl looked up at Yū, who leaned down in turn.

"You know, I've been meaning to talk to you this whole time. I'm sorry I haven't found a moment."

Staring through her thick curly locks at Yū with her big emerald eyes, the girl smiled sheepishly. "It's okay, Sibling Yū. What do you want to talk to me about?"

"I just wanted to tell you how proud of you I am. You're being incredibly brave today. We're going through some big scary stuff, and you haven't tried to run or hide or anything. You've been standing by us through it all. I'm very impressed. You know who you remind me of?"

"Who?" the girl giggled.

"My daughter," Yū replied.

"Is she here on the ship, too?" the girl asked eagerly.

"No, my dear," Sibling Yū sighed. "She died a very long time ago."

"Oh," the girl whispered. "What happened to her?"

"I don't know if you remember or heard this, but I used to work as a doctor on Ganymede. Do you know where that is?"

The girl shook her head.

"Ganymede is one of Jupiter's moons. Well, when I went to work there many, many years ago, my partner and I thought that Ganymede might be a good place to start a family. So, we adopted this beautiful little girl, and, wouldn't you know it, she grew up in a flash and decided that she wanted to be a doctor just like me. So, she went to school, scored tremendously on her aptitudes, and graduated at the top of her class."

The no-name girl stared into Yū's eyes, enraptured by their story.

"She could have gone to work anywhere," Yū continued, "even on Earth. She was that good. But do you know what she decided?"

"Nuh-uh," the girl answered, shaking her head.

"She decided to volunteer at the trauma centers all around

Ganymede. You see, Ganymede can be a pretty scary place. There are gangs and lots of danger and violence, and we never seemed to have enough doctors to help all the sick and injured people that needed it."

The no-name girl nodded her head. "Then what happened?"

"One day, she got called into the hospital where I worked. It was the first time we got to work side by side. I was so proud of her and what she had become. She was a better doctor than I had ever dreamed I could be. I was so in awe of her. But then, we got reports of an attack in one of the poorer dormitories, where people and their families live, near the hospital. Pretty soon after that, patients began to pour into the hospital and, in trying to help as many people as we could, we were separated."

The girl inched forward, extending a hand toward Yū. Yū took the girl's hand in their own, gently brushing their thumb across the girl's tiny knuckles.

"While I was in a trauma suite, that means I was performing surgery, she had gone back out into the waiting room to see if there was anyone in need of urgent help. But when she got out there, a gang of thugs, the same ones responsible for the attack at the dormitories, were in the waiting room, causing a ruckus. They had heard that our hospital was where most of the victims were being taken, and they were searching for someone, a man. And they wanted to kill him. But my daughter stood between the thugs and the injured man they were after. It didn't matter who he was or what he had done. To my daughter, he was just another person that needed help. So, they shot her."

The girl lifted her other hand up to Yū's cheek, wiping a tear away.

Yū continued, "She was still alive when I got out of surgery, but it was too late to save her. She told me what happened, that the thugs had been scared off by security right afterward. She had saved that man, even though he probably didn't deserve it. And she paid for his life with her own."

"Is that why you left Ganymede?" the girl asked.

"One of the reasons, yes," Yū answered. "Part of me died that day, too. Not long after, my partner and I split up, and there was nothing left for me there. So, I chose to leave and become someone else. A fresh start. And that's what brought me here."

"I'm sorry that happened to your daughter."

"Oh, that's okay. It was so long ago, but sometimes it still hurts like it was yesterday."

"What was her name?" The girl brushed her hair aside and, for the first time, Yū saw the little no-name girl's face.

"Leila." Yū smiled. "We called her Leila."

Finally, Penelope returned to the front of the group, signaling for Yū and the girl to follow. Only this time, Mailman's towering exoskeleton didn't follow them, instead trudging off back in the direction they had come.

☿

Phineas Ames, known simply as Fink by friend and foe alike, was not about to be marooned on a ship he had spent so much time and effort trying to get away from—either of them. But since he couldn't figure out how to release *The Tardigrade* from *Gaia*'s lockdown, he hatched another plan. He was going to collect all the supplies he could find and commandeer one of the ORC pods, riding the damn thing back to Deadwood where he could find another ship to take him as far from

Organic Humanists, Contractors, and anyone else who knew his name as possible.

Knowing the chaos he had wrought in freeing his fellow prisoners, he was well aware that his time was limited. If Foxhound had survived this long, she and her automaton companion were sure to return to the ship, along with God knows who else, as soon as they could manage. And while the AI aboard the hulking automaton might be able to bypass the OH mothership's security and release the lockdown, the pair wasn't likely to welcome him with open arms. In fact, they might just launch him out into the blackness of space for what he had done. Hell, depending on whoever put the bounty on his head in the first place, the contract might not even stipulate that he needed to be brought in alive. Fink preferred not to find out.

Of course, that was only one of the potentially negative outcomes. It was also just as likely that the ship might start evacuations and, were that to happen, someone aboard would surely recognize him from his time masquerading as Brother Phineas. Then, they might put two and two together and figure out that this whole mess was his doing. Or worse, they might enlist his assistance in evacuating the ship.

What did happen, however, was the one thing Fink hadn't counted on.

"Fink, honey, I'm home!" Hecate Neumar sang as she entered the ORC pod bay.

Having just loaded a crate of foodstuffs and medical supplies from *The Tardigrade*'s living areas, the man sat in one of *Gaia*'s ORC pods, catching his breath. But upon hearing Neumar's voice, Fink clapped a hand over his own mouth, quieting his panting.

His lips pursed and nostrils flared, the man reached down for the rivet gun at his side. But the makeshift weapon wasn't there. He checked for the plasma torch on his other hip, but it, too, was missing. In fact, the belt to which he had attached them was gone entirely. And then Fink remembered: he had left it sitting on the deck of *The Tardigrade*'s cargo bay.

As he had been packing up supplies, Fink realized that the large, heavy belt was slowing him down. So, with the intention of grabbing it once he had everything he needed loaded into the ORC pod he had claimed for himself, he had left it lying there, out in the open, certain that nobody would catch him unawares.

Hecate Neumar, the Widow of Venus, had proven him utterly wrong.

And now he had left himself practically defenseless against a woman known for her guile, viciousness, and a particularly perverse love of venoms, toxins, and poisons.

With only one path of recourse, Fink decided to do one of the things he did best. He hid.

But he also knew it was only a matter of time until Neumar found him. Then he'd have to figure out another plan.

Fink reached into the pocket of his jumpsuit, the one he had stolen from the security substation on Deadwood, and wrapped his bony fingers around the four shit sticks he had stashed in his pockets. The ones he had taken right out of the Contractor's own ship after escaping his cell.

If he could get Neumar close enough without alerting her to his presence, the shit sticks might just give him the edge he needed to take her down. He just had to wait for the right moment.

He wasn't excited about dealing with that comedown a

second time, and he didn't have Billie and their fully stocked apothecary to help him through it this time, but it was still a better option for him than death.

☿

Compared to the lower decks, especially toward the aft of *Gaia*, the corridors near the ship's bridge were downright crowded. Brother Loch and his wayward companion even had to sidestep between groups of armed guards at certain points.

Loch had believed in Mother's path for the Organic Humanists. He had even learned to accept that violence might be inevitable if they wanted to retain their sovereignty and maintain religious freedoms in an increasingly repressive system. But this, the army of men protecting the bridge at the expense of the rest of his Siblings and all the children they had saved, he found deeply unsettling.

Numerous parts of the ship, their one and only home, were burning. And there were criminal maniacs running free, murdering all who crossed their path and leaving destruction in their wake. Yet here were so many able-bodied men who were capable of helping those in need, and they were doing nothing. Worse, they were protecting a so-called leader who prioritized their own safety over that of the meek.

This was not a simple case of adapting to the solar system at large. This was full-blown corruption. And Brother Loch had just about enough of it. Having felt so much despair in the trek from the staterooms-turned-holding-cells, passing body after body, Loch now felt resolute in his purpose. Someone had to do something, to take a stand for what was right and just, and who better than him?

We can't change humanity, he remembered the words that Sister Penelope had once told him, *but we can do our best to help as many in need as possible, especially those who cannot ask for it themselves.*

It all seemed so long ago, but it rang truer now than ever.

I should have helped her, he thought, a pang of regret nagging at his mind. *She deserved better than my misguided blindness. And she was right. What we've become, what we're doing. This is all so wrong. So many dead already, and for what? To protect Mother so that they might lead us toward more bloodshed? I should have said something, done something sooner.*

But that was all behind him. Now, all he could do was focus on what was ahead.

"Why are there so many guards up here?" The almost whispered question came from behind. Lost in thought, Brother Loch had forgotten about the man he was leading to the bridge. And with whom he hadn't shared the information he had gleaned from the dead guard's communicator. Between groups of guards, Loch halted and turned to the man.

"Treason," he said, surprised at his own candor. He knew, as soon as the word left his lips, that he might be making a fatal mistake. This man, after all, had told him at their first meeting that he wished to pledge himself and his service to Mother's purpose. But Loch also knew that this man, his Sibling, had a right to know the truth so that he might decide for himself whether Mother's crusade was to be his own.

"I see," the man said, his eyes scanning the hallway in either direction.

"Listen to me," Loch said in a panic, "this is not our path. This is not what we are. What Mother is doing is selfish and

195

dangerous, and it flies in the face of the tenets of the Organic Humanists."

Warrick Kano rested a hand gently on Brother Loch's shoulder and smiled, saying, "I know. It's okay."

Loch exhaled, not realizing he had been holding his breath.

"I have to do something," Loch continued. "I have to confront Mother, but I can't ask you to join me in this fool's errand."

"You don't have to," Kano replied. "I'm coming with you."

Feeling something wet roll down the side of his face, Loch wiped his cheek. It was a tear. Loch had started to cry. But it wasn't out of sadness or fear. It was relief. He was about to do the hardest thing he had ever done, and when he did, he wouldn't be alone. That made all the difference.

♀

"I have to say, I'm pretty disappointed," Eris Enyo, the Blood Queen of Titan, roared as she approached Foxhound's body, lying in a heap against the still-smoking combine wreckage. "I knew you were a coward, but I thought you'd put up at least a bit of a fight. To kill you now, like this, seems almost too cruel, even for me. Almost."

Enyo marched up to the Contractor and stopped for a moment to admire her work. But when she saw just how still Foxhound's body remained, a frown formed on her face. With one of her enormous boots, she gave the armored woman's helmet a nudge.

Nothing.

Another nudge

And still nothing.

Finally, with frustration, Eris wound her leg up and kicked Foxhound straight in the chest.

This time, the Contractor began to cough, heave, and groan.

"Oh good," Enyo said, "You're still alive. Had me worried there for a second. Can you hear me? Raise your hand if you can hear me."

Foxhound's arms remained limp, hanging at her sides.

Eris Enyo let out a chuckle. "Ah, I'm just messing with you. I know you can't lift those little noodles. With how bad you're looking, I doubt we've got much time left together, so I'm gonna tell you a little story, but I'll make it quick."

With a grunt, the enormous woman got down on one knee and leaned forward, propping herself up on an elbow. With a deep breath, she continued, "I grew up on one of Earth's colony barges in the South Pacific, about as poor as poor gets. Even with my mom's Guaranteed Income, the slumlords and the gangs meant we were barely scraping by. What I didn't know at the time was that she was also spending some of that government credit on whatever pills she could find, saving them up for trade while I was going hungry. On my tenth birthday, I found her body. She was already cold. No note, no inheritance, no nothing. I was out on my own. So, I did what most kids on the barges did. I joined one of those gangs and started doing work for the slumlords."

Enyo winced, pressing her free hand to her stomach. When she pulled away, it was covered in blood. "Looks like you might've gotten me better than I thought. That's okay, I've survived worse. Plus, as you know, I've got this cool little trick to keep me going."

With her bloodied hand, she made a tight fist, and her knuckles popped. She closed her eyes and took a deep breath as the adrenaline and painkillers flooded her system once more. She opened her eyes and gave Foxhound a wink.

"Anyhow, where was I? Right. Poor, dead mom, joined a gang. Lied, cheated, stole, you know the drill. Got in a lot of fights, started most of them, even killed a few folks. Felt good. All of it. So, I kept at it. Rose through the ranks and saved up just barely enough to take a little trip to one of the continents to get some real dirt beneath my feet for the first time ever. And since I was eighteen at the time and I never really had any intention of ever going back to that shithole I crawled out of, I enlisted with the Omniphage Security Force. Went through basic, scored high enough marks that my XOs mostly overlooked all the troublemaking but not high enough to avoid punishment altogether. So, I got better at hiding, learned who to trust and who to watch out for, that sort of thing. Eventually, I got noticed by some higher-ups who saw fit to put me into the Aegis Guard program, stuck me alongside the most elite soldiers in the whole of Earth's military. And, goddamn, I was good at the work. Became an officer, got promoted. Even got to take my own little strike force out around the outer planets. Until that little shit-stirrer, Private—"

Enyo saw the Contractor convulse and paused. Foxhound let out a weak cough and, once it subsided, a whisper that Enyo couldn't quite make out. The giant woman leaned a little closer.

"Get to the fucking point," the Contractor wheezed.

With a roar, Eris Enyo brought one of her fists down onto Foxhound's helmet, sending a spiderweb of cracks across her visor.

"I was a god!" the gargantuan warrior howled, "A god among insects! And you, one of those very insects, thought that you

could cage me?!"

Foxhound's left hand, the one missing its B.A.N.G. module, lay palm-down against the ground at her side. And though she was struggling to stay awake—her significant injuries numerous and Eris Enyo pontificating at great length above her—she thought she felt a familiar, steady vibration quaking the soil that touched her fingers. But Enyo hadn't seemed to notice, as her fervor didn't wane.

"—so cowardly a method, too, spiking my entire store of Jovian wine. And such a high dosage it must've been. How many of my men did you have to kill as collateral? You think *you're* righteous, and *I'm* the criminal? You're a lapdog of Earth, and you'll never be more than that. You're no better than me."

The Blood Queen of Titan spit at the Contractor at her feet and, with a deep inhale, paused. She looked down, confused.

So, it's not just me, Foxhound thought, noticing that the thundering vibrations had increased in intensity. She even thought, for a moment, that she could actually hear them. Had Eris Enyo managed to rip her helmet off as planned, the former Aegis Guardsman would have seen the smallest hint of a smile on the Contractor's lips.

Instead, she turned around just in time to see a lumbering bipedal skeleton, even larger than she, charging straight at her. Enyo attempted to brace herself, knowing the automaton was too close to avoid.

Just feet from its target and running at full speed, Mailman dove at Eris Enyo, tackling her into the combine wreckage just behind Foxhound. Together, the automaton and Enyo crashed through the machine's center, ripping through it like a meteorite and sending debris and shrapnel soaring across

Gaia's central chamber in an explosion of smoke and metal.

Enyo and Mailman, their limbs entwined, rolled through flames and over bodies, neither releasing their grip until finally Enyo managed to shift Mailman's mechanical body under her and held the automaton beneath her weight as they slid to a stop, leaving a tremendous gouge in the soil beneath them.

"A fucking robot?!" Eris Enyo growled as she braced her legs, straddling Mailman and digging her toes into the ground beneath them. She pinned Mailman's exoskeleton down with one arm and, leaning as much of her weight down on top of the automaton, punched as hard as she could over and over at the module locked in its center.

"You think your fucking robot can stop me?!" She hammered down on Mailman's control unit with everything she had. Mailman shifted beneath Enyo's weight, trying to gain purchase and right itself, but, with a shove, the former Aegis Guardsman pinned the automaton back down into the dirt.

"I'm not a robot," Mailman said, as chipper as ever.

"I don't care what you are!" Enyo screamed in response, her rage fueling her to strike at the AI automaton's control unit even harder. With each hit, the pair shifted deeper and deeper into the soil, the shock waves loosening the rich dirt around them.

Mailman continued, unfettered by Enyo's assault, "I'm a Modular Automaton Intended for Labor—"

Eris punched Mailman's control unit. They sunk deeper.

"—in Manufacturing—"

Another punch. And deeper still.

"—Agriculture—"

Another punch. Deeper.

"—and Navigation." With one of its enormous claws shut

tight, Mailman pistoned its arm into Enyo's still-bleeding belly, right at the same spot in which Foxhound had unleashed a volley of projectiles, ripping straight through the soft flesh, missing all the woman's titanium skeletal reinforcements, and out the other side.

Her eyes widened in shock. Enyo knew, in that moment, that there was no amount of adrenaline or painkillers that could save her anymore. She coughed, spraying blood onto the automaton below. With nothing left but fury, she raised her fist and continued striking at Mailman, each swing weaker than before until, finally, she fell limp against the automaton.

Mailman retracted its arm through the enormous woman's lifeless body, unceremoniously shoved her aside, and rose to its feet. Then, the automaton marched back over to Foxhound, bits of soil falling from the exoskeleton with each thundering step.

Despite her injuries, the Contractor had managed to prop herself up, giving Mailman a nod as it approached.

"Good to see you, buddy," she said. "You okay? For a second there, I thought I might lose you."

"I am sensing one minor stress fracture in my control unit," the AI automaton responded. "Otherwise, I am happy to report that I am in good working order. However, were my control unit destroyed, I would have simply returned to *The Tardigrade*. How are you?"

"Right, fail-safes. Handy, that. I've...been better," the Contractor wheezed. "Why did you come back, anyway? I told you to go."

"At first, Mistress Penelope explained she was worried about your well-being."

"Well, that was nice of her."

"I thought so, too. But I informed her that it wasn't a good enough reason to ignore your order."

Foxhound let out a pained laugh.

"Then, she informed me that my size and volume were so great that I might be endangering them more than helping. And after careful consideration and an unfortunate encounter with some armed guards, I came to agree that she might be correct. So, instead, I chose to come back and help you."

"I very much appreciate the assistance. But I think I'm gonna need a little more help."

"What can I do?"

"Can you carry me back to *The Tardigrade?*" Foxhound barely got the question out before she lost consciousness.

"It would be my pleasure, mum."

Intermission

Survive.

The young woman woke to blindingly bright strobing red lights and the blare of emergency sirens. She rubbed her eyes and looked around but didn't recognize the small room she was in. She did notice that the ceiling and walls were all made of satin-finished metal—a signature of just about any small spacecraft traversing the solar system. She could also see the undersides of tables mounted to the walls flanking her, all made from the same metal. She was aboard a ship—probably in the crew's common area—she was sure of that much. And if she could see the underside of the tables, that meant she was lying on the floor. But that wasn't what concerned her most.

It's cold, she thought. *Why am I so cold?*

She brought her arms close to her chest with a shiver and, feeling her fingers brush against her bare skin, answered her own question.

Because I'm naked.

And that led her to another question.

Why am I naked?

But the flashing lights and ear-piercing sirens cut through her disorientation, reminding her that there were much more pressing matters to attend to. She hopped to her feet and gave the rest of the room a once-over.

She saw a line of integrated lockers on one wall, all with their doors ajar. Inside one hung a drab green jumpsuit and, sitting just below it, a pair of boots.

She slipped into the jumpsuit and zipped it up, noticing an embroidered logo on one shoulder. It was an image of a snarling animal—one the young woman had never seen before, even in pictures—with floppy brown ears, a white snout, and a black button nose. And below it, a single word.

"Foxhound," She read with a shrug. "Huh."

She stepped into the boots and turned around, spying a door on the opposite wall.

Move.

She ran for the door, slapping the panel beside it to open it up, and stepped out into the adjoining passageway. To her right, she saw another larger door with the words "ORC Pod Bay" emblazoned over it. To her left was a ladder.

Observe. Examine. Analyze. Extrapolate.

If that's the pod bay, she thought, *the cockpit must be up top.*

She ran to the ladder and climbed the rungs two at a time. Passing through the small portal, she stood in the center of a cramped pilot compartment. Squinting against the emergency lights and sirens that, somehow, seemed even louder in the cockpit, She tried to make sense of all the myriad displays and control panels.

She leaned over the captain's chair—if you could even call it that, the tattered old sling—and tapped at the central display.

On the screen, a message blinked in concert with the siren: *Structural Integrity Compromised, Catastrophic Decompression Imminent.*

And below that, a timer counted down. There were only minutes left.

React. Retreat.

With a gasp, the young woman jumped back down the portal, this time skipping the ladder entirely. But she landed awkwardly, twisting her ankle. With a wince and a gasp, her body crumpled to the deck.

Now hobbled, she rose to her feet once more and limped down the hallway, shielding her eyes from the bright lights and bracing her weight on the walls. She knew that each labored step meant she was that much closer to safety—so long as there were actually any ORC pods left in the bay—and that each passing second also brought her closer to an agonizing, albeit quick death.

She hopped and stumbled, staggered and shuffled until she stood before the larger double doors of the ORC pod bay, slapping her hand against the panel beside the door. But the doors didn't budge.

Above the panel, on a small display, the words *Keycard Required* flashed in tandem with the emergency lights.

"Oh, come on." The young woman groaned.

She looked down at her jumpsuit, patting its half-dozen-or-so pockets in the off chance its previous owner had been careless enough to leave their keycard.

And then she felt it. In the breast pocket just below the embroidered logo, she found a small, rectangular card. She pulled it out of the pocket and flipped it over in her hands, but it had no markings on either side. She squinted as she pressed the card to the door panel and, with a chime and a groan, the doors slid open.

Inside the bay, there were four airlocks, three of which were devoid of pods. But on the fourth, tucked into the farthest corner, one ORC pod remained.

Survive.

The young woman ran to the pod, the pain in her ankle fading as adrenaline coursed through her body, and hopped inside. As quickly as she could, she strapped herself in and smashed the *Emergency Launch* button beside the pod's central controls.

The pod sealed shut, and she felt her ears pop as the pressure normalized. Then, with a jolt, it launched into the vacuum of space.

The young woman let out a deep sigh. She had done it. She escaped the disaster. She was finally safe.

And then, the debris from the imploding ship collided with the ORC pod, and everything went dark.

♂

"Hello, hello, anybody home?"

The young woman opened her eyes to find a filthy, burly man leaning over her, his giant paw smacking her on the cheek. She screamed and shoved the man, sending him doubling over with a crash.

"What the hell, you maniac?" He groaned and scowled at her from the cold deck below. "I'm trying to help you, ungrateful brat."

She looked around and realized she was still strapped into her seat in the ORC pod she had used to escape the imploding ship. Except she wasn't careening through space anymore. Through the egress of the pod, she could see dozens of pod airlocks, each with its own gangway and each surrounded by all manner of scrap metal, spare parts, and other space debris. And sifting through the debris, she saw others dressed in similar fashion, just as filthy as the man lying before her.

"Where am I?" She asked the man, who still sat on the deck before her.

"You're safe," he answered. "That's what I was trying to tell you before you assaulted me. This is the thanks I get for trying to do my duty as a citizen."

"A citizen of where?"

"The Old Tin Can, obviously." He gestured to the scrap scattered around.

"And where is that, exactly?"

"Are you serious? The salvage station in orbit around Haumea. It's the biggest scrapper colony in this part of The Reach."

She stared at him.

"...In the Kuiper Belt. Have you really never heard of The Old Tin Can?"

Ignoring the man, the young woman released herself from the jumpseat, rose to her feet, and took a step forward.

"Hey, hey, hold on," the man protested, righting himself. "You can't just leave. I saved your ass. You were just floating out there, and I towed you in. I think I deserve a little compensation for that. And since you don't have anything to trade, we're going to have to work something else out."

The man stretched his arm across the pod's egress, blocking her exit.

"You owe me." He smiled, flashing a mouthful of crooked, rotting teeth.

The young woman ducked under his arm and stepped out of the ORC pod. Out of the corner of her eye, she saw the man reach for her with his free hand.

Dodge. Guard. Protect.

The young woman's instincts kicked in. She leaned back, evading the huge man's grasp, and stepped back, planting her heel on the deck behind her and slapping the man's paw, setting him off-balance. He fell again, this time bashing his shoulder into the ORC pod's egress.

"That's about enough of that," he said through gritted teeth. "You wanna do this the hard way? We can do it the hard way."

As the man regained his balance and turned to face the young woman. This time, with both arms, he reached for her and lunged.

Faster.

The young woman stepped to the side and extended one of her legs, letting the man tumble to the deck for a third time. This time, he howled with rage, drawing the attention of some of the other scrappers in the pod bay. A few dropped what they were doing and began to creep toward the ruckus.

The man stood back up, brandishing a metal rod he had picked up from the scrap pile he had tumbled into.

Advance. Attack. Annihilate.

The man raised the rod above his head. But before he could swing it back down, the young woman jolted forward, balling her hand into a fist and punching him straight in the throat.

The man choked, dropping the rod to the ground and stumbling backward. He wheezed and coughed, trying to take a breath, and his eyes bulged from their sockets.

Seeing their compatriot in trouble, the other scrappers closed in even faster.

Survive.

Looking around, the young woman saw the mob closing in on her and decided to make a break for it. But they had already surrounded her, and she couldn't see a reasonable means of escape. So she backed into the ORC pod once more. But as she retreated, a little voice in the back of her head screamed, drowning out her fear and hesitation.

Slash. Maim. Rip. Crack. Devour.

The young woman leaped forth, tackling the scrapper closest to her, smashing his entire body against the deck with an echoing clang. In the blink of an eye, she was back on her feet. She shot an arm toward the next closest scrapper, grabbing them by the throat. She squeezed harder and harder until she felt a pop and then threw the scrapper's body into the crowd.

Someone screamed, and the rest of the scrappers began to panic, running away from the young woman. But she was too fast, sprinting between the terrified, retreating scrappers, breaking limbs and ripping flesh from their bones.

Once the remaining scrappers had been dispatched and she halted her assault, the young woman took in the scene around her. Tens of bodies littered the deck, and blood pooled between them. And at her feet, she found someone's hand. It had been ripped off their body just above the wrist, and blood still dripped from the flesh.

Jutting out from the flesh, the young woman could see jagged, white bones and, at the center of those bones, glistening marrow.

Her stomach growled as she lifted the bone closer to her mouth.

She licked her lips and dropped the hand to the deck at her feet.

☿

Her stomach still growling, the young woman wandered around the cluttered, overcrowded space station—The Old Tin Can, the giant man had called it.

After an hour or two, she concluded that the station's authorities weren't after her. Either the scrappers were too scared to go tell anyone—either in fear of her or the thought that nobody would believe what they had seen—or this wasn't the kind of place where one *could* ask the authorities for help.

Either way, it didn't matter to her. She was safe again, and that was enough. But the hunger was starting to get the better of her.

She wandered the corridors of the scrapper colony, following her nose to one of the station's mercantile sectors—a corridor lined with merchant stations selling everything from weaponry—of questionable legality, from the look of it—to exotic foodstuffs.

The young woman stopped at a small cart advertising several dozen dishes for sale, all made with the same smoky, nostril-singing mock beef—a synthetic protein made to give the impression of meat from an Ancient Earth animal that had gone extinct centuries earlier. The elderly woman working the counter, hunched and frail, eyeballed her.

"Can I help you, dearie?" The old woman beckoned her forward.

The young woman stepped up to the counter and pulled the small card from her jumpsuit, the one she had used to open the ORC pod bay door.

"This is all I have," she said, handing the card to the old woman.

"This is a keycard," the woman replied with a laugh. "You can't buy anything with this."

Suddenly feeling sheepish, the young woman looked down at her feet.

"Oh…Well, thank you anyway." She turned to leave.

"Wait, dearie," the old woman said. "Let me make something up for you. We're near closing time anyway, and I'd hate to have to toss all of this food in the trash. Plus, you look famished."

"You don't have to do that," the young woman said.

"Think nothing of it."

"Thank you."

"It's my pleasure, dearie. Have you got a name? I can call you when it's ready."

The young woman furrowed her brow and shook her head.

She couldn't remember. She couldn't remember anything from before she woke up on that ship. Whoever she was, wherever she came from, what she had been doing out there alone floating through space—it was all a mystery.

She looked down at the drab green jumpsuit and remembered the embroidered logo.

"Foxhound," she said. "My name is Foxhound."

"And so it is." The old woman smiled.

Digest.

The young woman hardly took a breath between bites, gulping down the food as though she had never eaten a meal before in her life. Which, since she had no memory of her past, might as well be true.

As she ate, she watched the elderly woman close up her cart. Once it was all locked up, the kind shopkeeper came to sit down beside her.

"So, Foxhound," she said, "how is it?"

"The best meal I've ever had, ma'am," Foxhound answered with her mouth still full of food.

The elderly woman laughed. "That's quite the endorsement. Too bad all my customers aren't as generous as you."

Foxhound shoveled another bite of food into her mouth, savoring the dry, astringent synthetic protein.

Satisfy. Nourish. Sustain.

"Where to next?"

This time, Foxhound finished chewing and swallowing her food before answering.

"I...don't know," she said.

"Look, this might not be your thing—hell, it's not my thing, nor is it really the thing for most folks out here in The Reach—but The Church has a chapter out here. If you can get past all the science-as-god mumbo-jumbo, I'm sure they'd give you a place to sleep, even just for tonight."

"Church?"

"The Divine Church of the Omniphage," the elderly woman responded. "The most powerful governing body in the entirety of the solar system? You really don't remember anything, do you?"

Foxhound ignored the elderly woman's question. "Where is it?"

"Just down there," she pointed through the crowd.

Foxhound peered down the corridor and, peeking between the bodies clogging the passageway, could see a white-and-gold facade.

"You know," the elderly woman continued, "I hear they even offer jobs to some of the younger, more able-bodied people out here in The Reach. You might want to try your luck. From what I've heard, it can be quite comfortable working for The Church. They might even train you and, if you're good enough for what they want, they may even give you your own ship...so long as you don't mind the whole totalitarian regime thing."

"I'm not sure I do mind," Foxhound answered. "Thanks for the intel."

Foxhound, finally finished with her meal, looked around the market. On the far side, where she first entered, she saw a group of scrappers gathering—some that looked familiar enough that they were probably the same folks she tangled with in the ORC pod bay. And they looked like they were searching for her.

Evacuate. Escape.

"Looks like I need to be on my way," Foxhound said to the elderly woman sitting beside her.

"So it does," the elderly woman agreed, seeing the growing mob of scrappers. "Take care of yourself."

Foxhound nodded at the elderly woman as she rose to her feet.

Survive.

Foxhound slipped into the crowd, headed straight for The Church.

Chapter Eleven

"Belay all nonessential emergency requests, that includes security and medical. If it's not an imminent hull breach or a cascading life-support failure, I don't want to hear about it!" Mother's voice boomed over the panic of the bridge, aided by their halo-shaped crown that allowed their voice to reverberate through the bridge's overhead speakers. As they stood before their throne, a mob of crew members moved from station to station, responding to as many incoming alerts as possible. It was an impossible task and they were failing at it spectacularly.

The bridge had devolved into near complete chaos by the time Brother Loch and his companion walked in. And that meant that nobody was paying enough attention to stop them as they cut through the crowd toward Mother.

As Loch and Kano approached, the leader of the Organic Humanists spotted them. There was a look of frustrated confusion in Mother's eyes.

"What are you doing?" Mother and Loch asked one another in unison.

Mother continued, "You've abandoned your post. You were meant to be watching our prisoners. Gauging from the chaos you can plainly see here and the numerous reports of violence spread throughout my ship, I'm forced to assume you've failed me."

"Your ship?" Loch asked indignantly. "You sent in a death squad and I was to be collateral."

"I did nothing of the sort," Mother gasped unconvincingly. "First of all, I have no idea what you're talking about. Second, I cannot be held responsible for the poor choices my children might have made in the heat of the moment."

"I heard your message," Loch continued.

"Yes," Mother interjected confidently. "We're clearly in a state of emergency here. I instructed everyone to get to safety while we work our hardest to get everything under control."

"I mean the other one," Loch growled. "You don't care about helping any of those people out there. You only care about protecting yourself."

One by one, the crew members of *Gaia*'s bridge stopped what they were doing to watch Brother Loch, once one of Mother's most trusted children, accost their leader in full view of the entire bridge.

"Do they know?" Loch gestured to the other Siblings on the bridge, most watching the scene unfold with mouths agape. "Do they know you planned to invade Deadwood Station?"

Loch turned to address the crowd, raising his voice so he was sure they could all hear.

"It's true," he continued. "That's why we're here. That's why we haven't left orbit. That's why we saved those children, because we knew they wouldn't have another chance once Mother's plan was put into motion. That's why all those poorly trained armed guards are wandering *Gaia*'s corridors. This isn't security. It's an invading force. Sibling Yū knew it and Mother, with my help, silenced them. We are all complicit, myself included, in a plot that would have amounted to genocide. And then we'd be no better than those who have raised their hands against us in ignorance and rage. Nay, we'd be worse, because we'd be putting our blind, unquestioning faith into the hands of an unworthy ruler. We have been misled, I tell you."

Loch looked into the eyes of his Siblings, one by one, before turning back to Mother, whose teeth were bared.

"Detain Brother Loch," they rasped.

None of the bridge crew made a move, nor did the armed guards watching from the outside corridor.

"Myself especially," Loch resumed, sadness in his voice. "I believed what you said, that *Gaia* was dying and that we needed a new home. That violence was an unfortunate inevitability. I helped you to these ends. But, after what I've seen, what I've heard, I know that this was never about the Organic Humanists. This isn't about family and finding us a permanent home. This is about you and some sick quest for power."

"Lies!" Mother screamed, slapping Loch across the face. "You can't believe the poisonous falsehoods spilling from the mouth of this...this apostate!"

But Loch held his ground, continuing to stare directly into Mother's eyes defiantly.

"You all heard Mother's empty words, an announcement promising aid to those who patiently sit and wait. But there was another announcement sent out only to armed security, isn't that right?"

"More deceit," Mother began to say. But another voice interrupted her. It was the meek comms officer Mother had accosted earlier.

"It's-it's true," she sputtered. "Mother ordered me to call all remaining armed guards to the forward section of *Gaia* to protect the bridge. They said that sacrifices must be made. But my children are out there…"

"I need to show you all something else," Loch said. "Can someone bring up the repair and procurement logs?"

"One moment," another Sibling answered. "I've got them here."

Reticent to look upon what he already knew, Brother Loch drifted slowly over to the crew member's station. As the display came into view, he saw it all there, as plain as day. Nearly every repair and procurement request over the past few months had been denied by Mother themself. All but one: a recurring procurement request marked "Security Assets." The cost amounted to the entirety of the other requests combined. And in the authorization slot, the name read "Mother."

"Do you see, Brother?" Brother Loch turned around to face the bridge crew, spreading his arms wide and raising his voice once more. "Corruption!"

"He speaks the truth," the man said, tapping his console and sending the chart to every station on the bridge. "See for yourselves."

Each and every bridge crew member looked at their workstation displays, some with mouths agape, others growling with anger, and a few even crying out in shame.

"Mother has misled all of us, purchasing weapons instead of making necessary repairs to *Gaia*. We have all been made victims of their shortsighted avarice. They are unfit, not just to lead us but to count themselves among us as a member of the Organic Humanists. None of us are innocent, but we can still make this right. There are people out there that need us right now."

"Fine," Mother shouted, turning around and tapping a panel on their throne that opened a storage slot set into one of the armrests, "I'll do it myself."

Mother reached into the slot in the armrest of their throne, pulled out a small pistol, and spun on their heels to aim it at Brother Loch.

It was the moment that Warrick Kano, the Savage of Europa, had been waiting for. In one swift motion, Kano dropped his robes and lunged forward, knocking Mother's extended arm, pistol still in hand, upward. The weapon discharged harmlessly into the ceiling of the bridge, but the loud report elicited a wave of gasps and yelps from the surrounding crew, many of whom dropped to the deck instinctively.

In the confusion and fear, Kano pulled the leader of the Organic Humanists close, his left hand still holding their right wrist up in the air while his right hand gripped the back of their neck.

"It is with the authority of the Divine Church of the Omniphage," he whispered into Mother's ear so nobody else on the bridge could hear, "that I, Warrick Kano, must inform you that your life is forfeit. May your energy and atoms return to the universe, restoring balance."

As he spoke, a tiny spring-loaded blade emerged from the inside of his right forearm, slashing through Mother's throat before retracting seamlessly back into his wrist.

As blood poured from their throat, dripping down and coating their stark white robes, Mother gargled and choked, the sounds echoing through the bridge's overhead speakers via their halo-shaped crown.

Gently, Warrick Kano set Mother down on their throne before taking a step back. Still, nobody on the bridge made a move, all watching as their leader expired before them, bleeding out and gagging, their eyes wide and full of panic.

As horrific as it was, it reminded Brother Loch of some of the religious artworks of Ancient Earth, which he had studied all those years ago, long before he left his post as an academic researcher to join the Organic Humanists.

Warrick Kano, his task complete, returned to Brother Loch's side and lowered his head.

"I'm sorry," he said. "I took advantage of your trust. I'm willing and ready to accept judgment as the laws of your organization require."

But Brother Loch was unconcerned with Kano's apology, instead stepping forward to pry the pistol from Mother's hand.

"She tried to kill me," he said, cradling the weapon in his palms. He turned back to Warrick Kano and handed him the gun. "Can you dispose of this?"

Confused, Kano looked at Loch. "Of course, but—"

Ignoring Kano, Loch turned back around to Mother and removed the halo from their head, placing it on his own. This time, when he spoke, the deep baritone of his voice echoed throughout the bridge.

"Stand down," he said, gesturing toward Kano. "This man is not to be harmed. He has freed us from Mother's corrupt grasp. The Organic Humanists shall no longer be used as a tool of a selfish despot. Today, we start over in earnest."

"But who will lead us?" It was the meek comms officer from before.

Loch considered her question before speaking again. "Not me. I am unfit. I was complicit in Mother's plot. Perhaps

220

none of us. Perhaps it is time for the Organic Humanists to become a true family, where every voice is measured equal to one another."

"And the assassin, what about him?" This time it was one of the armed guards standing nervously in the entryway to the bridge.

"He is not to be harmed," Brother Loch declared. "You all saw that, upon my revealing of their true intent, Mother attempted to kill me. This man, a Sibling or not, as deceitful as he may have been, saved my life…and perhaps many more in the grand scheme. It is my opinion that he should be free to go. Do any of you object?"

A silence fell over the bridge.

Loch turned back to Kano. "Take Mother's personal ORC pod. It's in a separate launch bay near here. One of my men will show you the way. It will get you wherever you need to go safely. And thank you. I wasn't sure I'd be able to do what needed to be done."

Warrick Kano, knowing better than to question the good graces of Brother Loch and his compatriots, nodded in thanks before slinking through the crowd, leaving the bridge as quietly as he had arrived. Within minutes, he was aboard Mother's ORC pod, rocketing away from *Gaia*. That was the last time any of the Organic Humanists would lay their eyes on the Savage of Europa.

His vigor restored, Brother Loch addressed the meek comms officer once again, "Can we send a new announcement out across the ship and work toward getting the lockdown lifted?"

"Yes, of course," she answered, sitting back down at her station and punching in several commands. "Ready when you are."

Brother Loch's conscience still weighed heavily on him. He had, after all, betrayed his closest confidante, Sister Penelope—even going so far as to jail her, strip her of her title, and exile her from the Organic Humanists. And he had done the same to Sibling Yū, who had stood up to Mother long before he had the confidence to do the same. And that was to say nothing of the long-term consequences of his complicity in Mother's betrayal of the whole of the Organic Humanists. But, seeing his Siblings on *Gaia*'s bridge eagerly await his next words, the gravity of this new responsibility far exceeded the shame he felt. He knew that this was his chance to start to make things right, even if he didn't believe it was possible to truly rebalance the scales.

Brother Loch closed his eyes, carefully considering the next words he would utter, words that would echo across the whole of *Gaia*, the mothership of the Organic Humanists and his home.

☿

Attention all Siblings and Children of the Organic Humanists, this is Brother Loch speaking. I regret to inform all of you that Mother is dead. I repeat, Mother is dead. Furthermore, I am deeply saddened to share with all of you the reasons for our leader's passing. Acting solely in their own interests and ignoring the tenets of the Organic Humanists, Mother betrayed us all, choosing to use their power for selfish gain rather than the betterment of the entire OH.

As many of you know, Mother had taken it upon themself to arm many of us. And we, blind in our faith, chose to believe the falsehood that in the current climate of the solar system, violence was not just unavoidable but necessary for our survival. I, like many of you, chose to believe this lie, despite my better judgment.

What I did not know and wish to illuminate for all of you now is that the state of Gaia as you presently know it, the disrepair and the decline of large parts of our mothership, nay our home, was entirely avoidable. Our former leader, in their greed, was using our resources, what little we had, to procure the weapons many of you now carry. And with them, Mother intended to coerce us all to invade Deadwood Station to take it for ourselves.

Upon revealing these facts to your Siblings here on the bridge, Mother made an attempt on my life and, in defending myself, I killed Mother. I regret the violence of my actions and my cardinal sin, allowing all of this to transpire under my watch. I will accept any punishment put forth by you, my Siblings in the Organic Humanists.

But before your judgment comes to pass, I make one request. Our former leader's avarice, this hatred, this sin flies in the face of everything we stand for, everything we are as Organic Humanists. And it must be put to an end. I call on all of you now: lay down your arms and cease this madness. Abandon your weapons and instead lift one another up, help those of us in need—I know there are many. Restore our collective humanity through love and empathy. We have suffered enough, both at the hands of Mother and as the result of our own inaction. Only together can we set things right. Together, we can save Gaia. We can save our home. And we can save our family.

$$\stackrel{+}{\mathrm{O}}$$

Mailman, carrying Foxhound's limp, battered body, had just made it to the edge of *Gaia's* central chamber when a group of armed guards burst through the door to which they were headed. The automaton stopped in its tracks.

In a panic, the guards halted and brought their rifles to bear. But none fired as Loch's announcement rang over the chamber's loudspeakers, filling the enormous enclosure with the man's deep, booming baritone.

There they stood, the Contractor-carrying automaton and the guards facing one another, neither making a move as the message came to its end. Then, as it repeated a second time, one of the guards lowered his firearm and released it, letting it swing at his side. Another guard, upon seeing the first, followed suit. And then another and another until all had lowered their arms. Then, they stepped aside.

Mailman continued in its trek, passing the men and entering *Gaia*'s lower corridors once more, heading back through the maze of passageways toward the ORC pod bay where *The Tardigrade* awaited them.

"Was that real?" Foxhound groaned.

"Mum, you're awake," Mailman answered.

"Just barely. Thought I was dreaming. Is that...Loch's voice?"

"Yes," said Mailman. "It seems a lot has happened since we last saw him. A welcome change, I'm sure."

"We're not out of the woods yet," the Contractor coughed.

"Woods, mum? There are no forests aboard this ship."

"It's an old figure of speech, Mailman," Foxhound continued. "Neumar and Fink Ames are still unaccounted for."

"Actually," Mailman interjected. "Sensors indicate that Hecate Neumar is back aboard *The Tardigrade*. Or she was a few minutes ago. Fink was there, as well, only a short while before that."

"Right where we sent Penelope, Yū, and the girl."

"That is correct. Although I do recall you mentioning that she is not, in fact, a girl."

"Yeah, yeah," Foxhound groaned. "You're missing the point."

"Being that you sent them right into the arms of two of the worst, most violent criminals this side of the asteroid belt?"

"That was a mean joke."

"Apologies, mum. I'm happy to adjust my humor matrix if you wish."

"No, no, it's fine," Foxhound sighed. "Just…can you get us there quicker?"

"You're in no shape to fight, I'm afraid."

"No, but you are."

"Very well," the AI automaton answered. "You may want to hang on. You're already badly injured, and this could hurt."

"Don't worry about me."

"As you wish."

The AI automaton picked up its pace from a steady march to a loping jog. And Foxhound felt shooting pain with each and every thundering step.

☿

Brother Loch's announcement boomed throughout *Gaia*'s ORC pod bay, just as it did across the rest of the ship, his words reverberating between the double-hulled walls.

"Ugh, how boring," Hecate Neumar, walking into *The Tardigrade*'s cargo bay, said to no one in particular. "Right when things were starting to get good. This is why you can't rely on peace-loving cultists. They never follow through."

She danced around the various crates and panels haphazardly strewn about, the same ones Fink had left in his wake while searching for supplies to tide him over in his escape from *Gaia*. And while most of it was useless rubbish to Neumar, one thing in particular stuck out.

There, just lying in the middle of the cargo bay deck, Hecate Neumar found a zero-gravity tool belt with a rivet gun and plasma torch still tethered to it. Fink, it seemed, was unarmed…unless he had found some other means of protecting himself, though Hecate doubted it–the man was in quite the hurry last she saw, and finding other weapons would have taken time he didn't have. That made him easier prey, which disappointed Neumar slightly, but it did make their foreplay all the more exciting, at least in the eyes of the Widow of Venus.

"Fink, my dear," she announced in her best singsongy voice, "Where, oh, where have you gone? Come on out so we can have some fun together. I promise to make it worth your while. Come out and play."

But Fink, still hiding in his ORC pod, remained as still and silent as possible.

With a twirl and a leap, Hecate Neumar danced out of *The Tardigrade* and back out into the middle of the ORC pod bay, continuing to sing to her quarry.

"Come out, come out, wherever you are," she said. "You and I both know it's only a matter of time before I find you. The lockdown is still in effect, and that means you're not going anywhere."

Her voice was growing louder, closer. Fink began to sweat, but he stayed put. He knew he would only have one chance, and he needed to make it count.

"Come now, don't you want to see all the wonderful things

I'm capable of?" Neumar asked. "Aren't you curious at all?"

Now he could hear her footsteps, as soft as they were. They tapped the deck below in rhythm with her words, giving her entire performance an almost lullaby-like quality. It reminded Fink of his own mother and the things she used to sing in her sickly voice for him when he was still a baby. Before she had succumbed to her illness. The thought terrified him. He almost didn't realize that, in his fear, he had begun to pant.

He cupped a hand over his mouth to silence his breathing, but the clap, as quiet as it was, echoed just loudly enough for Neumar to hear. She whipped her head in the direction of his ORC pod. She knew where Fink was hiding.

And so, she danced—a skill she had learned almost too many years ago to remember as a young girl growing up on the Arcadia-class Protectorates orbiting Venus.

A balancé to the left, a brisé to the right.

A traveling glissade into a pirouette.

And then, as elegantly as she could manage, she came to a stop before Fink's ORC pod with a deep bow.

"Where's my applause?" she harrumphed. "Do you not appreciate my dancing, dear Fink?"

Fink hid behind his supplies, but he knew his time was running out. Still, he had one more move yet to play, one that might give him just a little more time. He bluffed.

"Come any closer, and I'll blast a hole through your torso. Have you ever seen what a vacuum-ready rivet gun can do to a person?"

"No, I haven't," Hecate Neumar laughed. "But I don't think I have to worry about finding out. You left your little toys in that ship over there."

Idiot, Fink thought. *You knew how stupid it was, and you left them over there anyway.*

Neumar continued, "Can we please drop this charade and dance together like you know we were meant to?"

"Yeah, sure." Fink stood up and shrugged. "Look, I'm not much for ceremony, so can we make this quick?"

"Oh, honey," Neumar sighed, a sad smile on her lips, "I like playing with my food almost as much as eating it. I'd much prefer it if we took our time. What do you say?"

But Fink didn't have time to answer as the ORC pod bay doors, just a few meters beyond Hecate Neumar, opened. And through them stepped Sibling Yū, Penelope, and, hiding just behind Penelope, the no-name girl. Fink took the opportunity to drop back behind his supplies and bide his time. Seeing the svelte Hecate Neumar standing before them, a joyful look of surprise on her face, the trio froze.

"Well, hello there," the slender woman giggled. "My name is Hecate Neumar. Now, who might you be? Appetizers, perhaps?"

"Oh God," Yū said. "That's...no, it can't be."

"Who?" Penelope asked.

"On Ganymede, when I was a triage doctor, men started coming in that had been poisoned with a variety of highly deadly toxins, venoms, and the like. All men in positions of power. And they were all linked to this one woman. When we started digging, it turned out that men all over the System had shared a similar fate, but by the time anyone caught on, the killer had made off with large portions of their fortunes. Nobody could track her down. Each time she made landfall, she'd change her name and alter her appearance. Even her DNA was edited just enough to bypass most security systems. Everything about her was different, but her signature method of murder remained. They called her the Widow of Venus."

"Oh, how wonderful." Neumar clapped, her grin growing ever wider. "Finally, someone who appreciates my work. Tell me, do you have a favorite? I'm always flip-flopping myself, but I think the way that neurotoxins make men writhe...well, it really gets my juices flowing."

"We don't have time for this," Penelope said, lifting her arm and pointing the B.A.N.G. module at Neumar. With a squeeze, she unleashed a volley of pellets, all of which struck Neumar in the chest and shoulders, unleashing a thick purple cloud of gas.

But the thud of Neumar's body hitting the deck never came.

Instead, the woman breathed in deeply through her nostrils, sucking the purple gas into her lungs. Then, she let out a raucous laugh, puffs of the smoke emerging from her mouth with each chortle.

"Come, now," she said. "You must be able to do better than that."

Penelope swung her head around to look at Yū.

"What? Don't look at me," they protested. "All of that exposure to...whatever the hell she's put in and on her body must have made her immune to most of this stuff."

"Ding, ding, ding!" Neumar sang. "We have a winner. Oh, this is going to be fun. That is, unless you'd like to try something else first?"

Penelope whipped her head back around, scowling at Neumar.

"Yeah, we've got just one more thing." She stepped out from in front of the no-name girl and pointed toward Neumar. "Get her!"

The no-name girl took one look at Hecate Neumar and

scampered back behind Penelope, wrapping her arms around the woman's leg and erupting in tears.

"That was your big plan?" Sibling Yū asked. "You were gonna sic a little girl on her?"

"Okay, it was a bad plan," Penelope answered.

"It was a terrible plan!" Yū retorted.

"I don't see you coming up with anything!"

While Penelope and Yū bickered, Fink peeked over his mound of supplies to assess the situation. Only a few steps outside the ORC pod stood Hecate Neumar, her back turned to him. And beyond that, it was another few meters to the new trio.

Fink had expected the Contractor, Foxhound, to be behind them shortly. That is, if she was still alive and hadn't been crushed to death in the arms of Eris Enyo. And while the Contractor might've been able to make quick work of Hecate Neumar, it posed a new, distressing set of problems for Fink. That included but was not limited to being recaptured and transported, in the Contractor's custody, back to Earth. And that just wouldn't do.

This is it, he realized. *This is my chance. And then I'll be the big hero, and surely they'll have to let me go free. If not, I can always deal with them afterward. But if I'm going to do this, I have to do it now.*

Fink reached into his jumpsuit pocket and pulled out his four remaining shit sticks. Then, taking two in each hand, he rose from his hiding spot, stepped out from behind the mountain of supplies, and launched himself into a full sprint.

As the thin man emerged from the ORC pod, Penelope, shocked to see her former Sibling for the first time since Deadwood, shouted with disbelief.

"Brother Phineas?!"

It was enough warning that Hecate Neumar, with an elegant twirl to her left, easily dodged the man careening toward her. As he tumbled, sprawling onto the ground between Neumar and the trio that had just joined them, Fink lost his grip on the shit sticks, sending them skittering out of his reach.

"So close," she giggled and smacked her lips, dancing toward Fink as he struggled and failed to right himself, merely rolling over. "But weren't you listening? Poison doesn't work on me, darling. Stick me all you want, hotshot, but this little heart's gonna keep right on ticking. I bet it works wonders on you, though."

Balancing on one foot, the other leg reaching into the air to counterbalance her weight, she leaned forward and grabbed Fink by the lapels, jerking the pale, scrambling man forward to press her lips against his. But she pulled back with a frown on her face to find Fink pressing his lips as tightly as he could.

Just beyond the pair, Sibling Yū, the former trauma surgeon from Ganymede, looked down at her feet, where the shit sticks had skittered to a stop, and realized what it was that Fink had been trying to do.

"What's the matter, dear?" she snarled. "Why aren't you kissing me back?"

"It's not poison," Fink answered, just as Sibling Yū swung their fists like hammers down onto Neumar's shoulders. Then, they released, revealing the four shit sticks, their injectors embedded into Neumar's flesh.

Hecate Neumar screamed, lurching backward and convulsing, swatting at the needles in her side, but she was too late. The potent cocktail of drugs, designed to shut down soldiers' pain receptors and kick their adrenal glands into high gear,

231

was too much for her rail-thin body to handle. Like mainlining electricity, the drugs flooded her system, sending her weak heart into a frenzy before shutting down, leaving her body a twisted, writhing, twitching, foaming, drooling heap on *Gaia's* ORC pod bay deck.

Penelope rushed to Fink's side, lifting him up off the deck alongside Sibling Yū but, when they released him, he fell back down, unable to stand under his own weight.

"It's okay," he mumbled. "I'm just a...just a little shaken up. I don't think she...got...I don't think any got in..."

Fink tried to get up again, but his limbs failed him. He splayed out on the ground, trembling and convulsing.

"No, no, no, no," Yū muttered. "Oh God, I thought it was just a rumor. I thought it was only a story."

"What are you talking about?" Penelope demanded, dropping to her knees to embrace the man she once knew as her Sibling.

"Don't touch him!" Yū shouted.

At Yū's urging, Penelope kept her distance as she called out to Fink, "Brother Phineas, stay with me. Keep your eyes open. It's okay, we're gonna get you some help, just stay with—"

"Penelope, it's too late," Yū interjected, placing their hand on the woman's shoulder. "We can't save him. It's a neurotoxin. I thought it was just a myth, but back on Ganymede, some of the other residents said she...her augmentations...she can actually secrete the stuff. I just...I thought it was hearsay, conjecture, gossip."

By the time Yū finished talking and Penelope looked back down, Fink's eyes had rolled into the back of his head, and drool trickled from the side of his mouth. He was gone.

"You have to let him go," Yū reiterated. "Keep your hands

away from his face. We don't know how potent that stuff is."

Penelope rested Fink's head on the deck and released his body, scooting herself away.

Only moments later, an automated message in a robotic voice played through the ORC pod bay's speakers, repeating three times.

"Lockdown lifted," it said.

And just after that, the doors of the ORC pod bay opened once more. This time, Mailman's hulking automaton exoskeleton, carrying Foxhound in its arms, stepped through.

"What did I miss?" the Contractor asked.

☿

As the neurons in Phineas "Fink" Ames's brain fired for the last time, the fading electrical signals triggered his data management implant, issuing one final command: to send out a faint signal, one designed to piggyback on the comms systems of whatever vessel or colony his body was on.

The signal was so faint and insignificant that anyone monitoring the incoming and outgoing comms data would have registered it as nothing more than a glitch in the system, a blip of white noise.

That blip filtered through *Gaia*'s long-range comms and shot across the blackness of space, bouncing off relay buoys and pinging between the ships in orbit above Deadwood Station.

Then it made its way down to the colony, going unnoticed by the comms officers on Deadwood just as it had on *Gaia*, sneaking through the station's firewalls, flagged as nothing more than a harmless packet of data, and filtering into

Deadwood's larger communications array.

From there, it made its way through the station's fiber-optic cables, passing the ORC bay, bouncing between food vendor stalls, and finally making its way to a small dusty apothecary shop in a dark forgotten corner of Deadwood.

A small chime rang out from a data terminal sitting on a small side table next to a cot in the shop's storeroom. And on that cot, a body stirred. It was Billie Kane.

With a groan, the elder rolled over to look at the data terminal, squinting to make out what the tiny flashing alert said "New message."

Billie reached out a bony arm and tapped the screen, opening the message.

Thanks for everything.

That was all it said. No greeting, no sign-off, no sender.

Then, another alert popped up. This time, it was from the Deadwood Station Credit Union, the bank that owned the apothecary, just as it owned most commercial properties on the station.

"It's too early for this," Billie said to themselves as they tapped the message.

Valued Customer Billie Kane, it read. *We are happy to report that we have received your final payment and that you have successfully paid off your loan in full. Furthermore, we'd like to confirm a recent transfer to your account. Please check your balance to confirm that this information is correct.*

Billie sat up, pulling the blanket around their shoulders as they hunched over the data terminal. With a few taps and swipes, Billie had opened a page on the station's intranet connecting them to the DSCU system. They punched in their sign-in data and, once logged into their account, tapped a button that read *View My Balance*.

Glowing right in front of Billie Kane's eyes was a number larger than they had ever seen, at least in their own account. Not only was it big enough that they could buy back their old apartment in full and pay for it in cash, but it was big enough that Billie would never need to worry about money ever again.

There, alone in the back storage room of a dark, dusty, forgotten apothecary shop on one of the most isolated and distant rocks orbiting the sun, Billie Kane wept.

Chapter Twelve

Penelope, Yū, the no-name girl, Mailman, and Foxhound—
finally back on her own two feet—were standing around
Fink's body when Brother Loch and a complement of Organic
Humanists, this time carrying medical and repair supplies
instead of guns, joined them in the ORC pod bay. Leaving his
men to get to work, Loch joined them around Fink.

"It was stupid to lift the lockdown while my prisoners were
still running amok," Foxhound said to the man. "Who knows
where they could have made off to."

"That was exactly what I was counting on, truth be told,"
Loch answered with a shrug. "I needed them off this ship so
we could focus on getting medical attention to those who need
it and repairing our home. Clearly, we were never equipped
to combat them, so that seemed like the best option at the
time. And I thought that you might leave, too, but it looks like
it's good that you didn't. We owe you a debt of thanks…and
I owe you my deepest apologies. If there's anything that you
need to get your ship back up and running, let us know. We're
also having the body of Eris Enyo brought down here from
the central chamber, but her…mass has proved to be a bit of
an issue. Don't worry, though. We'll get it done. Hopefully,

there was a death clause in your contract you can still cash in on. Are these the last of them?"

"Not quite," Foxhound answered, "Warrick Kano is still unaccounted for."

"Actually," Loch interjected, "I can account for him."

"Pardon?" Foxhound sounded irritated.

"He was with me on the bridge when Mother... He saved my life. So, we let him go."

"You're shitting me," the Contractor said. "And where is he now?"

"Gone. He took Mother's personal ORC pod."

"You just let him go? Do you even know who he is? What he's done?" Foxhound's voice rose.

"What would you have had us do?" Loch's rose in return. "That man, the way he moved. He would have killed us all."

Foxhound stood, still and silent as a statue, considering Loch's words.

"You're right," she finally said. "That was the right call for you and your people. Do you have any idea where he went?"

"Ship telemetry showed he was headed sunward."

"Back toward Earth in a fucking pod," Foxhound confirmed. Pointing to the body of Hecate Neumar lying several meters away, she continued, "I'll take her off your hands. Get her loaded on my ship with the others. But I think this other one might be yours."

"Dear Brother Phineas," Loch exhaled. "So, that *was* you back on Deadwood who captured him."

"At your service," Foxhound groaned. "Should probably let you know...he went by *Fink* when he wasn't *Brother Phineas*. He was using you as a front."

"He wasn't alone there." Loch looked toward Penelope and

Yū. "Look, I-I don't really know how to tell you how sorry I—"

"It's okay," Penelope interrupted. "People make mistakes. Some bigger than others. It's up to us to recognize those mistakes and give them a chance to redeem themselves."

Brother Loch nodded his head, a sad smile on his face.

"Shouldn't you take his body, as well?" Loch finally asked Foxhound.

"Don't ask me," she answered, gesturing to Penelope and Yū. "His contract didn't come with a death clause, anyhow."

With that, Foxhound turned and hobbled away, followed closely by Mailman. The AI, its control module still housed in its mechanical exoskeleton, kept close behind the Contractor, its arms extended, ready to catch her should she lose her footing.

"Where are you going?" Penelope hollered.

"Don't worry. I'm not headed far." Foxhound waved her gauntleted hand in the air. She was still having trouble lifting the other one. "Suit's a little banged up. I know…hard to tell. Thought I might go finally take the damn thing off and get cleaned up. Come and find me on *The Tardigrade* when you're all done out here. And don't bring the girl. We need to talk. Alone."

☿

All throughout *Gaia*, people began emerging from their hiding places—their locked-down staterooms, storage closets, maintenance tunnels, cargo lockers, and more—and got back to work.

Together, they put out the fires in the ship's central chamber

238

and began clearing the various wrecks, debris, and shrapnel so that farming could once again resume.

They respectfully cleared the gray-robed bodies out of the corridors and the central chamber, identifying those who had passed, notifying their next of kin, and performing traditional Organic Humanist burial rites. Called Reclamation, the process involved recycling the bodies of the fallen and tilling their elements into the soil so that crops might grow from their remains and help to sustain all those still tethered to the mortal realm.

Several teams began to collect the firearms that had cost them all so much but very nearly had cost them so much more. Some would be melted down and converted into repair parts to help in however small a way with the monthslong maintenance backlog. And others would be begrudgingly sold, in as inert a form as possible, to help resupply *Gaia*'s storehouses and purchase new equipment to replace that which was destroyed.

And once all of this had concluded, the simple life of the Organic Humanists would resume in earnest, as simple, honest, and true as it was long before Mother's machinations. However, it would never be the same, for they had all learned a lesson they'd cherish and honor for generations: that trust between people is a sacred bond that needs to be honorably earned, never recklessly given.

And they'd all be better for it.

☿

"What would you have me do with him?" inquired Loch.

"He saved us, Brother," Sibling Yū answered. "Were it not

239

for him, we might all be dead, and the Widow of Venus would still be wandering around out there killing indiscriminately. He deserves the Organic Humanist burial rites just as much as any of us."

"He didn't save you," Loch winced. "He was trying to save himself. You admitted as much already."

"Did you not tell me yourself, Brother Loch," it was Penelope this time, "that actions are all we have to measure one another by, as words bear no weight?"

"Well, yes, but—"

"But nothing," Penelope continued. "His actions saved the three of us and perhaps many more."

Penelope looked down at the body lying on the floor. She knew now that the Sibling she remembered, Brother Phineas, was a fiction—a character invented by a madman designed to let him hide as a wolf among sheep. But she could not bring herself to see a monster. No matter how twisted and sick he may have truly been, she remembered the kindness and caring nature of Brother Phineas. And she knew, somewhere within that fiction, he was real.

"He's not even one of us," Loch griped. "He doesn't deserve to be respected as one of our family. Not after what's happened here today. And his quarters...the things we found upon searching them. What he's been hiding from us all about who he is and the things he's done."

"And what about what you did, Loch?" Sibling Yū snarled.

"Yū!" Penelope barked, turning her gaze toward Loch. "People make mistakes, right?"

Brother Loch lowered his head in shame, taking a moment to reflect. "You're...absolutely correct. By all accounts, this man deserves to be Reclaimed just as we all do. I'll see to it personally. Penelope, I need to talk with you for a moment, if that's all right."

Yū glanced at Penelope, who nodded back at them reassuringly. "It's okay. Just watch her for me, yeah?"

"Of course," Yū replied, kneeling down in front of the no-name girl as Penelope and Loch stepped aside.

☿

"You're serious?" Penelope beamed. "That's not at all what I thought you wanted to talk about. But yes, that might be the best idea you've had since… In a long time."

"I'm glad you agree." Loch smiled, this time with genuine warmth. "And I think it could do all of us some good, considering what's transpired. We'll just have to see what they think of it before moving forward. If I may, what was it you thought I was going to ask you?"

"Honestly, I thought you were going to invite me back into the flock, ask me to stay," Penelope answered.

"Would you have accepted?"

Penelope looked over at the little no-name girl, who was standing in front of Sibling Yū, enthralled by whatever it was the good doctor was saying.

"Absolutely not," she finally answered. "But not out of spite or disdain. Not for you or any of the other Siblings. I just… I think I've found my purpose."

"And now you know why I didn't ask." Loch rested a hand on Penelope's shoulder and joined her in watching Yū and the no-name girl. "Just…be careful with her, okay? What happened here on *Gaia*, what she did—"

"She's not a monster," Penelope snapped. "I-I'm sorry.

241

You're right. Of course, you're right. And I'm scared, but she's scared, too. Regardless of what she is, she needs someone to care for her and keep her safe. She needs me."

Loch sighed, "And perhaps you need her."

Penelope nodded her head.

"Should you ever change your mind and decide you want to come back…" Loch said, choking on the words.

"I know," Penelope answered. "We're not going anywhere just yet. Save the goodbyes for later, Brother."

"Right, of course. On to Sibling Yū. Trying to make amends is arduous work," Loch said, wiping his eyes.

"But you're the right man for the job."

☿

Penelope cautiously stepped into *The Tardigrade*'s cargo bay. She knew that the holding cells were already empty and the danger was long gone, but the idea that this ship had led to so many of her Siblings being killed was a hard image to shake.

While she wasn't sure what to expect—most of Penelope's experience sailing across the solar system had either been aboard *Gaia* or one of its ORC pods—she was still surprised by the disarray. Strewn about on the deck were storage containers, their lids torn off, bulkhead lockers with their doors ajar, and an array of maintenance supplies haphazardly scattered around. There was even a tool belt with a riveter and plasma torch still attached to it.

But the Contractor was nowhere to be found.

What Penelope did notice was that, at the forward bulkhead, a large mechanical exoskeleton was set into a depression in the hull. But the control module at its center, what she had come to know as Mailman, was also missing.

"Welcome aboard," a warm, maternal voice rang out over the ship's loudspeaker. It was Mailman. "This is *The Tardigrade*."

"It's...kind of a mess," Penelope laughed nervously.

"My apologies for the state of things. I'm afraid, in our absence, the man you know as Brother Phineas raided our supplies."

"Mailman, you don't have to apologize to me. I'd like to help clean up if that's okay."

"While I am grateful for the offer, Miss Penelope, I must decline. Foxhound has asked that you meet her in her quarters. At the forward bulkhead, you can find a ladder on the port side and a lift on the starboard side. Either will get you to the primary deck. You'll find her quarters toward the aft of the ship."

Penelope opted for the ladder, climbing up to the starship's main deck. Ahead, she saw *The Tardigrade*'s bridge, a dizzying assortment of sensor arrays, visual displays, and varying consoles, all arranged around a single pilot's chair.

In one of the consoles—a monolith of blinking lights, buttons, and switches—Penelope noticed a familiar shape. She stepped up to the console and reached out a hand, grazing her fingers over the cracked surface of the glowing oblong orb.

"Is this where you live?" she asked.

"While this is my primary server node," Mailman answered, "I am, technically, integrated throughout this ship's systems."

"You're inside the whole ship?"

"In a manner of speaking, yes."

"And what about on *Gaia*? That wasn't you?" Penelope had a puzzled look on her face.

"It was, and it wasn't," Mailman responded. "The orb in front of you is my control module, which can separate and operate independently of my greater systems. However, I can never truly leave the ship. *The Tardigrade* and I are one and the same. Two parts of a whole."

"If Fink or any of the other prisoners had managed to bypass the lockdown...they'd have kidnapped you?"

"Potentially, with the right technical aptitude. But I am also designed with a self-preservation directive. I can activate defensive measures to protect *The Tardigrade* and anyone aboard."

"And here I thought you were just some...robot."

"Modular Automaton Intended for Labor in Manufacturing, Agriculture, and Navigation, a M.A.I.L.M.A.N, if you would."

"That's a mouthful," Penelope chuckled.

"You were supposed to come to my cabin," with a hiss of static, a voice came from behind Penelope. She turned around to find Foxhound decked out from head to toe in what looked like a brand-new armored suit, nearly indistinguishable from the one that had been destroyed.

"You just have those suits lying around, do you?"

"Something like that."

"I thought we'd finally be meeting face-to-face." There was a pang of disappointment in Penelope's voice.

Foxhound ignored the comment. "I'm taking the girl with me back to Earth."

"Like hell you are." Penelope hissed, "She stays with me."

"I know," Foxhound retorted. "You're coming, too. You saw something in that girl. Something that nobody else did. And she trusts you. We both know what she's capable of, and with you there, she seems...soothed. Or at least less likely to go on a killing rampage."

Penelope stared at her own reflection in Foxhound's visor, choosing her next words carefully. "What did you see in her?"

"What do you mean?" Foxhound asked, puzzled.

"You're a Contractor, right? She was your contract. You agreed to bring her in, but you helped us instead. You could have told Yū that she was the Marrower, but you didn't. And with all your armor and weapons, you could have gotten rid of all of us or left us behind and made off with her. Why? That's what I keep asking myself. Why would you do that when it goes against everything you are?"

"A Contractor is not who I am," Foxhound answered. "It's what I do. And that's what's been bothering me ever since I came aboard that ship of yours and met that girl. I don't know who I am."

Foxhound looked down at her gauntleted hands, turning them over and back again. "It never mattered before. I honestly didn't even give it much thought. I had my ship, my AI, and a never-ending list of contracts to complete. Everything outside of that was…unimportant. And that's what I'd tell myself every time I looked in the mirror. It wasn't important that I didn't know who I was or where I came from. It wasn't important that I didn't have any concrete memories. There were flashes. Or maybe more like feelings. Places I'd been and people I knew. A forest and…someone, a woman who I think might have been my mother. But every time I'd get close to remembering, it would all just fade away like space dust on a solar wind."

"That's…awful," Penelope said. "I'm so sorry."

"Then I saw that girl…" Foxhound faltered.

The armored Contractor reached both her hands up to the

sides of her helmet and turned a pair of valves, one with each hand. The helmet's hermetic seal breached with a hiss, and the whole thing telescoped open.

Foxhound lifted the helmet off her head, a cascade of thick, curly brown locks of hair falling upon her shoulders. And through those locks, framed by dark skin, Penelope gazed into two vibrant emerald green eyes.

Penelope gasped and stepped back. She looked older, more grown up, but there was no mistaking that Foxhound and the little no-name girl shared the same face.

"I need to know where she came from," Foxhound said, "because that's where I came from, too."

Chapter Thirteen

Though she had left the Organic Humanists, first forcibly and then of her own volition, it still took some convincing for Penelope to agree to accompany the no-name girl and Foxhound to Earth. She, the Organic Humanists as a whole, and so many others at the far reaches of the solar system had built up humanity's home planet and the organization that controlled it, the Divine Church of the Omniphage, as something to be avoided and feared. To them, it was a draconian authority that valued control over all else and not the bastion of knowledge and science it presented itself as.

For so many, the OH included, the dangers and lawlessness of the Reach, which included the Kuiper Belt, a wide variety of slapdash space stations, a network of refurbished listening posts, and the Oort cloud beyond, was preferable to living under the thumb of Earth. Even the outer planets and their moons, which were patrolled by Earth's various military bodies, including the Aegis Guard, courtesy of a flimsy collection of defense treaties and security accords among the planets' respective governing bodies, were too close for comfort for those who valued their freedom beyond all else.

But Foxhound had eventually persuaded Penelope to put

her prejudice aside.

"Earth, the Omniphage, these are my employers," the Contractor had argued. "And the exclusive contract they gave me was abundantly clear that the Marrower was not to be harmed."

"What's an *exclusive* contract?"

"It means they didn't offer the job to any other Contractors. They wanted *me* to complete it and no one else."

"There was even a Contractor execution clause," added Mailman. "The Divine Church reserved the right to send other Contractors after Foxhound if she had failed in her mission. And with kill orders, no less."

"And you still agreed to take on the job?" Penelope had asked.

"I've never broken a contract before," Foxhound answered, "and I wasn't about to start. But it seems she wasn't all they wanted. They put me on the job because they wanted me, too. That means they have answers, and I plan to get them. If they wanted to get rid of one, either, or both of us, we wouldn't be having this conversation right now."

Although she was still skeptical, this—plus the promise that Foxhound would rain hellfire on anyone who tried to harm the girl—was enough to get Penelope and the girl aboard *The Tardigrade* for the monthslong trip back to Earth.

☿

The trip was awkward at the outset. Foxhound wasn't used to sharing her space with anyone other than her AI companion, so she mostly kept to herself on the primary deck, moving between her quarters and the cockpit as her wounds healed.

Penelope and the no-name girl took up residence in the cargo bay, the only other place aboard the ship that had any semblance of livable space.

Foxhound, at first, hadn't even revealed herself to the girl, choosing to continue wearing her armor whenever she wasn't in her own room.

"We don't know how she might react," the Contractor had reasoned.

"No," Penelope had answered. "That's not it. You know she trusts you. I think it's something else. You're afraid."

"As long as I'm in this suit, I can survive in a vacuum. Should she attack me, all I have to do is have Mailman vent the atmosphere. I'm not afraid. I'm prepared."

"It's a dark place inside that helmet of yours, you know that?" Penelope had replied, brushing off the thinly veiled threat. "But that's not what I meant. You're afraid of children."

"I am *not*," Foxhound retorted, appalled.

"You're afraid that she'll want to talk to you and spend more time with you."

For a time, Foxhound continued to wear her armor whenever outside her quarters and periodically reiterated to Penelope what a foolish, absurd idea it was that she, a Contractor, one of the most respected and feared warriors in the entire solar system, was afraid of interacting with a mere child. As time went on, however, Penelope's comments had stuck with Foxhound.

Eventually, she had sat the no-name girl down and, with guidance from Penelope, showed her that they shared the same features, from their emerald green eyes to their dark skin.

From that point forward, just as the former Organic Humanist had predicted, the no-name girl was practically glued to Foxhound's side.

The Contractor was reticent at first, spending large parts of the passing days locked in her quarters, the one place she kept to herself. But when she opened her door to come back out, without fail, the girl was waiting there for her.

Before long, Foxhound had embraced the situation in which she had found herself, ostensibly because it was convenient and useful to have another pair of willing hands around the ship. She had even taken to teaching the girl various maintenance tasks. But Penelope knew better. She could tell that the once stoic and solitary Contractor was warming up to her tiny doppelgänger.

Within only a few weeks, the trio began spending more and more time together. Penelope took to teaching the no-name girl an array of educational subjects, just as she had back aboard *Gaia* with the children she and Loch rescued. Foxhound focused on the more physical aspects of her enrichment, including some basic survival skills, hand-to-hand combat, and field maintenance, which the girl took to almost immediately, showing the same kind of aptitude for the work as Foxhound.

"This is nice," Penelope had said late one evening after they had finished dinner and were working on cleanup. "It feels almost normal, like being back aboard *Gaia*."

Still, Penelope found some days extremely difficult. She had, after all, whittled her family down from literal thousands to just two. And while she was grateful, she also missed her old life, her old Siblings, and her old home.

But there were things that, to a degree, helped ease that pain. Sometimes, the trio played games together. Penelope and the girl also listened to Foxhound tell stories, and they all celebrated milestones together. Penelope even crafted a makeshift birthday cake—little more than a handful of nutrient-dense cubes, standard rations aboard starships, mashed together and topped with freeze-dried synthetic fruit—when the girl had excitedly announced to them that she had finally picked the perfect name for herself.

One night, Penelope woke with a start to find herself alone in the cargo bay, with the newly-named girl nowhere to be found. In a panic, she began searching the ship. She checked the other cells, but they were all empty. She looked through the cargo storage cupboards but found nothing but supplies and repair parts. She climbed up to the cockpit but found only the same consoles, displays, and sensor arrays that were always there.

Finally, she made her way back to Foxhound's quarters and found, for the first time since she had come aboard, that the door had been left open. What she saw when she peered inside was almost enough for her to forget all that she had given up and left behind.

There, nested together, she found Foxhound and the girl asleep, a datapad clutched in the Contractor's hand.

Penelope was going to leave the pair in peace when, as she turned to leave, she saw that Foxhound had opened her eyes.

"I didn't mean to wake you," Penelope muttered.

"It's fine," Foxhound whispered back, the girl gently stirring, nuzzling her face in the crook of the woman's neck. "She said she was scared, had a bad dream or something. So, I was reading her a story. Must have fallen asleep."

"Do you want me to take her?"

"No, that's okay. I can bring her back down if she wakes up

again."

Penelope smiled and nodded before going back to the cargo bay to sleep.

☿

By the time *The Tardigrade* needed refueling, the ship had already made it well past the outer planets, stopping at Listening Post Theta—an old signal monitoring satellite, built when humanity was still convinced that it wasn't alone in the universe—that had been retrofitted into a refueling station for a resupply run.

While *The Tardigrade* refueled and Foxhound handled procuring foodstuffs, medical necessities, and anything else they might need for the rest of the trip sunward, Penelope and the girl remained aboard. And while the girl remained occupied by her studies, Penelope took some time to catch up on correspondence.

Sitting before the comms data terminal in the cockpit, Penelope thumbed through various messages, most from her former Siblings and the children once in her charge checking in to wish her well and share stories, milestones, and the like. But there were two others, ones she had been eagerly awaiting, from Brother Loch and Sibling Yū.

With a double tap, she opened the first video. An image of *Gaia's* cockpit, with Brother Loch standing at its center, filled the screen. But he wasn't sitting in the captain's chair, the gaudy throne once occupied by Mother. Rather, he sat at the forward comms station.

"Penelope," he said with a smile, "I hope all is well in your travels. And I trust, based on what I've heard from the other

Siblings, that Foxhound is treating you and the girl quite well. Here on *Gaia,* things are finally getting back to normal. Just as we planned, the guns are all gone, either melted down or sold off. The crops are growing again. We've even restored function to many of the systems in the lower decks."

Loch paused, the smile melting from his face.

"The work has been hard. And we've lost so many. I know they are all still with us, enriching the soil that feeds our crops and, thus, sustaining us all. It's bittersweet. I know we are meant to look forward to the future and not dwell on the past, but there is a weight on our shoulders. I see it every day. While there are smiles on our Siblings' faces, their eyes still bear a deep sorrow…"

He raised his head, the smile returning to his lips.

"Speaking of the future, I do have something wonderful to share. As we discussed before you departed, I spoke with Sibling Yū about taking up the mantle, the responsibility of being Mother of the Organic Humanists."

He laughed, the first genuine laugh Penelope had heard from him in a long time.

"They promptly declined the offer. But that's not the good news. Sibling Yū proposed an alternative, and we're giving it our best shot. Rather than installing a singular leader, a Mother, I am happy to announce that the Organic Humanists have embarked on a new journey. We have become a democracy in which every Sibling's voice is heard and given equal weight. In fact, only a few days ago, we had our first vote to elect a council of representatives, a kind of collective that will help us decide the future of our family. Much to their chagrin, Sibling Yū was elected to this council practically unanimously, especially after I shared with our Siblings Yū's bravery and foresight in sniffing out Mother's plot."

Brother Loch's eyebrows furrowed as he swallowed the lump in his throat.

"Your absence is felt every day, but I know you're following the path that was laid out for you. We miss you. I miss you. And I hope that, when this is all over, we might see one another again. Farewell, Sister."

Penelope sat for a long time after hearing Loch's message, processing all she had heard. She was full of sorrow at missing her family, but also overflowed with joy at the news of how things were progressing.

Finally, she double-tapped the second message. This time, the screen displayed a stateroom, and sitting in its center with a frown on their face was Sibling Yū.

"I suppose you had something to do with trying to make me the next Mother," Yū grumbled with the tiniest hint of a grin on their lips. "I didn't know you'd be this bitter about my not coming with you. Either that or you knew I'd say no, and this was your plan all along. But *Gaia* needed me...still needs me, so it seems. Whatever the case, that was a dirty trick, and I won't forget it. Next time you come to visit, I'll get you back."

They laughed, a warm smile on their face.

"I suspect Loch will tell you much the same in his message, but I said no. After a lot of discussions...perhaps more like shouting matches, especially among the older, more traditional Siblings...we've come to an accord. The Organic Humanists are officially democratic. We even held our first vote. As usual, Loch refused to take any credit for it...even though I distinctly remember hearing it was his idea. He's been telling everyone I came up with it. Can you believe that? As a result, and much to my chagrin, I was elected to this…*council of representatives*, I think we're calling it. The idea is that, through discussion and debate, we might collectively help guide the family down a path that best suits all of us. Loch told me I couldn't decline this time. Something about reticence being next to godliness and those not wanting power being the best to wield it. You know how he is. So, I guess you still got what you wanted, kind of."

Sibling Yū rubbed their eyes and took a deep breath.

"How's the girl? Has she picked a name yet? There is some crazy gossip going around *Gaia* that she was actually responsible for some of those gruesome deaths. You know how people can be, anything to keep the rumor wheel turning. Tell Foxhound and Mailman hello for me. I'll be eagerly awaiting your next message."

They looked into the camera, smirking.

"Representative Yū, signing off."

Penelope, through her tears and laughter, recorded her responses to both Loch and Yū. Shortly thereafter, Foxhound returned to the ship, loaded up *The Tardigrade*'s cargo bay, and they were off once more.

Epilogue

"We're approaching Earth's orbit," Mailman announced throughout *The Tardigrade*.

Foxhound was already sitting in the captain's chair. Penelope and the girl stood at either side of her, gazing into the monitor displaying a field of stars with a pale blue dot, growing ever larger, at its center.

"Welcome to Earth," Foxhound said.

With every second, the planet grew in both size and detail. First, the silvery crescent of the moon and its dark side—dotted with millions upon millions of points of light from its hundreds of thousands of settlements, refineries, and manufacturing plants—came into view. Next, the planet's continents and oceans took shape, all of which were covered, practically from edge to edge, with their own structures, barges, and other manmade architecture. Finally, as the display's star field had been almost entirely replaced by the planet below, the trio began to make out the millions upon millions of satellites, colony stations, starship dockyards and, of course, the never-ending stream of ORC pod traffic entering and leaving the planet's atmosphere.

"Magnificent," Penelope eventually blurted, her jaw hanging

open. "I've… I never imagined… There's just so much."

"Earth," the girl said. "It's huge!"

At that, Foxhound let out a laugh.

"You'll have plenty of time to gaze," the Contractor said. "Earth gets a lot of traffic and the Divine Church prioritizes it with an utterly perplexing need-based system. We're going to be pretty low on that list so we could be waiting up here for another few months."

Just as the words left her lips, an alert flashed on the comms screen. *Priority Atmospheric Entry Granted*, it read in huge letters. Foxhound tapped it, opening the full message.

"Or we can just land now, I guess," she corrected herself.

The Contractor scrutinized the message before turning to Penelope, her brow furrowed.

"What? What is it?"

"These coordinates…they're for Omniphage HQ."

"Isn't that where you always come? I thought the Church was your employer."

"Mostly, they just send out requests or have me meet with a priest on one of the church's orbital platforms."

"What, like those creepy automatons? No offense, Mail-man."

"None taken," the AI's maternal voice rang out over the ship's intercom, "as I am not a creepy automaton, as you put it."

"I've never actually been to Earth's surface," Foxhound finished. "At least not that I can remember."

"That would have been good information to share back on *Gaia*," Penelope growled.

"Do you want answers or not?" Foxhound barked back. "This was the only way to get them. Besides, we're already here. It doesn't matter now."

"No," Penelope agreed, "I guess it doesn't."

"So, we're going, right?" the girl bounced up and down excitedly.

"Yes." Penelope patted her on the head. "We're going."

☿

Crowded into *The Tardigrade*'s ORC pod, Foxhound, decked out once more from head to toe in her powered armor, the girl, Penelope, and Mailman's floating control module, this time without its hulking modular exoskeleton, headed for the coordinates provided by the Divine Church of the Omniphage.

Once they had cleared the upper atmosphere, the pod's wraparound screens blinked on, displaying Earth's North American continent, nearly entirely covered in the planet's signature shimmering white-and-gold architecture. But, as they approached their destination, the girl pointed to a spot on the screen—a pocket of lush green that stood in stark contrast to the rest of the continent.

As they got closer, Penelope realized what it was they were seeing. It was something she had heard about only in stories, seen only in paintings: a forest. Flanked by huge, gray-and-white-capped mountains, it was a forest valley that looked, to Penelope, as natural and pristine as she had always imagined Ancient Earth to be.

"I thought there were no more forests," Penelope said as she gawked.

"I can find no public record of this location in my database," Mailman responded. "Historical records, however, indicate that this location was once referred to as Yosemite National

258

Park."

"Look," the girl squealed, pointing to the horizon.

There at the edge of the valley, just barely visible between two of the valley's great peaks, was an enormous wall built from what looked to be the same stone as the mountains themselves. And atop those walls, staggered at regular intervals, Foxhound recognized something else: gargantuan point defense cannons—ones that used the same technology as ORC pod launchers to hurtle enormous metal slugs and warheads alike at anything remotely threatening, be that ships, space debris, or anything else, turning it into a fine, harmless dust.

"Whatever this place is," Foxhound whispered, "they don't want unexpected visitors."

Penelope scanned the horizon around them and, sure enough, the wall appeared to reach all the way around the valley, except for one spot at the south end. There, rising into the sky like the mountains themselves, stood an enormous, glistening tower surrounded by a throng of smaller edifices. Emblazoned on the side of the tower in shimmering gold was a massive emblem: a pyramid with an eye at its center surrounded by a serpent devouring its own tail—the symbol of the Divine Church of the Omniphage. And they were headed right for a landing pad jutting out from the side of the tower, almost at its apex.

"Prepare for landing," Mailman said as its floating control module embedded itself in a depression in the ORC pod's inner hull, magnetizing into place with a loud *shunk*.

Foxhound, Penelope, and the girl sat back in their seats as their safety belts tightened.

The ORC pod's retroboosters kicked on, sending a quake of

vibrations through the cabin. The girl reached out her hand and grabbed at Penelope's, squeezing her eyes shut as the pod shook.

"It's okay," Penelope reassured both the girl and herself.

It had been so long since she had traveled planetside that she had forgotten how violent ORC landings could be. But this, with Earth's unique combination of gravity and atmosphere, was beyond any turbulence she had experienced. Like the girl, she too squeezed her eyes shut right up until she felt the pod jostle and the vibration of the retroboosters cease.

"Landing sequence complete," Mailman confirmed. "Releasing safety restraints now."

Penelope's harness released, as did Foxhound's and the no-name girl's. Then, with a hiss, the pod's rear hatch opened, flooding the cabin with a warm breeze.

Penelope, the former Organic Humanist who had never even been to the inner colonies, let alone humanity's home planet, for the first time in her life, took a deep breath of fresh Earth air. And with it tears streamed down her cheeks.

The girl was already up and hopping around by the time Penelope finally attempted to rise. Stumbling unsteadily, the former Organic Humanist caught herself just before toppling over.

"I feel so heavy," the girl laughed, hopping from foot to foot.

"You may experience some disorientation," Mailman said, its control orb floating freely once more. "Please exit with caution."

"One second," Foxhound said to her AI companion as she turned to Penelope, still gripping her seat's armrests, and the girl. "I know we came here for answers, but I don't know who or what's out there waiting for us. I just want you to know that, whatever happens, I will do everything in my power to protect you both."

Penelope and the no-name girl nodded in unison.

Foxhound, as surefooted as ever, was the first to exit the pod, followed by the wobbly Penelope and the no-name girl, still bouncing up and down with each step.

But when they descended the pod's ramp, there was nobody and nothing waiting for them on the landing pad below other than one other ORC pod—a model that reminded Penelope of the ones back aboard *Gaia*, only far more ornate.

"This feels wrong," Penelope said, bracing herself on the side of the pod as she looked out across the vast expanse of trees far below the tower's pinnacle.

"I don't like it, either," Foxhound confirmed. "Maybe we should head inside."

It was more a question than a statement.

Penelope nodded, and together, the trio—followed by Mailman's floating orb—walked across the landing pad toward a massive pair of double doors carved into the tower's facade.

As they approached, without making so much as a hiss, the doors began to slide open, revealing a single white-robed figure standing at its center.

Penelope's heart raced. The figure looked just like Mother. *Impossible*, she thought. *No, this can't be.*

But as the figure approached, it removed its hood, revealing a featureless, stark, matte-white visage adorned with the same shimmering gold pyramid-and-serpent emblem they saw on the side of the tower as they approached. It was one of the Church's priests, a skeletal automaton that functioned as both a herald of Earth's governing body and its surreptitious leader.

"Huh," Foxhound said, puzzled. "They're usually black and

261

shiny."

"Allow me to extend my deepest apologies," the automaton said in what sounded like several voices at once. Just like its appearance, its voice also reminded Penelope of Mother in a deeply unsettling way. "Dr. Sage had intended to welcome you personally, but something unexpected arose that required her full attention. It would be my distinct pleasure to do the honors of showing you our facilities and delivering you to the doctor's personal quarters, after which you may accompany me to your rooms."

"Our rooms?" the Contractor puzzled.

"Yes," the automaton answered. "You will be staying with us for some time."

The automaton tilted its head in Penelope's direction.

"I'm afraid your arrival was unexpected. You are Sister Penelope of the Organic Humanists, is that correct?"

"*Former* Sister, actually," Penelope answered. "And how do you know that?"

"Pleased to meet you, Former Sister Penelope," the automaton said. "The Divine Church of the Omniphage prides itself in its accumulation of knowledge. While this includes a breadth of information, ranging from history to science and everything in between, we also collect data from across the solar system, including that of its citizenry, regardless of whether those lives fall under the purview of the Divine Church or not."

"The Church is always watching," Foxhound grumbled.

"In a manner of speaking," the automaton continued, "Yes."

Penelope wrung her hands nervously.

"My sensors indicate that your stress levels are rising, Former Sister Penelope. Allow me to put you at ease. The

Divine Church does not wish to do you or your former Siblings any harm. We value information, but it is not our intention to weaponize it."

"Tell that to the people in the slums and on the barges," Foxhound interjected.

"Every Earth citizen is afforded a Guaranteed Income equivalent to that which they would need to procure food, shelter, and medicine relative to their geographical location," the automaton responded. "The Divine Church provides all that it can to ensure that every Earthling lives a happy and comfortable life."

"As long as they don't oppose the Church's views, right?" It was Penelope this time.

"The Divine Church asks only that every citizen respect a concise set of rules and regulations that ensure peace and prosperity throughout Earth and its surrounding colonies, protectorates, and territories." The automaton turned back to Penelope. "If you do not wish to accept our invitation, you are free to leave whenever you so choose. We will neither stop you nor harm you so long as you are under the Divine Church's care."

Penelope looked down at the girl, still gazing with awe at the automaton and the tower behind it.

"No," she said. "I think I'll stay."

"Very well," the automaton said. "It is my pleasure to meet and serve all of you. Please follow me."

The gilded automaton turned around, its servos so smooth and quiet, it almost seemed to be floating. And together, the group entered the shimmering tower high above Omniphage HQ.

☿

Navigating through the tower's intricate interior with its lofty ceilings and the same gold-on-white motif as its facade, the automaton's torso pivoted to face the group to address its guests without missing a step.

"To the outside world, the Tower, as it is known, serves as a beacon, a monolith, a lighthouse meant to remind those far and wide just how much the Divine Church of the Omniphage has achieved and, in turn, shared with the people of our solar system."

Foxhound tilted her head toward Penelope just in time to catch the former Sister rolling her eyes. Still safely hidden behind her helmet's visor, the Contractor smirked. Unfazed, the automaton continued its zealous sermon.

"But it is much more than that. This edifice represents some of the greatest achievements of the Divine Church and, in fact, houses some of our most significant works." The automaton gestured downward. "There are hundreds of floors beneath our feet, and on each and every one, you will find the Omniphage's most vital and prolific laboratories, including centers dedicated to biological research, advanced cybernetics, astronomical data tracking and extrapolation, and even resource and population management."

"Do you grow people's children here, too?" Penelope grimaced. "And how much gene editing do you do without informing the families? How much of our unique human DNA is even passed on from parent to child? And how much of it is...conjured up by your warlocks?"

"I can assure you," the automaton said without skipping a beat, "the embryos matured and refined within the Divine

264

Church's Offspring Development Centers are completely human, and their DNA is comprised almost entirely of genetics taken directly from direct parental donations. We are not in the business of rewriting human genetics apart from eliminating things such as disease and deformity."

"That's the problem," Penelope snapped. "Who are you to decide which parts of humanity get to exist and which are done away with? This is eugenics, plain and simple—"

Foxhound placed a hand, as gently as she could, on Penelope's shoulder. Penelope turned with a jerk, seeing her own scowling face reflected in the Contractor's visor, before inhaling deeply and letting out a long sigh.

"We understand that one of the primary tenets of the Organic Humanists is the belief that humans are meant to be conceived, gestated, and birthed largely naturally, is this correct, *former* Sister?"

Penelope winced at the automaton's words. "Yes, that is correct."

"Is it not also true that the Organic Humanists utilize vaccines and other modern medical science to assist in keeping children healthy?"

"That's not the same thing!"

"In what way is it different?" the automaton asked coldly. "We do not and have never tampered with an embryo's race or gender and have never attempted to influence orientation or even things such as the potential for intelligence. We do not, as you say, engage in eugenics. So, in what way is what your people do all that different? Is it not simply a more rudimentary version of what the Divine Church has achieved?"

Penelope flushed.

"It's just… You're removing things that don't need to… You can't just decide what parts we get to keep and what we have to lose—"

"Penelope," Foxhound barked.

Penelope clammed up, understanding what the Contractor meant, even without her saying it aloud: *this isn't a fight we can win.* And Penelope knew she was right.

Foxhound, Penelope, the no-name girl, and Mailman's hovering control module followed the Omniphage's automaton envoy deeper into the facility, careful not to interrupt its propagandist lecture any further.

☿

By the time the automaton had announced that the group had arrived at its destination—a pair of imposing stone doors with the Omniphage's ouroboros-and-all-seeing-eye symbol carved deep into their surface—Foxhound's patience had worn thin.

As soon as they had entered the facility, she had activated her suit's breadcrumb tracker—the same tech she used to navigate asteroidal colonies and space stations with which she was unfamiliar. And she had quickly discovered that the automaton guiding them through the Omniphage tower hadn't been taking them on even a remotely direct route to where they were supposedly headed.

The path meandered to and fro, in and out of a hodgepodge of hallways and varying chambers, and even doubled back on itself at more than one point.

Even with the breadcrumb tracker activated, Foxhound wasn't sure how to make a quick exit should escape become necessary. It seemed, to her, that the tour was a means of distraction and disorientation. They were invited into the Tower, but they were not meant to leave.

It left the Contractor with an uneasy feeling but one she kept to herself.

It did bring her some comfort to see the awe and excitement still on the no-name girl's face. Yet, with that comfort, if she dwelt on it for too long, came more uneasiness.

In the months since leaving the Organic Humanist mothership and throughout the long, slow trek toward Earth, Foxhound had found it easy to forget all of the questions she had about who the no-named orphan girl was that shared her face, how such a seemingly innocent child could be capable of such tremendous violence, how they had come to encounter one another seemingly by chance in one of the most remote parts of the solar system, and what forces pushed them toward this end. But it also brought to the forefront of the Contractor's mind a question she had quarreled with for as long as she could remember:

Who am I?

Foxhound told herself, as she often did, that the question didn't matter if she couldn't find the answer. But that was before…all of this. Now she couldn't get the nagging query out of her head.

And it had only gotten worse since arriving on Earth, ushered into the Omniphage's mystifying headquarters like some kind of VIP when, before, she had only ever been granted permission to remain in orbit aboard her ship.

None of it made any sense. But maybe, just maybe, the answer was waiting beyond the great stone doors before her.

As if on cue, the automaton spoke once more, snapping

Foxhound back to attention.

"Please, step inside," it said. "There's someone who would very much like to meet you."

The doors creaked open. And the no-name girl ran inside.

☿

The girl couldn't wait any longer.

She had been so patient while the Divine Church's automaton had dragged everyone all around Omniphage headquarters but had been bored practically out of her mind for almost the entire time. There were only so many gold-accented rooms she could admire, after all. But it wasn't just that she was bored. It was eagerness. Something about this place, for the first time in as long as she could remember, seemed familiar.

On *The Tardigrade*, she had felt safe. And after a few weeks of spending time with Miss Penelope and *big-sis* Foxhound—a pet name the Contractor only barely tolerated—it had even started feeling like home. But now, on Earth and inside the Divine Church of the Omniphage's enormous lighthouse—that *was* what the automaton had called it, wasn't it?—she felt something else. It was more than home. It was where she belonged. She was certain of it.

So, when the enormous doors to Dr. Sage's personal quarters finally creaked open, she squeezed through the breach and sprinted inside...and immediately stopped dead in her tracks.

Before her, reaching all the way across the room, she gazed out of the largest panoramic window she had ever seen and onto—*what had Miss Penelope called it? A forest?* It was unbelievably beautiful, whatever it was. So green, so vast, so welcoming.

It hadn't even occurred to the girl to look around the rest of the room. She was mesmerized.

Behind her, Foxhound and Penelope entered the room. But they were both less entranced by the views out of the panoramic window and instead took stock of their surroundings.

Of all the rooms they had been taken through since arriving at the Tower, this space was by far the largest and most lavishly embellished. The walls were lined with art and artifacts, most of which looked decades, if not centuries old. The cold stone floors were covered in luxurious rugs. And there were what looked like crystal chandeliers hanging from the ceiling, the light coming in through the windows refracting through them and tossing brilliant, vibrant rainbows on practically every surface.

In one corner of the room sat an extravagant, ornate bed surrounded by stately furniture, all made from a dark, natural-looking material none of them recognized.

Penelope walked over to it, running her hand over the edges of what she believed to be a dresser, which she confirmed by opening one of the drawers and finding neatly folded clothing inside.

"It's made of black oak," a voice rang out from the other side of the room. Foxhound took a staggered stance, raising her B.A.N.G. modules in the direction of the voice, but neither she nor her companions could discern from where it came.

"Well, actually," the voice continued, "it's an approximation of black oak. As far as we know, the species died out some centuries ago. But we had enough data to build our own biological facsimile."

Opposite the bedroom furniture, at the far end of the room, there was an array of what appeared, to Foxhound, to be a number of laboratory devices, computer terminals, and various other workstations.

A small figure emerged from behind one of the stations and shuffled toward the quartet, Foxhound, Penelope, the no-name girl, and Mailman's floating orb.

Foxhound focused on the figure and let her suit's sensors do what they did best. Inside her helmet, readings started to pop up on her HUD. Whoever this person was, they were almost entirely human—no discernable cybernetic signatures—and somewhere between one hundred fifty to two hundred years old. Furthermore, they appeared to be quite healthy if their biometrics were to be believed.

But as the figure got closer, Foxhound could no longer focus on the sensor readings. Instead, her eyes locked on the figure's face.

Flanked by thick, silvery curls draped down over dark chestnut skin, surrounded by deep wrinkles, and situated above full lips and a button nose, Foxhound fixated on the figure's large emerald eyes.

They were the same eyes she had recognized on the no-name girl. The same eyes she gazed into every time she looked in the mirror. They were her own eyes.

"I'm so sorry I was unable to meet you at the landing pad," the woman said with a warm smile on her face. "I'm afraid I have a bad habit of getting far too deep in my research."

Foxhound took a step backward, keeping her arms raised, as the old woman continued forward.

"No need to be afraid," she continued. "My name is Odessa

Sage. Well, technically, I'm Odessa Sage the Ninth, but that sounds so...formal. You may call me Odessa if that makes things easier. Dr. Sage works, as well, if you're put off by being overly familiar."

Foxhound took another step back just as the no-name girl hopped in front of her.

"And you two," Dr. Sage's smile grew even wider as she regarded Foxhound and the girl. "How should I put this? You two are the closest thing I have to daughters. Welcome home."

The girl telescoped her own hand and gripped Dr. Sage's.

"It's a pleasure to meet you, Odessa," she said. "My name is Leila."

Intermission

Survive.
  Move.
  Survive.
  Observe. Examine. Analyze. Extrapolate.
  React. Retreat.
  Survive.
  Dodge. Guard. Protect.
  Faster.
  Advance. Attack. Annihilate.
  Survive.
  Slash. Maim. Rip. Crack. Devour.
  Digest.
  Satisfy. Nourish. Sustain.
  Evacuate. Escape.
  Survive.

Foxhound, Penelope, Leila, and more will return in The Marrower Saga: Books Two and Three…

About the Author

Sean M. Tirman is the author, creator, and custodian of the Marrower universe and has been published in both *Infinite Worlds Magazine* and *Infinite Horrors Magazine*. He lives in Rochester, New York, with his wife and two remarkably entitled, small, old dogs. *Hounds of Gaia* is his first novel.

A Note from the Author: If you've made it this far, I hope that means you've finished reading *Hounds of Gaia*. For that, I'd like to thank you from the bottom of my heart. It genuinely means the world to me that you'd take the time to read my work. Now that you're done, I'd love for you to take a moment to share your thoughts and leave a review. As a largely one-person operation, I can't properly express how important and impactful reader community evaluations are to me and my book.